KAIYO

THE LOST NATION

*The righteous one is aware of the soul of his animal,
and the evil withhold their compassions.*

Proverbs 12:10 Original Aramaic New Testament

D1511011

A NOVEL BY

CLIFF COCHRAN

ISBN 978-1-64114-841-2 (paperback)
ISBN 978-1-64114-842-9 (digital)

Christian Faith Publishing, Inc.
832 Park Avenue
Meadville, PA 16335
www.christianfaithpublishing.com

Illustrations by D. Bin Cochran
Cover design by MarketWake, LLC

Printed in the United States of America

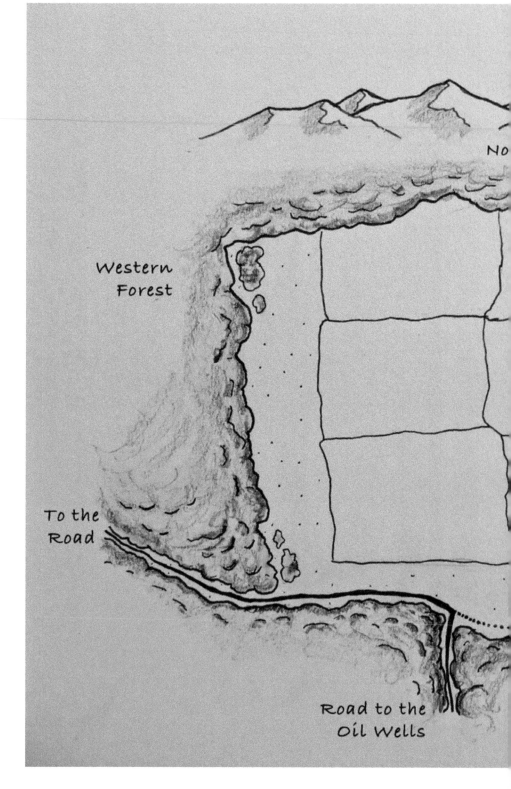

Western
Forest

To the
Road

Road to the
Oil Wells

No

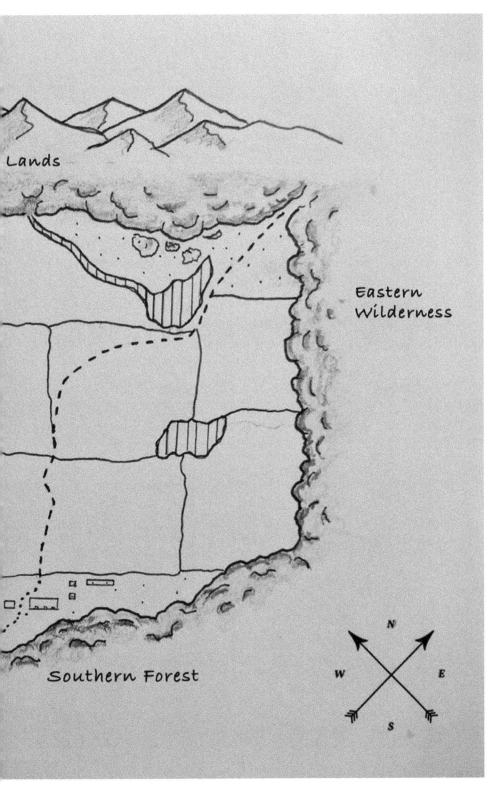

Lands

Eastern
Wilderness

Southern Forest

N

W   E

S

ACKNOWLEDGMENTS

Firstly, to my children, Brooke, Bin and Lily who dream big, creative dreams and step out on the precipice to achieve them. You three inspire many. I enjoy being in your audience. To my wife, Kriss, without your cheerful and constant encouragement to write, I would have lost my fire long before the first chapter was ever finished. To God, thank you always for loving the thief on the cross next to you. I will need no less grace.

INTRODUCTION

GRACE

No one has to remind me that we live in a fallen world. It is still God's creation, but it is fallen nonetheless. There is too much pain to believe otherwise. But it wasn't always that way. I now know a little of what it was like.

Almost everyone has some sympathy for animals. That is no accident. We want to be close with them because closeness is an ancient memory buried deep in our hearts. There once was a place where we had perfect communion with the animals. They weren't our pets; they were our friends. But man brought on the plague of death, and Eden fell out of sight. But Eden is not gone. It never was. And somehow, Eden found our family and we experienced at least some of what humanity lost long ago.

It has been many years since Kaiyo joined our family. He is my little brother, and this is his story.

PROLOGUE

LIBBY

It was a horrible thing to watch. A big male grizzly was attacking a female grizzly about seventy-five yards away from us. Our horses were nervous. I was scared. My dad was furious. We knew this male grizzly. He seemed to have been born with a chip on his shoulder. Dad had named him Goliath because he was huge, proud, and cruel. It was a perfect name. We watched as the big male killed the other bear. The noise was deafening. She wasn't much of a fighter, but she fought back fiercely to protect her cub. Just when Goliath was finishing off the mother grizzly, we saw the cub—a young one—start running for his life. He was racing toward the trees off to our right. Goliath saw him and roared, then he bolted for the cub. Dad cursed under his breath. He never cursed in front of us. I could tell Dad had enough from that bear.

He gave me a quick look. "Stay here, sweets!"

In the midst of the confusion, I thought how Dad often called me by nicknames. He rarely called me by my name, Elizabeth, and when he did, it was usually just Libby.

In a split second, Dad spurred his horse and headed full speed to intercept Goliath. In one move, Dad pulled his rifle out of its scabbard and he brought it to his shoulder. A shot rang out and dirt kicked up in front of the big bear. The big grizzly heard the shot and felt the dirt splatter in his face. Then he spotted my dad at the same second. He saw me, too, because I was chasing after my dad. Goliath knew we were trouble.

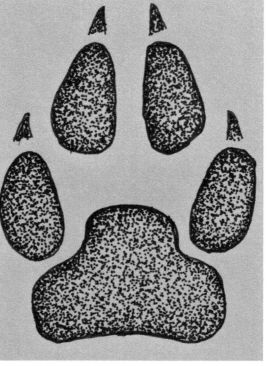

PART 1

HORRIBILIS

HOME – LIBBY

It all started on our farm in Montana. Something was different about this place and by living here; it was obvious to all of us. First of all, it was beautiful. To the north, we could see mountains. The mountains were almost always snow covered, at least the tops. Our land went for miles to the base of those mountains. To the south, our land dropped off into miles and miles of thick, low, swampy forest. In fact, the edge of that forest came pretty close to our house, and at night, sometimes it was creepy. This forest was called the Southern Forest, and we all knew it was spooky in there. I often felt something was watching us from within those woods. I learned later that sometimes something was watching, and it wasn't always a good thing.

To the east past the barns and the pastures, the land was a mix of open meadows and grassy parks surrounded by deep patches of tall timber. I have seen buffalo out there and antelope, too. It was that kind of place. Along with a lot of other grizzlies and black bears, it was also Goliath's home. Farther to the east, there were more mountains, but they were a long way off. We called this the Eastern Wilderness.

The western part of the farm was the part I knew best. We had a driveway that was almost six miles long. Starting from our house and barns and for about two miles, our driveway made the southern edge of our fields. Then, the fields gave way to what we call the Western

Forest. This part of our farm was open forest with tall trees and frequent rock outcroppings. Our driveway snaked its way through the beautiful forest until it finally reached the *Road*. That's what we called it. It was just the Road. Go to the left about forty miles and you go to the town of Radford, Montana. Go to the right and the Road heads north into the mountains, and then toward Canada.

Our mailbox was right at the Road. My friends from town would complain about them having to go get the mail. From my point of view, that sounded whiny. They had no idea. Just getting the mail for us took some real time.

But the horses loved getting the mail. My parents did not want me driving our four-wheelers or the UTV, even though they were easier and faster. Our UTV looked like a mix between a big four-seat golf cart and a small pickup. We all loved it. We had a few four-wheelers, too, but Dad and Mom never thought of them as very safe. We didn't use them nearly as much as the UTV. As for getting the mail, Dad said the horses needed the exercise (which was true) and no four-wheeler or UTV would ever warn us of danger. Dad was sure right on that one.

Sometimes, the horses would come to a quick stop and swing their ears forward and stare in a certain direction. We knew something was there. Sometimes it was a deer or elk, and we would move on. Other times, it was a bear or a cougar, and we would keep our eyes on them. They usually moved away pretty fast when we would come into view. Other times, we would know there was something watching us, but it wouldn't show itself. That was usually a little scary.

All of our horses were of good, strong stock, and I was fond of all of them. I rode several horses, but Jet was my favorite. She was black with a white star on her face and she was fast as the wind. It was Jet who was with me when we saw Goliath.

My parents farmed and ranched about six sections. A section is one square mile or 630 square acres. Some of the fields were for crops, and some of the land was pasture for cattle, horses, pigs, and alpacas. The fields were a mix of round fields and squared off fields depending on how much water they got. We also had chickens and some guinea fowl. Dad would rotate the crops from field to field, and every year, he would leave a different part of the land alone—no crops, no animals. He taught us how the land needed to rest, just like us. God told the ancient Hebrews to give the land a rest once every seven years. My dad often chuckled that if God thought it was a good idea, it probably was. It made sense to me.

My mom Susan McLeod was amazing. She was my dad's equal, and he knew it. He liked it that way. For an older woman in her mid thirties, she was also really pretty. He liked that, too. Mom could ride and shoot well, and she could also hunt if necessary. She could dance, too, and she saw beauty whenever it showed itself. For her, beauty was everywhere. I think beauty followed her around like a puppy. She had a way of looking at things that was different than Dad's way. They respected each other, and they both sought each other's advice.

Best of all, Mom understood me. She never seemed to forget she was a kid and a teenager once, too.

I have a little brother, Dean, and a little sister named Grace. Everybody called her Gracie. Dean is two years younger than me. Gracie is five years younger than Dean. I think my parents weren't the best planners in the world.

Mom was the type to do things now. Dad didn't like to procrastinate much either, but he tended to take more time getting to things. They were the very best of friends. They loved us, and we all knew it. We were also pretty sure they loved each other more than they loved us. We were okay with that, too.

Remember the bear cub we were talking about right at first? His name is Kaiyo, and this is where the story begins.

THE RESCUE – LIBBY

At the time we first met Kaiyo, he was running for his life and he wasn't running fast enough. He was terrified. His mother had just been killed and he had just a few seconds to live. He knew it, too, and he was bawling at the top of his lungs.

Goliath was just a dozen or so yards from catching and killing the cub when he saw me and my dad riding hard right at him. We had problems with him in the past, and we knew he hated us. Seeing my dad here was confusing to him, too. Goliath had learned the hard way to steer clear of the farm, at least during the day. Goliath rarely saw us way out here. Dad's first shot was a warning. Goliath quit the chase and stood to check us out. Standing about ten feet tall, Goliath had a good view. I turned Jet toward the running cub. Dad sat on his favorite horse, Hershel, and he placed himself and Hershel between me and the big bear. Dad gave his horses names that reminded him of his favorite football players. Hershel was smart, fast, and powerful. Hershel was also fearless, and he trusted Dad when it came to situations like this. Staring down a ferocious bear was something he and Dad had done before.

In his evil brain, Goliath knew Dad was dangerous and that Dad must have wanted the cub, too. He also knew the smell of guns. Goliath could see Dad's gun pointed right at him, and he could smell two others. He didn't like guns, and he probably knew Dad had two and I had one. By the way he acted, he probably thought that was a few guns too many. We also had bear spray which could cripple Goliath in searing pain. Goliath was a brutal bully, but he had been checked and he knew it. The big bear fell to his feet, roared at my dad, turned, and walked away from us. Slowly. Goliath was not scared. It was just time to leave.

I turned to chase the cub. He was too young to survive out here without his mother. The cub saw me coming, and he did something that astonished me. He stopped and waited. Wild animals don't do things like that. As he kept an eye on the drama of my dad dealing with his mom's killer, he came right at me. Even though he was very young, he was big enough to make Jet a little nervous. She didn't know yet they were about to be friends for life. I comforted Jet while the little bear climbed on a low stump and waited. When I came close, he hopped right on the saddle and into my lap. Jet shuddered. Both Jet and I were certain we would be clawed or bitten. What I got instead was a baby bear hug. He buried his head in my coat and seemed to cry. And he didn't let go.

I watched Dad ride up to the mother bear and take a few pictures on his cell phone. I thought that was a little odd. Then, Dad wheeled around and trotted up, smiled at the little bear, and said, "Let's get going before Goliath changes his mind. He's grumpy and can't be trusted."

I was a fifteen-year-old girl, and that's how it started.

Developments — Tracker

I could tell well before I got there she was probably dead. The circling vultures helped me figure that out. The smell confirmed it. That was not good because I was sent to bring her back. I am known as Tracker. That's not my real name, of course, but it is what I have become accustomed to. I am a hunter and a tracker. I find the lost, and I'm good at it. Some of my ability is because of the way I am made, some of it is just trying to think ahead. I'm also lucky sometimes, too. But this time, I was late, not lucky.

Why she decided to leave was not my concern. Some say it was grief. I understood, though, why she wanted to come back home. I don't know why some want to leave. Most understand leaving usually doesn't end well. Still, it's better not to ask too many questions. I do what I am told to do.

By the time I got there, she had been dead for most of a day. What a shame. I liked her, and she would be missed by so many. The area near her body was torn up. I had been following the tracks of a huge grizzly, and I could see where he had detected the presence of her. He was not a particularly thoughtful bear. It looked like he had simply caught her scent, and then broke into a run right at her. That seemed odd to me. Bears don't usually act that way. This must be some brainless brute of a male bear. By the time I got to the scene, it looked like she had put up a valiant fight. She was never much of a fighter. We all knew that. Her mate was a big male grizzly and a fierce fighter, but he had been killed months before. She didn't have a chance, but as I read the scene, I was proud of her. She fought as hard as she possibly could, and a lot harder than I thought she was capable of.

And then I knew why. There were the tracks of a cub. I didn't know there was a cub. I doubt any of us knew. And it was obvious from his tracks he had been running fast. The bigger bear probably wanted to kill the cub. Male bears do that sometimes.

Moving further away, I saw real trouble. Horses were part of the fight. That meant people were part of this, and I didn't much like it when people got involved. It made things tricky.

Reading the track, it looked like the people were brave, too. There was a big one and a little one. The tracks of the big one sunk deeper into the soil. That's just basic tracking. The little one was probably a child or a smallish female. He or she was at least a hundred pounds lighter. The tracks never lie, understanding what they say is the hard part. And those tracks told me the heavy one stood down the big grizzly and forced him to leave the scene. Those tracks also told me they probably had the cub. I would bet my life on it. They may have rescued it or captured the cub. It was hard to tell what they were doing.

I wouldn't be bringing the mother back, but I would have to bring the cub back even if it didn't want to go with me. The cub couldn't be very big, so it ought to be somewhat easy. The truth is, that little bear isn't made to live in ignorance. Nothing good could come out of lifelong captivity. It's certainly not made for slavery or to live out his life in a cage. And I could not let the cub get too used to people. The little bear would only be confused. That wouldn't do.

There were a couple of problems, though. First, I hate to deal with people. I prefer to work alone. Second, people are smart and arrogant, and they're nearly always trouble. I would have to think this one through. I knew, though, I had to get involved sooner rather than later. I didn't like to be forced into situations, but I was thinking that this time I had no choice.

On top of that, there was another problem. Those folks should have shot and killed that killer grizzly. It looked like he was following them.

CAN I KEEP HIM? – SAM

We made sure the cub was nestled into one of Jet's saddlebags. The cub didn't want to leave Libby, but I was afraid he would fall off the saddle and get trampled by the horses' hooves. Also, I didn't like the idea of Libby having just one hand on the reins. So, we put him in the saddlebag with a blanket, and we set out for home. The farm was a long way off, but Jet and Hershel were good for it. We set a pretty fast pace just to put some distance between us and Goliath. For some reason, Goliath wanted to kill the mother bear. He may be mean, but he has been out here for years, coexisting, more or less, with the other bears. I suspected there was a reason.

Libby probably didn't appreciate how close we came to getting killed. What I did was actually stupid on my part and mighty dangerous for both of us. It is almost always better to let nature take its course. Nature can be brutal and it often is. The English poet Tennyson once wrote that nature was "red in tooth and claw." He was spot on right.

Some people, especially those in the towns, tend to overlook that part. They think nature is something it is not. They think nature is sweet, but in reality, it's brutal. Several times, I have been asked by Captain Hamby of the State Patrol or Sheriff Tuttle to search for hikers who haven't come back. Hershel and I have found a number of those lost hikers. Several times, there wasn't much left of them because either the weather killed them or some animal took them out.

Of the ones I found alive, I was usually aghast at how ill prepared they were. They had food enough to eat, and around here, the creeks are clean enough to drink from, but all they usually had to protect themselves was a bell, a whistle, or a pocket knife. That is pure foolishness. The lands around here have grizzly bears and black bears, wolves, cougars, moose, elk, poisonous snakes, bad bugs, and some big coyotes. If people who come out here don't like firearms, they ought to at least have a few cans of bear spray. Bear spray usually works a lot better than guns, and it doesn't kill the bear. It works on other types of dangerous animals, too. To come out here poorly prepared invites tragedy.

The grizzly bear has had a hard time of it. They have been hunted from the beginning of time, and most people have misunderstood them. Some folks believe they are sweet and kind, others think they are the devil incarnate. They are neither. Grizzly bears are bears, and they have bear thoughts. Some are more pleasant than others, some are cranky like Goliath. Most bear problems, though, would go away if people didn't love them or hate them but just respected them. I always give them room, and they usually do the same for me.

The big mistake people make is to think bears are like dogs and that feeding them is okay. It's not. In fact, it's just outright crazy. Why anyone would want an 800-pound animal to view them as a food source is beyond me. It breaks my heart when I see folks out here feed bears in their back yards, and then call the FWP when they keep coming back for food. Those poor bears just become dead bears.

I have hunted all my life and have decided bear hunting is not for me. Other people do and I cast no judgment on them. But as for me, I enjoy watching these smart beasts, though always from a distance. That doesn't mean I haven't had to shoot a few bears. I have. And I hated every second of it. But I preferred my life to theirs.

After about an hour of some hard riding, I looked over at Libby and at the little cub. He had managed to stick his head out of the saddlebag. There he was, cute as a speckled pup, standing in the saddle-bag with his head out in the wind. He was staring straight ahead with his ears perked up and his nose working the breeze. I would swear he felt he was safe. Then, I watched as he looked at Libby. He stared at her with his brown fur blowing around, and I saw her fall in love with that little grizzly. *That's going to be a problem*, I said to myself.

A few hours from home, we stopped in a nice setting called the Elk Pen. The Elk Pen was a beautiful meadow where elk would gather before winters. We crossed through a cold, crystal clear stream, and stopped to let the horses get some water and cool off and to give ourselves a rest. I hopped off and held the little bear, while Libby got off Jet. I thought he would try to bite me or to get away; that's what wild animals do. This little guy was different, though. Even though he was young, he was still strong. But he didn't fight me. In fact, he acted more like a puppy. I liked that.

I walked around, glassed the area with my binoculars, and watched our back trail again. I watched the back trail because it was a smart thing to do. If something or somebody is tailing me, I need to know about it. As for our stopping place, I was looking for more bears, of course, but even an elk or a moose could ruin your day. They could also run off the horses. I don't think Hershel would run off on me, but I didn't want to be careless and find out. I would hate to have to walk home cradling a bear, even a little one.

After a few minutes, we both felt safe enough to sit and relax for a while. Jet and Hershel drank their fill and moved out of the creek onto the bank close to us. They looked at us, and then started cropping the thick green grass that grew next to the creek. Libby and I stared at the cub. He was a good-looking little bear. Libby described him as *adorable*. She was right. He was a cutie.

He stayed very close to us and wouldn't leave. Finally, he wandered over to the creek and got a drink, then he turned and ran right back to us. Even the horses seemed to like this little guy, and neither of them were fans of bears. Except for a few of our dogs, the horses were pretty biased against all meat eaters. All of a sudden, Libby gushed, "Dad. He is such an amazing bear. Can we keep him?"

There. She said it. I was waiting for it. It was out there now. How we could begin to keep and shelter a growing bear was something I had no clue about. In fact, most people knew next to nothing about raising grizzly bear cubs. Even I knew very little about the care and feeding of grizzly bears.

I didn't answer. If we did keep him, we could probably only keep him for a few weeks. I just sat watching the little guy play at our feet. Finally, I looked at Libby and said, "You are right about him being an amazing bear. What about a name for him?"

Libby looked at me. I continued, "The pioneers and trappers of the old west called grizzlies by the name of Old Ephraim and Moccasin Joe. They would say something like 'Moccasin Joe came by the creek this morning.' Everyone would know what that meant. Blackfeet tribal lands used to be near here. They had a few words for bears. I remember the words *kaiyi* or *kaiyo*. Those words also meant 'one who is lost,' and that little guy is sure lost. I'm not wild about the names Old Ephraim or Moccasin Joe, but I like the Blackfoot names. Let's call him one of those. What do you think?"

The little bear perked up when he heard me talking.

"Dad," Libby stated as respectfully as possible. "How you know stuff like that is just weird. I'm not even sure you're not making it up. But even if you're right, those aren't the right names. They're okay, but they don't mean much to me or probably to anybody but to you and the Blackfoot tribe. Do you remember my first teddy bear, the one I called Happy Bear? Well, I want to call him Happy Bear. Can we?"

I looked at my sweet daughter looking back at me. She was growing up so fast. If that was what she wanted, then it was okay by me, but it sure didn't seem right. "It's your call, Libby, but do you think that name will stick with him as he gets bigger? He's a cute cub right now, but it won't last. He's still a grizzly, and they are pretty ferocious animals."

Libby looked at him and said, "I like Happy Bear."

I laughed and said, "Good thing he doesn't understand English. I think he'd be insulted."

The Ride Home — Libby

Nearly every farming family has rules about naming the farm animals. The first rule is never give a name to any of the farm animals you might end up eating. It's weird and really sad when it happens. "Oh Libby, the hamburger you're eating used to be Bessie." That is just about as bad as it sounds.

The second rule is if you do name an animal, then they're really hard to get rid of. So, if you raise a lamb to show in the county fair and give her a name and spend lots of time with her to make her ready to show, well, before long, you're going to be pretty fond of her. At that point, eating her is out of the question, and selling her is just too hard. Watching them get carted away is heartbreaking.

Best of all, Dad just named the bear. Well, he tried to. I named him. He didn't say no about keeping it, either. He didn't say yes, but things were definitely looking up.

When that little bear stood in the saddlebag and looked out, he was so cute. Watching him here play in the grass, he was even cuter. My mind raced. The Latin name for grizzly bears is *Ursus arctos horribilis*. Dad taught us the grizzly bear is the same as the brown bears that live in Europe, Asia, and here in North America. The European settlers who were only accustomed to black bears had a lot more trouble with the grizzlies. Grizzlies were bigger, stronger, faster, and didn't always run. Lewis and Clark had trouble with a few of them, as well. Rightly or wrongly, the grizzly bears got a nasty reputation, and somebody added the word *horribilis* to describe grizzlies. I guess, if they ran into a bear like Goliath, it would make sense. But I've lived in grizzly country all my life and the name *horribilis* is, for the most part, undeserved. I looked at the cub and he looked back at me. I laughed out loud. That was no horrible bear. Dad looked at me and smiled. It was like he knew what I was thinking.

HOME – SUSAN

Sam and Libby had been gone overnight, and I was a little nervous. That was not unusual. Mothers get nervous about things like that. Cell phones don't work way out here yet, and not hearing from them for over twenty-four hours was just disconcerting. But it was certainly not a rare thing. Sam has had to leave overnight frequently. But Sam's taking my firstborn with him was a relatively new thing. I wasn't used to it and I didn't know if I ever would be. Libby was mature for her age and she had always been extremely independent. Keeping her here at home with me *just because* was not going to happen. I comforted myself knowing everything would be fine, and that this trip would not be any different than the others.

Dean came and had that look on his face. Dean was only thirteen, but he was as gifted as a lawyer at explaining why he should get his way. Conversations with him were nearly always interesting. I could usually see where he was headed and would prepare myself. I marveled that he was only thirteen. I could only imagine what he would be like as an older teenager. I just hoped I could hold my own.

He started. "Hi Mom. Wow, you look great today."

Uh oh, I thought. *Here it comes.*

He then said, "I know you are proud of me doing my chores and most of Dad's, too."

Hmmm. "Okay," I replied. "I guess I'm proud of you."

He continued, "And it's only two o'clock and the cows don't need milking until five. So that means I will be doing Libby's chores, too, if she doesn't get back in time. So in the next three hours, I can watch some TV or help you clean the house which would mean I have to work all day. I could also maybe play some violent video games. Or, I could go fishing. I'll even catch our dinner."

He looked at me for a second, but he didn't let me respond. He rarely did.

"And even better, why don't we all go? I can tell you are worried about Libby and Dad, and you and Gracie joining me would keep your mind off those unnecessary worries. They'll get here, but your pacing around the house is no good."

Oh, he was good. I smiled and congratulated his well-reasoned argument. I also didn't comment on his flattery, but I did appreciate it.

Our family is as emotional as any other family, but Sam and I have learned that a reasoned argument is always less hurtful and more productive than arguments based on emotion. Appealing to reason was also like exercise for the brain. We also knew emotions can't be trusted. So, if our children wanted something we were not inclined to give them, they knew getting mad or throwing a tantrum was going to get them nowhere and really fast at that. So, they have been taught the best way to get their way is via a reasoned argument. And Dean was a master of the reasoned presentation.

On top of that, a little outdoor time was actually a good idea, too. I needed to be distracted from thinking about Libby and Sam, and being with the kids fishing on this beautiful day would work nicely.

Dean was as cute a boy as they come. He was intensely loyal to the family and very protective of his sisters. For a thirteen-year-old, he was tall, very strong, and mighty quick both in body and in mind. He did have an ornery streak, and sometimes he and his sisters fussed, but that was fully manageable. My one big concern was that he was also far too brave for a boy of his age. That was a tremendous concern to his father, too. Sam's desire was to train the bravery while discouraging his foolhardy behavior. Well, that was sure easier said than done.

"Go get the poles," I said.

Dean was gone in a flash. I cleaned the kitchen, as Dean clomped around the house. This kitchen had been completely remodeled a few years back. Now it was big, open, friendly, and beautiful. I did love this place.

A little whimper broke my daydream. There before me was my eight-year-old, Gracie. Dean had awakened her from a nap and told her we were going fishing. I wasn't pleased with his timing, but she looked so cute. There's nothing like bedhead in the afternoon to make a mother's heart skip a beat or two.

Gracie is best described as walking, talking, self-aware joy. She rarely whined, but she always managed, somehow, to get me, her dad, or her brother or sister to do her chores, or make her meals, or find her misplaced items. Sam and I saw this in her. We just marveled at how we crumbled under her good-natured assaults on our resolve to get her to be more self-sufficient. Sam would often chuckle that Gracie would be the most successful of all of us. I didn't doubt that for a minute. While she was a pretty little girl, her gas tank was filled with pure, high-test personality.

"We goin' fishin'?" she asked.

"Yep," I said back to her. "We goin' fishing. Go get dressed."

Gracie looked around, and then back at me. "Mom, can you help me find my boots?"

I laughed because I knew it was coming. Pretty soon thereafter, our two dogs Moose and Major, let me know that it was time to go. They saw Dean walking in and out of the barn, getting ready. Both dogs were powerfully built and they were made for this life. Moose was a mix between an Argentine Dogo and an Anatolian Shepherd. He looked like, and was, the perfect watchdog. Sam called Moose our *designer dog*. We needed a mix of size, strength, and the desire to hunt and herd. Moose was ordered that way. He also was very protective. Several times, he kept Gracie from heading toward the forest just to the south of the house. It was here the forest stood closest to the house. All the children were told to stay clear of those woods. Sometimes I would watch Moose and Major catch a scent, and both would move quickly and stand between the house and the forest. There they would just look into the forest and growl. It didn't happen much, but it was still creepy enough for Sam to lay down the rule that no one goes into the Southern Forest without an adult. In fact, leaving the farm at any place without an adult was not allowed.

Major was a different breed and he was equally tough, though not as big as Moose. Sam called Major the miracle mutt. Major was a rescue dog. They told us he was a shepherd mixed with something else. We had him tested, and they were right. Major was a mix between a large German Shepherd and a Carolina Dog. Carolina Dogs are also called American Dingoes. That part enabled Major to run for hours and trail the faintest scent trail. Major was a hunter first and a shepherd second. When Sam would leave the farm, it was Major who usually went with him. Moose protected us here, and Major protected Sam out there.

Within a few minutes, Dean had loaded the UTV and had pulled it around to the back door. Our UTV was like a golf cart on steroids. The dogs had already hopped in the back. It always looked funny when they rode the UTV side by side. It made me laugh. I looked back at Dean and marveled how he had started to look like a grown-up. "Gracie," he yelled past me. "Don't forget the duck food. The ducks will be waiting."

"Okay," she said. "But can you get them for me?"

"Of course!" he said. He looked at me and winked. We were all just bit players in Gracie's world.

Living on a farm out here in the west was a delightful thing. But it was not necessarily a safe place. Along with the fishing gear, I packed bear spray and a rifle. We live in wild country, so we have to be aware of bears, cougars, and wolves. These lands can also have the most dangerous animal of all—people. Most people we see out here are generally okay. They're usually oil company workers or lost hikers. We see hikers a lot in the summer. But some of the people are drifters, some are poachers, and some are worse. Sam had close call years ago with a couple who tried to ambush him while he was out hunting. So I am prepared for the worst. What else can I do? We are a safety first type of family. The closest policeman is usually more than thirty miles away, and that simply won't do.

About a mile and a half from the house is one of the three good-sized ponds we use to water the cattle, goats, and alpacas. Each pond is creek fed, and they are all deep and somewhat clean. I wouldn't drink out of them, especially the pond the cattle use, but the fish that come out of them are big and good to eat. We also don't swim in the cow ponds. Cows just aren't particularly clean animals. Anyway, we stocked the ponds with bass, bream, and catfish a few years back, and let nature take its course.

The minute the UTV pulled up to the pond, a short parade of wild ducks and our own farm ducks came waddling up. The wild ones know this farm is a safe place. Sam never, ever hunts on the part of the property that is within a mile radius of any of our cultivated fields or pastures. The dogs have been trained, so there is no chasing of bears, deer, moose, or elk unless they are in the fields. But the woods around us are thick with wildlife. For the most part, the wild animals have learned to avoid those places where they get harassed by the dogs. Wild animals will also move out of areas where they are hunted, if they have a choice. Sam said someday we may be bottled up here, and we may need to hunt here. I didn't know what could possibly bottle us up out here, but if it mattered to him, it mattered to me. Also, I love the fact our place resembled a wild life sanctuary.

While I was enjoying the time with Gracie and Dean, in the back of my mind, I was worried. Where were Libby and Sam? They were already two hours late.

2

NAMES MATTER — LIBBY

I hate being late. And we were late. Mom was always patient and forgiving, but Dad and I understood we should never selfishly cause her to worry. If we tell Mom we'll be back at two o'clock, or three o'clock, or whatever, it's up to us to meet that time. Besides, I also hate being late. Being late is a sign of a sloppy mind. I read that somewhere.

We took our time at the creek resting because we were only a few hours from home. While we were there, I was still thinking about the name. I liked the name Happy Bear despite what Dad thought. Happy Bear was every bit as cute as a teddy bear. As it turned out, I didn't call the cub by the name Happy Bear for long. We changed his name to Kaiyo, and with good reason. Strangely enough, it changed because of the arrival of an aggressive mob of thirsty, creek-wallowing bison.

We didn't know anything about the bison at first. I did notice that Kaiyo had gotten really antsy and very vocal. He tried to push me up and off the grass. I didn't know what he was doing then, of course. Dad and I thought he was just being a bear cub, and was hungry or just playful. Kaiyo even went over to where Jet was grazing, grabbed the reins in his little mouth, and tried to lead Jet over to me. Jet didn't appreciate that and she pulled back quickly. That quick move sent the poor little cub tumbling backward. Kaiyo stood and growled at Jet. Dad and I looked at each other. Kaiyo tried to grab Jet's reigns again, and Jet gave him the same treatment. Kaiyo bawled but quickly turned his attention back to us.

As we were watching Kaiyo and trying to figure out what he was doing, Jet and Hershel both pricked their ears up, turned their heads quickly, and looked over us to the west. A few quick moments later, we heard grunts and the low rumble of hooves. Dad didn't even look. He shot to his feet, and while grabbing Kaiyo, he looked back at me and said sternly, "We gotta go!"

I looked behind me and saw a wall of dust, hooves, and horns coming our way. Dad was right. Gotta go!

I was scared, but I knew what to do. I leapt to my feet and darted to Jet. Hats off to good horses. Jet saw the herd of bison coming and she still waited for me. Jet had to have been scared. What a great horse.

Dad was cradling Kaiyo, and with a quick jump, he was already up on Hershel. Dad turned Hershel, raced toward me, and in one quick motion, he passed Kaiyo to me. It was like a hand off in football. He pulled out his rifle and charged toward the bison. I heard him shoot twice to get their attention and slow them up. I spurred Jet, and we went fast back through the creek and kept running in the only direction that had no bison in view. Kaiyo was in my lap, facing me and holding on to me. He was looking past me at the bison coming our way. He was tense. After a few seconds of hard running, I could sense he had relaxed. I knew then we were safe.

Soon, Dad came riding up next to me to make sure I was okay. We kept riding eastward just to get a little more distance between us and the bison. They had claimed the creek for their own. They spread out in the creek and started drinking their fill and cooling off. They were no longer interested in us. I just started to laugh. It was nerves, I guess, but then Dad started laughing, too. We needed a good laugh and we enjoyed ourselves. Close calls are pretty normal, but this one was probably more frightening than close. Those big, dim-witted beasts just wanted some water and to force some distance between us and them. And they got it.

After our laughing died down, we had no option but to wait for the buffs to clear out. They were between us and home. And they were in no hurry. While waiting, Dad looked at Kaiyo. Then Dad said something interesting. "That little bear tried to warn us."

We quickly recalled what Kaiyo had done just before those buffaloes so rudely asked us to leave. We were both convinced that Kaiyo had indeed tried to warn us. Dad continued. "In fact, he did everything in his power to tell us we were in danger. If he had run away, that would have made sense. But he didn't. He stayed and risked getting trampled and killed. Wild animals simply do not ever do things like that. Shoot, even dogs rarely ever do things like that. And he was mad at Jet for pulling back, remember that? This little guy here is a hero."

Dad got quiet and looked over at Kaiyo. Then he looked back at me, and said "There is something very different about that bear. I don't think any other cub or any other animal would have done such a thing. Amazing."

Dad's voice trailed off. He just sat on Hershel and watched Kaiyo sit on my saddle and look back at him. "He may not get it, but he deserves a stronger name than Happy Bear."

I had to agree with Dad. When the cub reared back in anger at Jet, he didn't seem like a teddy bear type. And he didn't run when he could have gotten safely away. "So Dad," I said. "I think I like Kaiyo better than Kaiyi. It's easier to say and it means the same thing, right?"

"I think it does," Dad answered.

From then on, *Kaiyo* it would be. I felt better about the name, too. Names matter. Maybe not so much for animals, but they matter for people. Parents should be careful about the names they choose for their children.

About an hour later, the bison started drifting back to the far meadow to graze. We picked our way through the few remaining beasts, and started our way back home. We were going to be late. I hated being late. But tell that to a few hundred bison because they don't care.

THE ADOPTION – LIBBY

It wasn't long before our farm came into view off to the west. We had been gone for a long time, and I was tired. Kaiyo was asleep in my saddlebag. Much had happened in the last twenty-four hours, that's for sure. Seeing my home was about the best thing I could see right now. I was tired, dirty, and hungry. I wanted a shower and something to eat.

Both Dad and I were concerned about Kaiyo. He had to be hungry. It had been hours since he was with his mother. He was probably very sad, too. I spent time praying we could take care of him. I didn't know how to feed him or even what we could do for him today.

The house and barn were about two miles away, but seeing home even in the distance gave me a much needed shot of energy. I looked at Dad, and he was looking off to the left. I followed his gaze and saw the UTV off in the distance, racing toward us. Well, racing is probably the wrong word. The UTV isn't particularly fast. But boy did it look full.

Dean was in the driver's seat, Mom was next to him, Gracie was in the back, and Moose and Major were standing on the back of the UTV with their tongues hanging out. I really didn't want to see those dogs right now. They were good dogs and obedient, but they have never been friends with bears. They have been trained to chase off anything that gets on the farm, and especially anything that could hurt any of us or any of the farm animals. They do a great job of keeping the farm clear of coyotes, foxes, the lone wolf or two, mountain lions, and bears. They are fearless and have chased off big grizzlies and treed mountain lions. Only rarely have I seen them somewhat fearful, and that happens when they stand guard against whatever it is that sneaks around the edges of the Southern Forest. It is rare enough when that happens, though, and I don't like to think of it.

Anyway, here they all came. Dad looked at me and said, "Stay here." He then spurred Hershel, and cantered directly at the family.

He met them about a hundred yards away. I watched as Dad hopped off Hershel and walked to the now stopped UTV. It looked like they were talking. I looked at Kaiyo who was wide awake and paying a lot of attention to the conference. He pulled himself out of the saddle-bag and onto my lap.

A gust of wind came from behind me and blew right at the UTV. I watched the dogs catch Kaiyo's scent. I didn't like what I saw, but I expected it. The dog's attitudes switched immediately. They went right into hunt mode, and they tried to jump off the UTV. Dad must have figured that was going to happen, so he had already tied them to the UTV. That probably saved Kaiyo's life. They were just doing what they were accustomed and trained to do.

In just the past few hours, Kaiyo had experienced some close encounters. Poor thing. He actually looked fine, though. I looked back up and watched. Dad took up their leashes, hopped back up on Hershel, and stayed put. That freed up the humans in the UTV, and they came right up at us. Kaiyo and I sat and waited. As they got closer, it was obvious from their expressions that Dad told them about Kaiyo.

The UTV had barely come to a stop when Dean bounded off and ran over. He knew enough about wild animals to slow down a few yards before he got to us. He knew animals tend to run away from anything fast that comes at them. But not Gracie. She ran right past him. She apparently didn't know about animal fear at all. I expected Kaiyo to try to get away or hide from them, but once again, I under-estimated the little bear. He was clearly interested in the unfolding scene. Gracie was first with "Can I hold him?"

And from behind her, Mom replied, "Not so fast. Nobody holds that bear!"

Dean then calmly stated out loud to no one in particular, "Except for Libby, Dad, or me!"

Mom came and looked at Kaiyo. There he was, sitting on the saddle in front of me as he looked down at Mom. "So," said Mom. "This must be the little bear that tried to save you two from the buffalo."

I must have looked confused. "Dad told us," she said.

"He didn't try to save our lives, he did save our lives," I quickly replied back to Mom.

After a few seconds, Kaiyo reached out to Mom and cried out. Instinctively, Mom extended her arms toward the little bear. I watched as Kaiyo jumped off of Jet and right into Mom's heart. Kaiyo was apparently good at that. As Kaiyo buried his face into Mom's chest and snuggled tight, Mom said out loud, "We need to get this poor baby some food!"

Then, Gracie and Dean sat in the field, cross-legged. They knew the drill. Mom brought over Kaiyo to each of them. Kaiyo clearly enjoyed sitting in both of their laps. It was odd how Mom's maternal instinct had just kicked in so fast. But there she was, cooing and talking baby talk. As for me, I was afraid Mom would have nothing to do with Kaiyo. I laugh that I ever worried about that.

Introductions – Sam

Standing there with the dogs allowed me to continue thinking about Kaiyo. If he wasn't hungry, he would be soon. It looked like he was too young to only eat meat or other solid food, so he would have to be bottle-fed. That was becoming obvious. But we had no bear milk, and probably no one else did either. I did know that plenty of folks and organizations had fed baby bears, and the answer was probably online.

I know it is an everyday thing, but I am old enough to still be astonished with my little cell phone. I have ready access to the accumulated and increasing knowledge of the world. The fact I can get it in seconds is just as amazing. Some idiot has probably put the plans for an atomic bomb on the web, and if I wanted to, I could probably print them out. Scary.

With all that, the good news is I know I can probably pull up dozens of good recipes to safely feed a grizzly bear cub. But first things must come first. I needed to reach out to our veterinarian Dr. Cindy. Her name was actually Dr. Cindy Rich, but everybody around here and in Radford just called her Dr. Cindy.

After their introductions, Susan, Kaiyo, and the kids came riding the UTV. Moose and Major just looked confused and started growling. The hair on their backs was up. That was a problem that had to be addressed.

I had Dean come over and hold the dog's leashes. I hopped off Hershel, and took Moose's leash and separated him from Major. Dogs are pack animals and are far braver in numbers than they are alone. They also don't think things out when they are in the pack. I know that sounds odd, but dogs think thoughts. They don't think people thoughts. They think dog thoughts. But they do think. We don't understand their thoughts, but they have them. Importantly, their thoughts support their natures. And I knew the dogs were protective of our family and of the farm animals. And they liked their roles. I could see it in their happiness.

Moose's nature was as a protector and a herder. I needed him to protect Kaiyo for as long as we had him. I didn't think Kaiyo would be here with us for very long, but I didn't want Moose or Major to tear the cub apart. That would just break everybody's hearts. So, Moose needed to meet Kaiyo.

I told Moose to sit, and Susan brought Kaiyo over. Major barked from his position with Dean, and I quickly chastised him. Dean took him farther back and away. Susan walked over to me and Moose. As Susan let Moose smell the cub, I was speaking to Moose to be calm. Then, Susan sat with Kaiyo in her lap. While Kaiyo was pretty cuddly with us, he was on his guard. Who could blame him? It took a few minutes, but Moose got the idea Kaiyo was family. And I think Kaiyo got the idea he needed to keep an eye on Moose.

We repeated the process with Major. This was a little different because Major was less of a herding dog and more of a hunter. It took him a little longer to get the message. But he got it.

That was important. I released the dogs, and told everybody I had to get to the house fast to figure out how to feed the baby bear. I hopped back on Hershel and raced toward the house. Moose stayed with the UTV. Major, being true to form, came with me. I needed access to our satellite connection and I needed it fast. Kaiyo needed to eat. Hopefully, Dr. Cindy would answer her phone.

HASSLES – LIBBY

Within two hours after Dad got home, Dr. Cindy drove from town with a supply of formula for Kaiyo. Having raised lots of infant and orphaned livestock, we had bottles and nipples galore. That sounds weird, but that's part of life on the farm. Unfortunately, some farm animals don't always make good mothers. So when a mother farm animal rejects her offspring, then it is up to us to feed and raise them.

Doctor Cindy was in the kitchen. There she explained that natural bear milk is higher in fat than nearly all other land mammals. Bear milk is about twenty-five percent fat. Whole cow's milk is only about six percent fat. So, feeding Kaiyo took some thought.

By the time Dr. Cindy got here, Dad had already ordered about a month's worth of ingredients for bear formula. Yes! That meant Dad was thinking Kaiyo would be with us for a while. I had already heard Mom and Dad talking about the difficulty of keeping a bear, and I understood. A grizzly is not a dog. Once they start to get big, they're not even as safe as a black bear, and black bears are not safe. I knew that. But I didn't want to think of it.

I watched as Dad, Mom, and Dr. Cindy prepared the formula. Kaiyo was playing with Gracie on the kitchen floor. The dogs would come and go, and I was pleased to see them come and nuzzle Kaiyo. Kaiyo was also watching the grown-ups make his dinner. He was enjoying Gracie. They were both babies, and they were being especially gentle with one another. Again, I was astonished he just didn't behave like a wild animal. It was also obvious he was very hungry.

Dad turned around and held the bottle. It was full. Immediately, Dean and Gracie said they wanted to feed him. He looked at me, and said to all of us, "I think it is only fair that the one who rescued Kaiyo ought to be the first one to feed him."

For a second, I thought he was talking about himself. Dad was the one who actually saved him. But Dad handed the bottle off to me.

I took the bottle and sat down. Kaiyo bounded out of Gracie's lap and jumped in my lap. In a second, he pulled the bottle to him and started right in. A moment or two later, he flipped on his back and held the bottle in his beautiful little paws. I steadied the bottle, but Kaiyo was in control. We all watched. The dogs sat and watched. Even the vet didn't leave. I think everybody and every animal in the kitchen was enchanted by the spell cast by this little bear. Doctor Cindy said what we all knew. "There's something different about that cute little bear."

We all knew that was true.

Within a few minutes, the bottle was drained. Kaiyo got up, burped, and crawled over and into Dean's lap. In a moment, he was fast asleep. Dean looked like he would do anything to protect the little bear. Little did Dean or any of us know that it would be all of us that would be protected by that bear. Right now, though, he just looked helpless.

HASSLES AND PROBLEMS — SAM

The scene in the kitchen was amazing, but reality crept in. Dr. Cindy motioned us to talk privately. She looked serious.

Dr. Cindy, Susan, and I headed out to the front porch. We had a wraparound porch that was a perfect place to sit and take in the world. It went all the way around the house. Even the dogs tended to sleep out there. Being protectors, that was where they felt the most comfortable.

Dr. Cindy spoke first. "I hope that you all don't get too attached to that little bear. There are laws that are in play here. In fact, keeping a bear is illegal unless you have a license. And getting a license for an American brown bear, a grizzly, is practically impossible."

I had been thinking about that. In truth, I didn't see us keeping a full-grown grizzly. That would be crazy. Those bears can be unpredictable, and they can kill even when they think they're playing. A well-known trainer was killed a few years back when his grizzly bit him on the back of his neck. One bite and it was all over. Only a few people, like Casey Anderson or Doug Sues, had bears for companions, but they had some amazing skills. We didn't have those skills. I just didn't want to turn him over to the authorities just yet. I didn't know when *just yet* would come, but it wasn't then.

"By law, I am going to have to notify the State Department of Natural Resources and Conservation," said Dr. Cindy.

Susan asked her what they would do. "Well, good question. I suspect they'll put him in a cage, pack him into a truck, and take him to a licensed rescue facility. There, they will keep him until a decision is made about placing him back in the wild or finding a zoo that might want him."

Susan was quick to respond, "That won't work. Kaiyo is obviously too little to be returned to the wild, and no zoo wants a cub that is so young. They need constant attention. They ought to be fed five times a day. The zoos have no staff to do that, and they are full of orphan bears."

I was pretty sure she was making that stuff up, but at least it sounded like she knew what she was talking about. I was impressed.

"And most of the places around here couldn't hold a big grizzly. I have seen them. They can barely contain the black bears."

Susan had a point there. Keeping a big grizzly in a cage was not an easy thing to do, especially because big grizzlies always want out of their cages. There was nothing like that around here. I saw Dr. Cindy nodding her head. She was thinking.

"Well," said Dr. Cindy. "There is one thing that might work. Go ahead and apply for a license. That means you will need to go to

Helena, and you will have to do it soon. I will hold off a day or two from reporting while you put together the application. Hopefully, the DNRC will treat the case differently. They will have to come out and visit and see what you have here to take care of the bear. That will take some time. They just might let you keep him, at least for a while. And I will support you fully. A bear needs open spaces, and you all have plenty of open space here. I would hate to see the little guy in a cage for the rest of his days."

"Done," I said.

We then thanked Dr. Cindy, and she headed back to Radford. We were lucky to have someone like Dr. Cindy pulling for us. She was a terrific veterinarian and was well-respected in town. Her credibility would be needed.

I called a friend and told him what we were doing. He wanted to be a part of it all. That was great. Tomorrow, he would pick me up and take me to the capitol. Tonight, I would print out the application, and Susan and I would get to work.

THE END OF DAY ONE – SUSAN

We sat out on the porch and talked for a while. Sam had filled out the applications and gathered all the documents he thought he would need. He was exhausted. Just this morning, he and Libby had woken up in the Eastern Wilderness and wondered what the day would bring. Now, nearing midnight, my three children and a baby grizzly were curled up in Libby's room fast asleep. Moose was also in there standing guard. Major was out here with us.

We sat together and listened to the night. It was a moonless night and quite still. Off in the distance, coyotes called out to one another. I heard a wolf call out farther away still. Wolves don't like coyotes and will kill them. The wolf's howl shut the coyotes up, at least for a while. A few whip-poor-wills called to the night. It was our music. We also heard the far away low hum of motors and metal clanking. The slightest breeze could hide that sound. Sam looked at me, chuckled, and said, "That sound never gets old."

True. I thought finding oil on our property would change our lives for the better, and it did. Sam was able to buy some of the neighboring lands, and that allowed us to farm a much bigger parcel of land. There were a few tracts that were next to ours we didn't own yet, but we were surely blessed. I had always heard residual income was a good thing, and it is. We get paid something every month from those oil wells. The income from the wells isn't so much we could just quit. Farming is still our main activity. While we aren't super rich in money, we are super rich in so many other things. Still, those oil wells have changed our lives. Something told me Kaiyo was going to change our lives even more.

Sam and I then prayed. We gave thanks that Sam and Libby survived their run in with Goliath, we gave thanks for the tremendous opportunities we had, and we prayed for Kaiyo's happiness. Our being able to keep him, even for a short time, was a long shot. Then we prayed for protection from our enemies, known and unknown.

It was good we did, too. Enemies were coming. And we would need God's help.

The End of the Day — Tracker

It had been a long day and the light was beginning to fade. Slipping past the big grizzly hours earlier, I followed the riders. Their tracks eventually led me to a farm. Following them was simple. They did nothing to hide their tracks. Most people don't. But I could see where the big one would pull aside and watch his back trail. A man who watches his back trail is a smart man. A man who hides and waits while watching his back trail is a smart man that lives. Neither man nor animal can ever safely assume they are not being followed. And based on the tracks, the big one was careful. He was also teaching the little one to slide behind a patch of trees or behind a bramble bush and watch the back trail. They obviously didn't see the big bear. But he had been hanging way back, probably well out of sight. I was hoping the big bear would change its mind and leave them alone.

I needed to figure out what sort of place we had here. It looked like a farm, a big farm. I decided to spend some time getting to know this place. It could take a few days, but that was fine with me. I didn't want to go back just then anyway. And I was really tired.

3

THE WAKE UP – LIBBY

Do you have any idea what it's like to wake up on a summer morning with a bear cub sleeping in your arms? In your own room? Well, it's amazing.

Dean had woken up and crawled to the edge of the bed. Gracie was probably good for another two to three hours of shut-eye. She hated to wake up. Not even a grizzly bear cub in the room could coax her out of her slumber. Gracie didn't even like to wake up for Christmas. Dean and I would be up by 5:00 a.m., ready to get Christmas started, but not Gracie. My parents told us we couldn't come get them or go downstairs until Gracie woke up by herself. I think they did that on purpose.

Dean and I whispered because Gracie was crabby as a bear in the mornings. We were just hoping Kaiyo wouldn't be as crabby as Gracie when he woke up. We just couldn't deal with two life forms being as crabby as a bear when they woke up, especially when one of them was a real bear. Kaiyo was destined to grow quickly. Both Dean and I prayed he would be sweet, not only when he woke up, but the rest of the time, too.

Dean reached out and scratched Kaiyo behind the ears. Kaiyo rolled on his back, grabbed Dean's hand with his paws, and then put Dean's fingers in his mouth. Kaiyo sucked his fingers, and fell back asleep. Dean just loved it. He looked like a proud little daddy. To be honest, I think Dean would be a good big brother to Kaiyo. I just hoped he got the chance. I kept watching Kaiyo, and I fell in love. Again.

I could hear Dad and Mom downstairs. I heard them last night working on putting together documents so we could keep Kaiyo, at least for a while. I heard Mom tiptoe up the back steps and softly come down the hall. Mom was so light, she could almost avoid the creaking of the hardwood floors. When Dad came down the hall, everybody knew it. Even when he was barefoot or in socks, the wood planks just creaked and groaned under his weight. He couldn't sneak up on anyone upstairs.

Mom came to the door and opened it slowly. She had a bottle full of Kaiyo's breakfast in her hands. She handed the bottle to Dean, and he held it so Kaiyo couldn't see it. Then, she gently woke up Kaiyo. We held our breath. Our fear was the sweet bear of yesterday would have changed into something else, something more like the wild animal he was. He sat up, opened his eyes, shook his head, and yawned. He looked around and he crawled over to Mom and gave her a big kiss. He came to me and did the same. Then he sat and looked at Dean. I swear he knew Dean had the bottle. Kaiyo sat on his tiny haunches and held his paws high. Dean pulled out the bottle, handed it to the little bear, and Kaiyo fell back on his back and got to work on the bottle. He seemed to have woken up both sweet and hungry. Wow.

After ten minutes or so, Gracie woke up and quietly watched Kaiyo finish breakfast. She woke up nicely, and that was a small miracle. Dean, Kaiyo, and I had just dodged a bullet.

After Kaiyo was done, I picked him up and took him downstairs to go outside and go potty. Yep, that's what we called it. I figured if the dogs could figure it out, Kaiyo could figure it out. Dad saw us and he came out with us. Dad and I sat on the steps in the cool of the morning. We had done this hundreds of times before. It was our time. Many times, Dean would join us. Sometimes even

Gracie would come out, but that was rare. We just sat and watched Kaiyo investigate our front yard.

Dad looked at me. "You know what I am trying to get done today is a long shot, right?"

I told him I did. He described his conversation with Dr. Cindy and what we were trying to accomplish. He told me Davey Carter would be flying in by eight o'clock to ferry him to Helena. He asked if I had any questions, so I asked if Davey was any good as a pilot. We both got a good laugh at that. I told Dad I trusted his judgment and Mom's judgment. And it really did make sense to try everything we could.

Dad called Dean over and asked him the same thing. Dean, being Dean, wanted to go with Dad. Dean wasn't afraid of very much, and flying with Davey didn't faze him one bit. I didn't trust Davey's old plane as much as everybody else. I truly believed his wife was going to call us some night to say Davey never made it back, and could we go out and try to find him. Sometimes, I think Davey's plane had enough duct tape on it to load it down. He loved that plane, though. My prayer was it would make at least two more trips.

"Dear Lord," I prayed. "Please bring my daddy home."

Dean saw me pray. He winked and said he had already done so. Dean always encouraged me when I really needed it.

Dad then told Dean to get the UTV. Dean ran around the house and was gone in a blur. Kaiyo watched him go. I could tell he wanted to follow Dean, but I said "No." He stayed.

Dad smiled, hugged me, and headed inside to get his stuff.

Pretty soon, I heard Davey's plane coming our way. It wasn't hard to hear it or identify it. Davey's plane sounded like a tractor. I scooped up Kaiyo, ran through the house, through the kitchen, out the back door, and climbed into the waiting UTV. Dad, Mom, and Gracie came out and hopped on. Dean was driving. Dad carried his briefcase, and he wore a tie, a sport coat, khakis, and shiny leather shoes. He looked good. Kaiyo crawled out of my arms and sat in Dad's lap. With a dog at either side of the vehicle, we headed out to our grass airstrip at the northern edge of the farm. It was about two miles away, but we got there pretty quick. The dogs loved escorting us. Kaiyo took it all in.

By the time we got there, Davey had taxied close and motioned us to stay away from the propeller. We parked about twenty-five yards shy of the plane. Dad handed Kaiyo to me. He kissed Mom and told her to pray for the favor of Pharaoh. Dad was referring to the story of Joseph the Hebrew and how he had been sold into slavery by his brothers and resold in Egypt. He was falsely accused of a terrible crime and was thrown in prison. After several years, God inclined Joseph's captors to give him favor. After a while, Joseph was second-in-command in Egypt.

Whenever Dad has to deal with the government, he always prays for the favor of Pharaoh. It usually seemed to help, and we definitely needed help. Getting a license to keep Kaiyo would be tough.

I Hate That Plane — Susan

Davey jumped out of the plane, and came over and gave me a hug. Davey and Lisa have been some of our closest friends for years, but I still hated his plane. Davey was great. His plane just didn't generate much confidence.

Sam grabbed his briefcase, kissed the kids, and patted Kaiyo on the head. Then, he gave Dean the *you're the man of the farm* look which caused Dean to clench his jaw and look serious.

Dad whirled around and pulled himself into the plane. Davey then walked around and hopped in, too. They turned, taxied back to the beginning of the airstrip, turned around again, and headed right back at us while picking up speed. By the time they got even with us, they were aloft. The plane banked to the south and headed out of view. I hated that sight.

I turned around and looked at the crew. Dean spoke before I could. "Mom," he said. "I know we have animals to feed and stalls to muck out, and we'll jump right on it."

So far, so good, I thought to myself. "Okay, so what are you thinking?"

"Well," said Dean. "We think we ought to have Kaiyo with us while we work. Gracie can watch him as we work, and that way, he will get to know the animals. If we get to keep him, maybe he won't kill them when he gets big."

Where does he come up with this kind of stuff?

I was just hoping they would get to their chores without me having to raise my voice. So, I was all in. But I had to add, "Well, kids, maybe you all could also convince the farm animals not to kill Kaiyo while he's little. That's more likely."

They were horrified. I held back my laughter.

And so began one of the best days I have ever had on the farm. That includes the fact I was worried about Sam, his being in an airplane, and the business in Helena.

The Farm Meets the Bear — Libby

Work is a constant fact of farm life. This is especially true when a farm has both crops and livestock. Both types of farming require a lot of work. Each spring, we plant corn and wheat, peas, and beans of some sort. We also have alfalfa hay fields and a large garden for vegetables that are just for us and friends. The planting is hard, but fortunately, we have good equipment to help us succeed. Once everything is planted, we have to be vigilant against a host of attackers. It seems everything in the area wants to eat what we plant. Dad and Mom do a lot of research to figure out what is the best way to protect the crops. Neither of them want to use chemicals to kill diseases or bugs, but they'll use them if they have to. We try to change out the crops, even in the garden, so the soil stays healthy and the bugs don't become too much of a problem. We move the farm animals around, too, so the pastures can recover.

Our biggest problem, though, is not bugs or disease, it's the bigger animals who think the corn, beans, wheat, and hay are theirs for the eating. Rabbits love the garden, deer and elk love the beans and peas and pretty much everything else. From crows to raccoons and bears, all like to munch on the corn. We have trained the dogs to patrol the fields to chase out the bigger animals. They are allowed to kill any rabbits they catch, and sometimes that makes me sad. They are also allowed to kill anything else they catch in the fields. Usually, though, that just means they chase the bigger animals out past the fields and into the woods.

The deal is, if an animal makes it to the woods, they are safe. Those are Dad's rules, and the dogs get it. I have seen elk get chased out of the corn and race into the closest forest while Moose and Major are right at their heels. Once they get into the woods, they will turn around and watch as the dogs stand there and bark. The deer and elk and a few black bears have it figured out, too. It's a game to them. Raccoons have learned, if they can't get to the trees really fast, then they will have to fight the dogs because they can't outrun them. Raccoons are pretty tough, but they have learned not to venture into the corn very far. A few of them who did paid for it. They became dog food.

Several times each day, the two dogs go on dog patrol. If the wind is blowing from the fields, they will know if something is in there because they can smell their scent. Just by sniffing the air, they can tell if it's a bear, a raccoon, a deer, or an elk. If the wind is not blowing or if it is blowing toward the fields, then they go on patrol and use their eyes and try to get upwind. Moose is better at spotting intruders, while Major could smell a mouse from a thousand yards. That's a good team. That day, because of Kaiyo, the dogs stayed home. I am sure they were just being protective. The wind was also drifting from the southeast to the northwest toward the fields, so anything in the fields would be downwind and the dogs couldn't smell them. That decision by the dogs to stay put just might have saved our lives.

Back to Kaiyo. Anyway, after Dad flew off, we took Kaiyo to the main barn. The main barn was a big, two-story building that was actually quite beautiful. Dad modeled it after the barns he saw in Pennsylvania. Dad and Mom have traveled throughout Pennsylvania many times. Dad would say "P. A. has the prettiest farms and some of the best folks in the country." He never called it Pennsylvania, he called it just *P. A.* Even the big painted star on the barn was a typical feature of P. A. barns.

Once inside, the barn was well lit. To the right against part of the south wall, we had the coops for the chickens and the guinea fowl. They had small, wooden door flaps in the outside wall, and openings in the cages to come and go both outside or in the barn. The guineas were the oddest of birds. They looked strange and acted stranger. Chickens were a little more independent. The guineas almost always would hang together in a flock. And the guineas were noisy. The males could sound like a donkey at times. And when a fox or a snake or some other predator would come close, they would make a ton of annoying, hard to listen to noise. Moose and Major knew that when the guineas freaked out, then they had something to do.

Guineas can fly, but they would rather run. They are fast and they can nearly outrun a horse. The best thing about the guineas was, they tasted so good. Their meat is dark and healthy. Dad didn't want to eat them, though, because they ate an enormous number of bugs, including ticks. We rarely had to pull ticks off of the dogs. Once the garden was planted and the plants started growing, the guineas were encouraged to wander in the garden and fields, as long as they didn't get too far. Sometimes, Moose had to go get them and bring them home.

Farther into the barn, Dad had stacks of feed, tools, equipment, and other things useful for the farm. To the left side of the barn on the north wall were the horse stalls. We had eight stalls, but only five horses. When Gracie gets older, Dad will get her a horse, too. Dean's horse was a beautiful dun mustang gelding named Solo. Dean named him Solo because he would prefer to be with us than the other horses. Next to Solo was my mare, Jet. Then came Hershel. He was a beautiful chestnut bay with a mane and tail that looked like blond flax.

Next to Hershel was Mom's horse Cali. Cali was a spirited palomino Quarter Horse and a talented barrel racer. A few years back, Mom and Cali entered several rodeos in town. Mom even placed in a few of those events. If they practiced, they would be awesome. Mom just likes having a horse that is fast and can turn on a dime. She loved to have the dogs chase her and try to catch her. Quarter Horses are the sprinters of the horse world, and Cali was a good Quarter Horse. If the dogs got close, Mom and Cali would turn around and be headed the other way before the dogs knew what was going on.

In the last and biggest stall was Peyton. Peyton was only four years old, and he was one of Dad's horses. Dad said he was named after another great football player. Peyton was a shire. Shires are enormous horses with long, flowing hair all around their hooves. They are not very fast, which Dad said was true of the football player, but shires are smart and very strong. Dad said that was also true of the football player. This animal was impressive. He could pull tremendous weights. In the winter, he could pull the sled for hours. He was gentle, though. He and Hershel were pals. Several times, Peyton worked the fields when they were too muddy for tractors, and Peyton often pulled out stuck equipment, trucks, or four-wheelers. Dad used him to pull out boulders and stumps or for dragging or pulling logs. He loved to work.

With each group of animals, we would hold Kaiyo while one of us tended to the animals. The cub watched, as we fed and watered the chickens and the guineas. The guineas were not impressed with Kaiyo. They saw him once and had enough. They ran outside and clucked loudly. The chickens ignored him. The horses, though, seemed to accept Kaiyo. Kaiyo was allowed to sniff each horse and watch as we brushed and fed the horses and cleaned out the stalls. I don't know what he was thinking, but it seemed like he was enjoying himself.

We approached Peyton's stall last. Peyton was so big we were concerned he would frighten Kaiyo. Sure enough, Peyton's size did cause Kaiyo to retreat into my arms. But Kaiyo was paying attention. Dean went and got a big scoop of oats and placed it into Peyton's feeder. Peyton sniffed the oats but didn't start eating. That was a first. Instead, Peyton kept his eye on Kaiyo. Peyton had dealt with bears before, and he didn't like them. He had dealt with wolves, too. Peyton had the scars to prove it. But to this day, he has never lost a fight. He still will give chase when he sees a bear or a wolf. They all run away.

Just then, Peyton stretched his massive neck and head out to sniff Kaiyo. Every time I got near that horse, I was impressed at his size. He was like a dinosaur. Peyton was about eighteen hands or six feet at the top of his withers. The withers are the part of a horse's back just over his shoulders where the neck meets the back. Peyton's head would be three or so feet past that. And there were bigger shire horses than Peyton. So imagine Kaiyo being all of thirty-six pounds, getting inspected by an animal that weighed at least 2,500 pounds. Peyton was usually gentle, and he sniffed Kaiyo. Kaiyo sniffed him back. That was nice, especially because of Peyton's generally bad experience with bears in the past.

While Kaiyo was a little bear, he was heavy, and I should never have let Gracie hold him. That's too much bear for a small girl like Gracie. But she wanted to, and Dean and I had some work to do in the barn. So, we sat Gracie down and put Kaiyo in her lap. We had to go and fork some hay and take it to the stalls. We both headed to the back of the barn. Here, we stashed seven or eight hay rolls right by the big back door. Most of the hay was kept in the hay barn, but we kept enough in here for the horses and to spread on the floor of the bird coops.

When we got back, Gracie was standing up. Kaiyo was gone. We followed her eyes. We saw Kaiyo standing in Peyton's food trough, which was about five feet above ground, only about half of Kaiyo showed. The other horses were all leaning out of their stalls watching. They all knew Peyton and bears didn't mix. I was ready for Peyton to head butt Kaiyo and send him crashing to the floor. But he didn't. He just sniffed him. Kaiyo gave him a little nuzzle, and then he climbed over and he dropped himself into the stall.

That was not good! The hooves on that horse were as big as dinner plates and heavier than anvils. I knew Kaiyo would be crushed.

Dean moved fast, and he raced over to Peyton's stall. We were never allowed in Peyton's stall alone because he was just so big. He was sweet to us, but he could crush us and not even know it. Dean, however, was going in. I couldn't watch.

Gracie ran to the stall and threw herself to the floor and to watch underneath the lowest planks of the stall. She saw it all happen. As Dean was struggling to unlock the stall door latch, she saw Kaiyo walk on the floor and sit next to the edge by the wall. She tried to call him, but he ignored her. I was crying. Then Gracie screamed, as she saw a mass of brown hair block her view.

The latch was a little complicated. Dad made it that way because he didn't want us in the stall alone. Cleaning out Peyton's stall always required two people, one to lead Peyton out and into the barn and one to scoop the poop. We took turns holding Peyton and cleaning Peyton's big poops.

Gracie was now crying, so was I. This was all happening so fast. The dogs had just run in, and Mom was right behind them. She saw what was going on, and for a moment, was paralyzed with fear. She stood there and couldn't talk. Had I actually known what was going on with Kaiyo and Peyton, I would have savored the moment. That woman is never without words. But there she stood, mute as a statue. I'm not sure she breathed.

Dean ignored us, worked the latch open, threw open the stall door, and stepped inside. He then stepped right back out. I was afraid Peyton had turned Kaiyo into something that looked like road kill. Gracie couldn't look, but Mom ran over and looked around Dean and into the stall. A moment passed, and Mom smiled. I cried even harder when she smiled. I knew Kaiyo must have been safe, but the relief was too much. With tears flowing, I came over and saw Peyton on the floor. Kaiyo had crawled onto Peyton's folded front legs and was nuzzling Peyton's muzzle and neck. "That's something you don't see every day," Mom said.

Kaiyo then climbed on Peyton's back, and the massive horse stood up. We just stood there with our mouths open. What could be next?

Well, from the lofty perch on Peyton's back, Kaiyo spent most of the rest of the day as we finished our chores. Mom came twice, and took him inside to feed him. Peyton followed them and waited for them at the back doorsteps both times. Each time after eating, Kaiyo would make it clear to us that he wanted to be put back upon Peyton, and Mom would reach up and put him there. Kaiyo was little and the horse was huge, but that's what they both seemed to want. Mom just laughed. Remember when I said beauty followed Mom like a puppy? This was a beautiful sight.

We introduced Kaiyo to the pigs and to the cattle. He seemed unimpressed with the pigs, and they seemed to ignore him. When he met the cattle, he obviously didn't seem to like them much. We don't know why. Gracie thought they probably reminded him of the bison that he had seen the day before. Those were some pretty smart words from an eight-year-old. I think she had a point.

When we got to the alpacas, Kaiyo was definitely curious. We kept about forty-five alpacas in a series of pastures that we moved them in and out of. Of all the farm animals, nothing is gentler than an alpaca. Now, that doesn't mean they can't or won't defend themselves because they can. But these precious animals have been domesticated for thousands of years. We never eat them and I was glad, though I have heard they are good eating. They were raised for their top quality wool. Mom had several commercial purchasers and some friends who would buy the wool. Sometimes they would stay over and spin the wool into yarn, and then weave the yarns into simple clothes. Nothing is warmer or more beautiful than an alpaca wool scarf. Just before they would get a haircut in the early summer, the alpacas looked so hairy, poufy, and funny. The sight of them just made us laugh. I think even they thought they looked silly.

Because the alpacas were not ever part of our dinner plans, we usually gave them names. Right now, my favorite alpaca was a young cria named Rosie. Cria is the name for a young llama or alpaca. The early explorers thought the baby llama types cried like human babies cry, so they were named crias. Alpacas are related to llamas but aren't as big or tall, so keeping them on the farm was easy. We did have some trouble with the carnivores trying to get at them, but except for some random coyotes, we haven't had too much trouble with bears or wolves. The mountain lions tend to leave us alone, too. And the coyotes know the dogs will try to kill them, and we will shoot them if they're found chasing our alpacas. We have several coyote families that live around the farm, and they have figured out they are welcome to live and hunt around the farm but never on it.

Rosie was a very young, beautiful little cria. She could cry like a baby, too. Her mother was named Sunny, and she was the friendliest of the bunch. When Peyton was led over with Kaiyo riding his big back, Sunny didn't run away like the rest of the alpacas. She and Rosie stayed and watched. Dean brought over some hay and placed some alpaca pellets in the trough to feed the herd. Sunny walked over to the hay and started munching. Kaiyo was fascinated at these gentle beasts. He wanted down. Mom came over, and he jumped into her arms. She tried to hold him, but he acted all boneless and slithered out of her grasp. In a second, he was under the fence, and into the pasture he went. Kaiyo then went straight at Rosie. Rosie drew back, but Kaiyo pushed forward and sniffed her face. Sunny took a few steps toward the little bear, but she didn't panic. She watched as Kaiyo and Rosie got to know each other. Within a few minutes, Rosie and Kaiyo were all alone, meeting the other alpacas. Most of the alpacas were curious, and they met Kaiyo. A few were a little skittish but they were certainly not hostile. As a whole, it seemed the alpacas were all in favor of us keeping Kaiyo. At least, while he was little.

Watching these two animal babies, the cria and the cub, spend their time playing was the best part of the day. They played for the next few hours, and it was great. Each of us would have to slip away to do something running a farm required, but one of us always stayed and watched. Several times, we tried to lead Peyton away back to the barn and out of the sun, but he let us know gently but firmly that he would rather stay and keep an eye on Kaiyo.

Watching all this caused me to pause and pray Dad would get permission to keep Kaiyo. And more importantly, I prayed Dad would get back home safely.

THE DOG PATROL – SUSAN

It was getting to be later in the afternoon, and it was time for another feeding for Kaiyo. He and Rosie had to be tired. They had played and chased each other for hours, so I managed to catch Kaiyo and bring him inside. Peyton was led out to the horse pasture by Libby where he was able to graze and relax for a while. The kids had been busy working, and even Gracie had put in a hard day. It was time for a late lunch, and I heard nobody complaining about that.

Dean had made the bear cub formula, and he and Kaiyo were on the floor eating and watching TV. Both of them looked dead-tired and I suspected they were. Gracie had eaten and was curled up on the recliner. Libby came in and was smiling at seeing Kaiyo so comfortable. Just then, the phone rang. It was Sam.

Hearing from Sam was great. It certainly wasn't the first time he had been gone overnight, and everything was good here. He told me about the meetings he had today. He had two more meetings, but the most important one got pushed off for tomorrow. He would have to stay overnight. He was upbeat, though, and I was just excited listening to him. Davey had no problem staying another night, so it was all good. The only thing that bugged him was that both he and Davey had been in such a hurry this morning, they forgot their phone chargers. I told him nicely to go buy one. I hated the thought of not being able to call him. That was scary. He promised if he had enough time he would swing by the store. He was focused on the next meeting, and I wasn't confident he would go get the charger. I don't know why I cared. When Sam and Hershel go off hunting or exploring out wherever, they don't have cell phone coverage. I guess, to me, big towns are scarier places than way out here.

While I was talking to Sam, Libby made both of us lunch. Libby was sweet that way. She had a tendency to think of others. "Let's go to the front porch," she said. "It's nice outside." That sounded great.

Our wraparound porch was nice and wide, and it went around the entire house. From the porch to the ground, it was only about four steps, but cows don't like steps. Occasionally, the cows have gotten out of the pasture and some have found their way into the front yard. For whatever reason, the steps seem to stop them from coming onto the porch. Nobody ever said cows were smart. Anyway, our favorite place was the front porch. When sitting there, we could see down the driveway lined with power poles as it disappeared into the Western Forest two miles away. The Southern Forest was to the left, and to the right we could see the fields and the Northern Mountains in the distance.

Lunch was terrific. Who doesn't like an egg salad sandwich and plain potato chips? That was just pure comfort food. The weather was just short of perfect. Out here in the west, we were always thankful the humidity of our long-ago Georgia home didn't follow us. It is so true about it not being the heat but the humidity that could ruin an otherwise nice day. It was summer, the temperature was probably in the low eighties, and it was delightful, at least while we were in the shade. The sun sparkled as cotton ball clouds moseyed through the summer sky. The birds were fussy, but everything else was just another part of a peace filled day. Sitting here with my oldest daughter, I was just thankful. We talked together for at least an hour. The rest of the family was sound asleep. What a nice afternoon.

Our delightful time was rudely interrupted when Moose and Major came racing from the back of the house, down the driveway, and then right by the front steps and the two of us. They were barking at the tops of their lungs. Their speed was astonishing. Within a few seconds, they had cleared sixty yards of green lawn and then plunged headlong into the corn.

My parents were from Iowa, and I was born there. When my dad and mom were kids, they used to hear farmers say that if the corn was knee high by the Fourth of July, then the corn crop was on schedule. That sure wasn't true these days. Our corn stalks were already over four feet tall, and in some places, it was five feet high. It was thick, too. And Independence Day was only a few weeks ago.

Libby looked at me and said flatly, "Dog patrol. Hard at work."

The sight we just saw with the dogs was something we saw a lot of out here. The wind had shifted, and they had probably smelled a deer or an elk in the corn or in the fields beyond them. It was their job to keep the fields clear, and they seemed to love the work. It always gave me the creeps, though, watching them run into the corn. I think I had read too many scary books as a kid. Corn fields were usually profitable, but they sure were creepy. Having good dogs was definitely a necessity out here.

After a minute or so, I heard the dogs in a way I hadn't heard in a while. They sounded scared. A scared dog will still do its job, but their howls and barking will give them away. We listened, as we could tell a chase was on. A few moments later, we could tell whatever they were chasing had stopped to face the dogs. The dogs sounded like they were locked in a battle to the death. Our relaxed moods changed. Then, I looked at Libby. "Stay here with the kids, and keep the doors closed but not locked. I might need back in, fast! And don't wake up the kids but keep your rifle handy."

Libby looked resolute. I trusted her and was so proud of her.

I reached in the front door, grabbed my rifle, and ran down the side of the house to the barn. The UTV would be quicker, but I didn't want to go into the corn on foot. I needed a horse. Cali saw me coming and she was ready. I opened her stall, grabbed a bridle, placed it on Cali, grabbed the reins, and hopped on bareback. We often rode bareback. Saddles and stirrups were better, but it all took time and I had no time to spare. General Custer once described the bareback riding Sioux warriors as the best horsemen in the world. General Crook called them the finest light cavalry in the world. They didn't need saddles, and neither would I. I slung my rifle over my shoulder and headed out fast toward the far pastures. The horse pasture was close on my right, and Peyton was there at the fence listening to the dogs. He looked nervous and fierce at the same time. What was going on?

Off to northwest, I heard the dogs farther than they were when we first heard them. It sounded as if the fight had moved out of the corn and was making its way past the fields and toward the Western Forest. I turned into the tractor path and headed due west at top speed. Tall corn was on either side of me, as Cali and I flew down the grassy lane. The barking of the dogs started to get louder. I could hear them off to my two o'clock. I unslung my rifle and turned right at an intersecting tractor path and headed north. I checked my rifle. It was loaded and the safety was on. Just then, the dogs quit barking. I stopped and called out to them. I instinctively moved the safety in the off position. Sitting atop Cali, I had a good view. We were in the northwest section of the farm and a little over two miles from the house. It was just to the south of the rifle range. The western and northern edges of the forest were not far.

I called out to the dogs, and heard Major barking. He was chasing something big into the woods about a hundred yards to the west. Whatever it was, I heard it crashing through the forest. It sounded like a freight train. I was scared. But where was Moose? Then from about twenty yards away, I heard Moose. He was obviously hurt. After a few seconds, both he and Major came out of the corn. Major looked fine. He was bloody about the mouth but I am pretty sure it wasn't his blood. Moose didn't look so good. He had some rough-looking cuts along his ribs and one eye was already swollen. He could walk, at least. And I had seen him worse off.

I told them both to stay. Cali and I waded into the corn. I had to see what was causing this ruckus. I was scared, but I needed to know. Shortly, I came upon the scene of the battle. Whatever it was had decided to fight it out right here. The corn was torn up. Looking closer, I could see some clear tracks. They were the biggest bear tracks I had ever seen. Could this be Goliath? If so, it meant trouble. Even more important, why was he here?

I decided to back track Goliath's tracks. I assumed he was watching me right now, but I had faith Major and Cali could get me out of bear trouble if necessary. Now that I knew what I was doing, backtracking Goliath was not hard. He was very heavy and his tracks were deep and he had been running really fast. He also crushed a lot of the corn stalks. That made me mad. He was clearly running from the dogs when these tracks were made.

I followed his tracks for about a mile. Three times he had to pass tractor paths, but he had stayed in the corn. The thing that bothered me was that his tracks were leading me closer to the house. I followed his path back through to where he started, and I shuddered. When the dogs got wind of him, he was only sixty-five yards from our house. A big bear like Goliath could cover that distance in a few seconds. He was up to something. He wasn't trying to eat the corn. Not only were the corn cobs small right now, it was clear he was using the corn for cover. And he had been watching us. That alone was frightening. How long? I just don't know. Gosh, I loved those dogs.

Could a bear, even a mean, ill-tempered bear like Goliath hold a grudge? We had a few hours until nightfall and much to do. I wish Sam was here.

THE DOG PATROL – TRACKER

I had hidden myself all night and all day. Those dogs of theirs were big and fast, and they probably had some good noses. With the wind coming from southeast to northwest, I had headed to the north part of the farm to stay downwind. This was fine with me. The north part of the farm was higher than the rest of farm, and it gave me a lot of places to keep watch and stay hidden. The forest here gradually got higher and rockier as it got closer to the mountains. Small cliff sides appeared here and there, boulders and rock outcroppings were intermixed with the trees. The farther the land was from the farm the more rugged it got.

I started the day to the east of the pastures, and hid in the dense woods that surrounded most of the eastern and southern sides of the farm. I kept being amazed at the animal signs around here. It was obvious deer, elk, and moose were commonplace. I saw signs of a mountain lion and several bears. They looked like black bear tracks. That was good. I had not seen the tracks of the big killer grizzly, and I thought that was a good thing. I was hoping he had turned back.

The people who lived at this farm were definitely unusual. People are people, I know that. But people and farmers in general don't usually put up with wild animals. I don't agree, but I understand. The meat eaters can and will kill sheep or cows. The plant eaters can ruin a crop in just a day. An unprotected farm could be ruined in short order. Farmers who want to survive will often respond by shooting and poisoning. It is a war of sorts. But this place was different. I liked that. And it seemed, for some reason, the bigger animals stayed out of the farm. Past the pastures to the west, I could see what appeared to be several miles of corn and beans. Keeping that area clear of animals had to be a chore. Something told me those big dogs had something to do with it. I like dogs. They have a hard time figuring me out, but I have always felt a kinship with them.

From the beginning of time, man and dogs have lived together. It would seem they were made for each other. The word I heard when growing up was that man and dog were best friends right from the start. After the divorce, they somehow stayed friends. Perhaps, ordinary dogs learned men were messy and left scraps of food where they came or went. Maybe men caught and tamed wolf cubs and bred them with other dogs. Or perhaps, dogs decided hanging around a man and his campfire was just good company. We don't know how it has worked so well on this side, but what we do know is, for whatever reason, a dog would prefer the company of a man or woman to other dogs. There is no other animal like a dog. Even the other domesticated animals can go wild and happily avoid man. That makes sense. An ordinary bear likes to be alone. The typical wolf is ferocious and too powerful for most men to keep. They all have no need of man. But a dog? It's almost as if they were all emigrants from the homeland.

A cow gets used to people but they can't be trusted like a dog. And cows can go wild. It's not unusual for me to find tracks of cows and horses miles away from people. And pigs? They can go wild really quick. I saw pig tracks a few days before I started this search. I don't like pigs. They multiply like rabbits, and eat anything they can get their snouts on. They can be pretty mean, too. Several times, I have had to deal with a big boar and his slashing tusks. They definitely taste good, but they also make my job as a tracker even harder. They tear up the ground wherever they go. I find more and more wild pigs in my job as a tracker. It looked like it wouldn't be too long before they become a problem here. Eventually, they might need more than a dog or two to protect their farm.

Well, I have learned the farmers here and the local animals seemed to have figured out a way to live together, at least, so far. From where I was hiding, I could look past the huge pastures and see the barn and other out buildings. It looked like there were four or five of them. I could see part of the back and the north side of the house. It was very early, though, and no people were stirring. I could see the cows starting to wake up and some sheep and a small herd of alpacas. I like alpacas, especially to eat. They are gentle beasts and they taste good. They couldn't live without man's protection. If they ever decided to leave the pasture and venture out, every meat eater in the land would catch, kill, and eat them to the last one. My stomach growled.

I knew I couldn't go much farther south, and with the wind coming out of the southeast, a subtle shift in the wind might reveal my position to those dogs. That's why I went to the north side of the farm. It was farther away from the house but it was higher and downwind. Being downwind was critical.

The tricky part was, I would have to leave the protection of the forest and cross about a half mile of open ground. That shouldn't be too much of a problem because I was about two miles from the farm house and too far for the animals in the pastures to notice me. I would still have to be careful. If someone did see me out here, I definitely would be noticed.

I had found a few low ridges after leaving the forest that helped hide me. I was pretty fast and took advantage of my speed and stayed low and behind the low, grassy ridges. I have learned to never walk on a ridge. Doing that is called skylining and it allows your silhouette to stand out to anyone who's looking. You can get shot that way, too.

Everything was going nicely and I was about to cross the open grassland without worry. Then two things happened. As I headed north, I came across the trail that the farm people and their horses and vehicles use to go into and out of the Eastern Wilderness. The trail was muddy, and it clearly showed what I didn't want to see. Bear tracks, big bear tracks. I recognized these as belonging to the killer bear. I guessed he was still working out his little grudge. It looked like he was headed into the same northern woods as I was. I knew I would have to keep my distance from him. I suspect he would try to kill me if he caught me. But having him here may actually work to my advantage, especially if he has no idea I'm here. And I didn't think he did. But even if he sees me, I sort of look like I belong out here. But if I was to have a chance at catching that little bear cub, I would have to work fast.

The second thing that happened was the sound of a small airplane. With me out in the open, that was definitely not good. I abandoned any thought of hiding, and just depended on my speed and my distance from the farm house to stay unseen. I ran as fast as possible and made it to the edge of the tree line to the north, as the small plane came low over the trees at the western edge of the farm. While that part of the farm was still a few miles away, planes are fast. Most airplanes are fine, but I don't like all of them. I have seen them before many times, but it's the really small ones I don't much like. Several times when I was out on patrol in this or that wilderness, a plane would fly over really low and somebody would lean out of the window and take a shot at me. Crazy.

Then from my hidden spot behind the tree line to the north, I watched a small vehicle leave from the house. It had several people on it. Their dogs were running along it. The airplane circled and then landed some distance away. It taxied close to the vehicle. When it stopped, I saw the big one, the father, leave the family and get on the plane. After a few moments, the plane revved its engine, taxied back, turned around, gathered speed, and headed my way. It lifted off, gained altitude, turned away from the mountains behind me, and headed off. I crouched underneath my hiding spot and watched it disappear. The rest of the family and their dogs headed back home

Interesting. This might be my chance to snag that little bear and get us back home before I had to spend another night out here. Finding the way home would be easy for me. For the most part, I liked it. It would be the best thing for that cub. Some leave our homeland out of a sometimes fatal mix of curiosity, a thirst for more freedom, or a desire to experience danger. Both curiosity and freedom are virtues, but anything that is good can also be used for something bad. As a tracker, my job is to find them and help them find their way back. Most are happy to see me. It's tough out here. Some are so lost even I cannot find them. And of course, some get captured and some don't survive. Occasionally, some leave home because they are banished. My job is to find the lost and guide them home. And pretty soon, I knew I would need to go back.

I didn't have much of a choice about that big grizzly. I wasn't afraid of it. I had dealt with bad bears before, but this one seemed different. I had no doubt that if this bear caught me, it would try to kill me. Normally, that wouldn't be a problem. I am made and trained to detect bears well before they get to me. I am capable of dealing with a bear if we stumble upon one another. Most bears don't want to mess with me. I have forced many a black bear up a tree. Even grizzlies usually try to leave me alone. I try to leave them alone, too. Looking for trouble with a bear is a stupid rookie mistake. I have known a few trackers like me who either underestimated the speed and strength of bears or they made the mistake of thinking that a bear could be a friend. That sort of thinking gets one killed. And I did not plan on dying, at least, not today. But having that cub with me would slow me down and would make me interesting to all bears. That's problem enough, but this killer bear also seemed determined to kill the cub.

He apparently slipped past me last night and he might have caught my scent. I am betting all the smells of the farm covered any recognition of my presence. He probably had no idea I was here.

I climbed higher. I figured out the big bear was away from me, lower and closer to the farm. I suspect the plane spooked him, too. I assumed he was hiding in a thick patch of willows, and I wasn't wrong. I kept climbing higher and got a little more distance from where I thought he was, and I came to rest on the wide ledge of a short straight cliff. Here, I could remain hidden and keep my eyes on both the bear and the farm.

After the people left the airstrip and went back to the farm, I saw the grizzly slip out of his hiding place and head straight into the corn. He was huge, but the corn was just tall enough to conceal him completely. He would take some steps, stop, and then move forward. Eventually, he crossed a couple miles of corn fields and waited and watched from a spot close to the house. Things were definitely getting dangerous.

In the hours that the bear took to get in position near the house, I watched the family introduce the cub to the rest of the farm animals. He seemed to be especially close to a tremendous horse. It seemed the big horse liked him, too. The cub was getting attached to his human captors. If I didn't act soon, those folks would figure out the cub was no ordinary bear. Oh, he was a real bear all right. He was just special.

I watched him play for hours with a little alpaca. The family would come and go, and somebody was always on watch. But they let the little bear play. Truth be told, I was accustomed to seeing people put bears in cages. These folks were different.

The big bear just watched. Something held him back and I suspect it was the dogs, that enormous horse, and the fact that people who probably had guns surrounded the little cub. That big bear had patience, and that is one thing I thought he had none of. A patient bear is a smart bear. He figured to be a bigger problem for me and for them than I first thought.

Later in the afternoon, the wind started to shift. That made me only a little concerned, but I was pretty deep in the forest. From the animal sign I saw in the woods, the dogs didn't harass anything that kept out of the farm. I couldn't count on it, but I was pretty sure of it. I also wasn't concerned because there was about 1,000 pounds of dank, smelly grizzly bear hunkered in the corn over there that would be really interesting to those dogs. With the shift in the wind, it was inevitable.

Almost like clockwork, I saw it all go down. The speed of sound is actually pretty slow, at least, when compared to the speed of light. I saw the dogs peel around the house at top speed well before I could hear them. They ran right toward the bear. They had some pretty good sniffers because they ran right to where he was. I watched the big bear turn and run. He apparently wasn't ready to do whatever he was thinking of doing, so he got up and headed out really fast. The dogs were fast, too, and they were soon on his heels. The bear kept in the corn. Bears will do things like that. They know the smaller and lighter dogs can't plow through the underbrush so easy. In the Appalachians, a plant grows there that has a lot of interweaving branches, and if a bear is chased by dogs, it will power through it and the dogs will get hung up in it. The locals gave the plant the name of *dog hobble*. That big bear could use some of that right now.

The dogs fell in line behind the running bear because the bear trampled the corn. The smaller dog was getting in some good bites on the bear's haunches. That dog was tough. The bigger dog was trying to get in a bite or two, as well. About a hundred yards or so from the western forest, the big bear had enough. He whirled around and the fight began. The noise was deafening. The bear's roars were intermixed with the constant barking of the dogs. Bears are mighty good fighters, and they can easily kill a persistent dog, but two dogs are a problem. While the bear paid attention to the bigger dog, the smaller one would wheel around and try to bite the bear's backside.

It was obviously painful, and it kept the bear from retreating into the forest. The bear hadn't figured out the woods were probably a dog-free safe zone. Too bad for him. Personally, I was pulling for the dogs.

The fight was vicious. The bear would swat with his huge front paws, and the dogs would dart in and out. At first, there was a lot more action than there was blood. The dogs were able to stay away from the bear's vicious claws, and the bear was, for the most part, keeping the dogs at bay. But that started to change, and both the bear and the dogs were getting in some punishment. As the fight kept on, of the three combatants, the big dog was definitely getting the worst of it. He looked tougher, but the smaller dog was actually a better fighter. Several times, the big bear had connected with his claws on the big dog's ribs. With a yelp, the big dog would be flung in the air and the bear would go in for the kill. But the smaller dog would grab the bear's rear end and bite hard, and the bear's attention would change. The little dog saved his friend several times. The bear's haunches were beginning to get bloody.

The three animals looked exhausted as they fought. The bigger dog would soon be needing some help. My attention was totally fixed on the fight when I saw her coming. The mother was on a horse I hadn't seen before. The horse was fast, and when it would turn into the alleyways made for the tractor, it did so without slowing down. The horse appeared well-trained. I watched the woman hold on to a rifle in one hand and the reigns in the other. She and the horse acted as one. The horse would turn, and she would lean in and stay in control. I was amazed when I realized she was riding bareback. She was headed full speed straight to the fight.

When she got closer, both the bear and the dogs knew it. She must have called out. That was too much for the bear. Two dogs and a human with a gun meant it was time to go. These people were not like the terrified campers that he was probably used to. They would cower in their tents while he ate their food and destroyed their camp. The big bear obviously figured out he was about to be in real danger. He took off for the woods and ignored the dog who was nipping at his big backsides. By the time the lady got to the scene of the fight, the bear had made it to the woods and he wasn't stopping. The smaller dog immediately broke off the chase once the bear hit the forest. Well, he did what he was told. I guess I do, too.

For the next thirty minutes or so, I watched as the mother made her way in the corn to the scene of the mighty battle. She stayed on her horse and surveyed the site. I expected her to run back off to her home. She had to be scared. But she surprised me again. She followed the bear's back trail through the corn fields all the way to where he had been watching her and her family and the cub. That took some time. When she got there, she looked about and then took off toward the barn. She didn't run because she was scared, even though she had to be at least a little bit. She ran off because she was getting ready for that bear to come back.

She was one brave woman. She was probably just as dangerous as her mate, too. That was a fact that I had better not forget.

For the next several hours, I watched the family get ready for nightfall and a possible fight. I also watched that big bear slide to the edge of the forest and wait. Night would be his friend, and he knew it. His hatred had started to blind him.

So, we had a showdown between a dangerous bear and a dangerous woman defending her own cubs. The big bear had already killed one mother defending her cub, but something tells me this woman was not like her bear counterpart. The cub's mother was a poor fighter. I think this lady is far more dangerous.

And if I was smart, I should probably stay out of this one.

5

PREPPING − LIBBY

Mom came home and called me outside. Dean and Gracie and Kaiyo were awake and had been playing in the TV room. Right when Mom got home, Dean had given Kaiyo another bottle and then took him outside. When he did, Dean saw me, Mom, and Major sitting on the grass looking closely at Moose. Moose was laying down, but his ears were still perked up.

Moose looked pretty bad, but we had seen him worse. Moose's ribs were cut and he had a pretty bad bite in the skin above his shoulders. Kaiyo squirmed out of Dean's grip and ran on over. He looked at Moose's wounds and licked his face. Moose's tail thumped in the grass. Kaiyo sniffed Moose thoroughly. As good a nose as dogs have, a bear's nose is much better. Their ability to catch a scent from far distances is renowned. Just try cooking bacon and leaving the pan uncleaned in Yellowstone Park. Do that and you will have some hungry, unwelcome visitors, and some of those would have traveled for miles.

Kaiyo sniffed Moose and stood back. He knew who had bitten and clawed Moose. Kaiyo then went over to Major. Most of Goliath's blood had been self-licked off of Major's muzzle, but Kaiyo still found some. Kaiyo licked the remaining blood off of Major's muzzle. Watching this little guy try to process all of this was sad. He had to be thinking of his mother. I was impressed at how Kaiyo had no fear of the dogs, even though the dogs had bear blood on them. I guess because it was Goliath's blood he was okay with it all. Kaiyo wandered over to me, stood, and let out a little cry. I picked him up and he was shaking. He hid his face and held on tight.

Mom believed in first things first. She announced, "Family meeting. Now!"

Dean ran in and got Gracie. His look told her it was serious, and she came without complaint. The three of us sat on the ground in front of Mom. Major left the group and walked off about twenty yards and sat on the lawn. He worked the breeze with his nose while he kept his eyes on the corn. Major was our early warning system. Then, Mom told us what had happened. I was stunned when she told us the story. First, I was impressed at Mom's bravery. But the fact that this was Goliath meant this was no nomadic bear that would move on and never come back. Goliath was here for a reason.

I looked at Dean and Gracie, while Mom told the story. Gracie was obviously frightened. But she had some strong stuff in her and she didn't cry. She was paying attention and that was notable. Dean, on the other hand, almost looked like he was going to play in a football game. I think things like this just get him going. I am sure he was afraid, but he was also a born fighter. As for me, I was afraid because I already knew Goliath. I had seen him look right at me and hate me. And I was pretty sure he would remember hating me. I started to weep.

Dean looked at me and gently put his hand on my shoulder, and said, "Don't worry Libby. He's just a bear and we can take him down."

Dean was already about three inches taller than me, and because of that, he seemed older than he was. I marveled at the confidence of this thirteen-year-old boy, but I knew with certainty that Goliath wasn't *just a bear*. I bit my lip, gave him a hug, and thanked him. Dean then looked at Mom and said, "What's next?"

Mom had obviously been thinking about things. Her plan, in short, was to shelter as many animals as possible in the barns and then stay in the house until morning. Then, if that bear was still here, we were to stay together and wait until Dad got home. It was a pretty good plan, and we said a quick prayer. We got up, looked at each other, and Mom said, "I have to call Dad." She each gave us some orders and went inside. She took Kaiyo and Gracie with her.

Dean and I went in and got our bear spray and our guns. I had a bolt action 270 rifle, and Dean had a 20-gauge shotgun loaded with slugs. Dean's shotgun was probably better for something like Goliath, but we were both under gunned. I was praying we had some time before Goliath got his courage back up.

My first job was to treat Moose's wounds. Moose had some loose skin above his shoulders and it had saved his life. If Goliath had crunched down on his skull or back bone, it would have been lights out for Moose. As it was, it looked like Goliath had given Moose a bad bite, but Goliath's sharp fangs only caught his skin. The swipes of Goliath's claws had done their damage, but some butterfly bandages worked just fine.

Dean and I cleaned the wounds, and we both felt for broken ribs. Neither of us felt any. We covered him with gauze, put one of Dad's tee shirts on him, and called it *good enough*. Moose would be sore for a while, but he could help us tonight if need be.

Now, it was time to split up and get those animals in the barns.

The Fortress – Susan

I tried to call Sam but his phone just rolled over. It was probably dead. I figured as much. I was hoping maybe he would get it charged later. I knew he was probably still in meetings, but you would think that your wife, who was taking care of a grizzly bear cub, just might have an issue or two that needed talking out. I fought back the tears and the anger. Neither tears nor anger were helpful right now. And they both made me want to do nothing to prepare or get ready, and that was as deadly as it was foolish.

I made a call and spoke to our friend Sheriff Lee Tuttle. Lee had been a lawman all his life in Atlanta and then in Dallas. He had been living here in our part of Montana for the past fifteen years. He started as a deputy, and after only a few years, he ran for sheriff and was elected. He had been sheriff for the last thirteen or so years. For a sheriff, Lee was young but prematurely gray. He was a good man with a good sense of humor, though he was not very diplomatic. He said a sheriff was about the only politician who can tell the truth and still get elected. The story around here is, Lee will tell the truth, and don't ask him for the truth if it might hurt. At the last election rally, he got in some trouble when some woman asked him if he thought her baby was cute. He told the truth, and she was crushed. Sam and I were there, and we just shook our heads.

His campaign manager managed to spin all that with a catchy little ditty. "Tuttle. He'll tell the truth whether you want it or not. A vote for Tuttle is a vote for truth."

I thought it was lame, but Lee got elected with over 70 percent of the vote. What did we know?

Lee's wife Ellie was as sweet and gracious as they come, and Lee adored her. The four of us were friends, and I knew I could call Lee for help. I told Lee what was going on and that I was scared. He told me he would drive out to the farm just after sundown. He said he would turn on his lights and siren when he got on our driveway and keep them on until he got to the house just to scare away anything that might be sneaking around the place. I liked the idea and I loved that he would come out. It made me feel better.

I hung up, and made sure Gracie and Kaiyo were together. Then, I headed outside to see what Dean and Libby were doing. When I got outside, I found out Dean had parked the cars and all of the tractors on the back lawn. I was stunned. I didn't even know Dean knew how to drive anything but the UTV and the four-wheelers. Something told me he and his dad didn't tell me everything. As I was standing there, I heard a truck door open behind me. I looked behind me and saw Dean as he hopped out of Sam's big, dually pickup truck he had just parked near the house on the grass in a *getaway* position. He said,

"I left the keys in there just in case we needed to hop in quick and get the heck out of here."

Then he winked at me and walked on past me to the barns. He was only thirteen years old, and he knew how to drive and I had no idea. I really need to spend more time with him.

Libby and Dean were working a plan. Dean would empty a building of as much stuff as he could roll or drive out, and Libby would make sure the hay or other food was out of reach. Libby filled the first cleaned out building with our goats. The building would need some cleaning in the morning, but the goats would be safe.

The next building was a big storage barn and it was crammed with the sheep. I liked the plan. We would be a fortress.

We had some hogs but not many. They already had a barn with birthing pens for the sows. The few that were out in the pasture were rounded up easily and sent inside.

The fourth building was our cattle barn, and we brought in the cows with calves. The rest of the cattle were on their own. There just wasn't enough room. I was okay with it because the herd had some tough old range steers who had grown up in the Eastern Wilderness. They had sharp horns, were good sized, and they could probably make Goliath think twice.

The main barn was cleared out, and it was filled with the gentle alpacas. Sunny and Rosie were first. The stalls held the horses; the alpacas spread out in the barn. This made them uneasy, but Gracie and Kaiyo came out and made them feel better. Rosie looked so happy.

We got through with a little daylight left. The sun was starting to sink and darkness started showing itself in the east. We all went into the house and prepared ourselves for the unknown. It was going to be a long night.

After about an hour or so, I heard a siren way off. Slowly, the sound got closer and after a while we could see the blue lights eerily glowing in the far off western forest. It was noisy and beautiful. And it made me feel so good. The kids loved it. We watched from inside as Lee got closer, and we stayed there until he got here. He parked the car, turned off the siren and the lights, and walked on up the stairs to the back door. Gracie opened the door before he could knock. He was a sight for sore eyes. We all sat in the kitchen, and I let Libby tell him what had happened the day before. Lee listened, and then picked up Kaiyo and scratched him under the ears. I told him about the fight with Moose and Major and Goliath and what I learned from my back tracking. He agreed Goliath was holding a grudge, and a grudge-holding bear was a problem. Lee then inspected the house and walked outside with Major and me and inspected the farm buildings.

While Lee was walking outside, he kept his eye on Dean and his shotgun, and when we got back home, Lee gave Libby and Dean a little lecture about gun safety. Once a sheriff, always a sheriff.

Then Lee and I went to the front and we talked for a while. During the talk, Sam called. Hallelujah, Sam bought a charger. We put the speaker on and told Sam what had happened and what we did to prep for tonight. We all felt the odds were pretty good that Goliath would leave the farm and move on. We also assumed that if Goliath attacked, he would probably take it out on the cows. It was possible he might try to break in the house, but very unlikely. Still, Sam wanted the family to sleep in our bedroom because it was big and it had a door that locked from the inside. Also, our bedroom was where we kept the most guns.

Sam told me he would call back in half an hour. Lee put on his hat, gave me a quick hug, headed out the back door, and out to his car. He stood by and he made me promise that if the bear came back I would call him. I promised.

When the bear did come back, I tried to call Lee. He didn't answer his cell phone. I learned later Lee never made it home.

NIGHT ONE – SAM

I hated being so far from my family. After talking it over with Susan, I felt better about everything, and felt tonight would be frightening for my family not because of what Goliath could do but just because he was roaming around out there. I told Susan to make sure all the motion detection lights surrounding the house were on and to leave every light in the house and in the farm buildings on. She was well ahead of me.

Tomorrow, I have one more meeting, and if all went well, we would get a visit from the local game warden. His job would be to report back on the conditions here at the farm, and whether we had the ability to keep a grizzly safe from people and people safe from a grizzly. He would make sure we have enough space and know-how to take care of bears. It would be sort of like a home visit. If the home visit went okay, I was assured we would be able to keep Kaiyo, at least, for a while. I think our place would then be listed as a menagerie.

I knew the local game warden who would be coming over. His name was Lowe Brigham and he was warden over this region. We had been friends for years, but he was a lawman first. If Lowe didn't believe we could handle raising a bear, he would make sure we didn't.

Lowe and I had worked together several times clearing poachers off of my land and in the lands of the Eastern Wilderness. Most poachers are not poor, hungry, rural folk just trying to put a little meat on the table. I have yet to meet that type of poacher. Poachers are usually slobs who just enjoy being animal killers or they're into it to make money. Regardless, they have no respect for the hunt or the animals they kill.

Some of those poachers were involved with the illegal trade in bear parts. Bear organs are highly prized in Asia. Man in general doesn't have such a good record about preserving wildlife, but certain countries in Asia are at the worst end of the spectrum. Their trade in endangered animal parts for ingredients for bogus medicines is awful, at least, it's awful to me and to Lowe.

Anyway, Lowe and I put an end to a lot of poaching out here. Several poachers ended up in jail. Both of us received threats from the poachers' families or friends. They wanted us to back off. Lowe and I wouldn't do that, but protecting wildlife comes at a cost. A few years back, somebody even shot out one of the windows at Lowe's house one night. Fortunately, we live way too far away from the road for somebody to try something like that.

There would be one more meeting at eight o'clock tomorrow morning, and then Davey and I would fly home. That last, final meeting was probably the most important of the many meetings. It should also be the shortest.

For a totally different reason, I looked forward to Lowe going to the farm. He should be getting there by the time I fly in, but if he got there even earlier, that would be fine. Not only would it be good to see him again, but having him around would make everybody at home feel safer.

LITTLE BEAR, BIG BEAR — LIBBY

Years ago when we first moved to the farm, we lived in a very small and very old cabin for a few years before our farm house was built. Gracie wasn't born yet, and Dean was a toddler. I think I was about four years old. I remember staying up at night, terrified of the nighttime sounds of the wild animals. In the years since we first moved here, I have gotten used to all of that and I have not been scared of the night. Until now.

It was 2:45 in the morning when Mom got a call. It was Ellie Tuttle looking for her husband. He had never come home, and he hadn't answered calls to his cell. Mom told her the sheriff had left here around 10:30. Mrs. Tuttle was upset, and they talked for a few moments longer. She thanked Mom and hung up. All of us were sleeping in Mom and Dad's room, but the call woke me and Mom up. Kaiyo and Dean stirred a little, but both were asleep before the end of the call. Gracie didn't budge, of course. Moose moaned in his pain. Major was sleeping downstairs.

I looked at Mom. She tried to reassure me that Sheriff Tuttle probably got a call from the sheriff's department to go check out a different situation somewhere else in the county. She also reminded me that being out of cell phone range was mighty easy out here and in a lot of other places in the county. It made sense because we didn't have cell phone coverage yet. Still, it bothered me. It bothered me because the sheriff had a police radio that worked fine. I heard it while he was here. That meant something was wrong, somewhere. I kept that to myself.

I looked out the window. Mom and Dad's bedroom was on the second floor in the back. It took the whole backside and about a third of the upstairs. They had a beautiful view of the mountains to the north and of the Southern Forest. Their back windows looked over the driveway circle and the main barn just beyond that to the east. It was all dimly lit because we left on all of the downstairs lights and left on the lights in the barns and buildings. I just wanted the night to slide into dawn.

This far to the north in the summer, days were longer than fifteen hours. Twilight would come around 5:00 in the morning, sunrise around 5:30. Right now, though, it was dark. Sunrise would bring comfort, and after that, Dad would get home. If Goliath was still out there when Dad got here, he would be hunted down. And good riddance.

Then we saw the glow of the first of the motion detector lights on the south side of the house turn on. It was the one up by the front of the house. Then, the light at the middle of the south side of the house came on. Those lights helped to illuminate the driveway if somebody drove by. I didn't hear a car. Then, the light at the back side of the house and right by our window came on. I ran over to the south window and looked out in time to see an enormous bear come strolling down the driveway moving by the house toward the barn. Mom flew over and was next to me. "Good Lord, he's huge!" she whispered.

Goliath paused and looked to his left and at our house. He was only about forty feet away. We watched as he studied the house. Then, he looked right up at our window and roared. He knew we were here. Our night of terror had just begun.

CHAPTER

6

THE ATTACK – DEAN

There's nothing quite like the roar of a giant bear and the crazed barking of dogs to wake you up. Fast, too. When I woke up, I saw Mom and Libby frozen and looking out the window. Gracie was on the floor, holding her ears and screaming and crying. Moose was going nuts and standing next to Mom looking out the window. Kaiyo was trying to hide under the bed. The noise of it all just made it hard to think. And that's what I needed to do. I needed to think and do it fast.

Some kids at school say I'm conceited, but it's not true. I play football, and I'm bigger and taller than many of my classmates, and if you're in eighth grade, that's about all that matters to most of them. One of my mom's brothers is tall, and both brothers are naturally powerful. When they were younger, they looked like Vikings. Mom told me her family was 100 percent Danish, and Denmark was the land of the Vikings. I take after them.

Dad was proud of my size and strength. He tries to coach me, and he usually makes sense. He once told me God made all men to be warriors. Some were warriors with their strength, some with their brains, and some with their cunning. He said when boys and men are not taught to be warriors, then they can become something useless and cowardly. Dad said the most important thing was to decide what kind of warrior I would be. Men, he said, had only two choices, and they wake up each day having to make that choice until it becomes their nature. We could be predators or we could be protectors. Both will fight with the strengths they have. Both will try to survive. One will live as a hero, the other will live as a bully and a coward. Dad said we had the choice to either be a wolf or a coyote. I would be a wolf. I had already decided to protect and defend others, and to be something better. That was a good thing, too, because right now, I had some defending to do.

Dealing with Goliath meant we had to be smarter. Nothing was as strong as him around here, except maybe Peyton. Mom and Libby were still looking out the window, and Moose was being ridiculous. I ran to the bedroom door and opened it so Moose could join Major downstairs. That would discourage Goliath, at least a little bit. Except for Gracie's soft crying, it got so much quieter. We could think.

Mom looked back at us. I looked at her, and whispered loudly, "Shoot him."

She gave me a blank look. I raised my voice. "Mom, now's our chance. Shoot him!"

Her wits returned and she got that determined look. I usually don't much like that look, especially when she's looking at me. But that look was just what Libby and Gracie needed to see. And right now, I liked it, too. Libby and Mom were looking out the back windows. I brought Mom's rifle to her. Mom had a semi-automatic Remington 30.06. That particular brand of gun is a favorite all around the country. It's a good one, and it has killed a lot of deer and even bigger animals, including big bears. Even though Goliath was no average sized bear, a well-placed shot from Mom's rifle would easily do the trick.

By this time, Goliath had passed the house and the courtyard and was at the front doors of the barn. He had figured out our animals were in there, and he started swinging those mighty paws into the doors. He was trying to smash his way in. We had to act fast! Mom ran to the back window, and I opened it. Mom looked over the sights of her rifle and saw the mountain of brown fur. And then, nothing.

Goliath had heard me open the window. He saw us in the window and probably smelled the scent of guns at about the same time. He ran off. I saw it. He turned quick and ran to the south side of the barn and headed away from us and out of our sight. I was amazed at his quickness and speed. Bears look clumsy when they run but they aren't. Bears are almost as fast as horses, sometimes faster. And Goliath was as fast as he was big.

We looked at each other. Gracie had quit crying and was looking out the window with all of us. Kaiyo had pulled himself up on the bed. The girls and Kaiyo were scared, but Goliath was nowhere to be seen. The dogs were downstairs still barking but not like before. We listened to the night. It was pretty quiet out there. We looked at each other again. Libby whispered, "This is too good to be true."

Still, we had our hopes. Goliath didn't want to be shot. Maybe running made sense even to a bully like him.

Then, we heard the banging. It sounded like a rapid wrecking ball. To our despair, Goliath had not run off. He had only gone to the barn's back door. He was out of our sight, but we heard him. We heard the doors start to give way under his attacks. Then, we heard the deafening screams of our terrified animals. Goliath was in and he had murder on his mind. What could I do? What would Dad do? I hated being only thirteen right now.

THE ATTACK – LIBBY

I couldn't help but scream out. There was a huge bear in my barn and he was busy killing. The guinea fowls and the chickens had fled their roosts, and they poured out of the barn by their outside chicken coup doors. They were in a full state of noisy panic. But the heartbreaking sound was the high-pitched alarm calls of the alpacas. I could hear the horses cry out while kicking at their stalls.

The noise was awful. By the noise, it seemed Goliath had the alpacas bunched against the horse stalls. Then the pitch and panic of the alpacas' screaming got even worse, and I knew he was wading in among them. They would all be dead in just a short period of time.

I turned and looked at Mom. I yelled out, "We have to do something! We can't just sit here!"

Mom was thinking. Gracie and Kaiyo were under the covers. Dean was standing by the bedroom door. He looked like he was trying to figure out a problem. But we were helpless. The only thing we could do was to hide up here and let that bear destroy nearly everything we loved. The animals were being killed. It sounded like he would grab an alpaca and take it outside and viciously kill it. Then, he would go get another one. I wept bitterly.

Mom looked at me, her eyes were fixed on the courtyard. "What the heck. The dogs are out! How did they get out? There they go!"

Wait. What? How did that happen? Those questions of ours were answered immediately when we saw Dean standing in the courtyard. He was clutching Dad's 12-gauge shotgun and was headed to the barn. Mom screamed at him to get back. She was mad at first. Then it dawned on her that Dean was going after that bear. She was overwhelmed with fear, and pleaded with him to come back. He kept going. I screamed and begged for him to come back. He kept going. Then when he was right at the barn, he stopped and looked at us and then he turned back to whatever it was he was trying to do.

I yelled out, "Grab your rifle, Mom!" I had mine. "We can cover him from here!"

Mom kept pleading with Dean, but her rifle was up and she was looking down the barrel for any sign of the bear. So was I.

I knew Dean had decided coming back was not an option. Good lord, that kid was brave. He went over to the barn doors. I think that was what Goliath was waiting for.

THE ATTACK — DEAN

I knew I could have stayed upstairs and still not have been a coward. But I was just so mad. And I had a plan. I thought over the distracting clamor of Mom's and Libby's yells, and walked quickly to the barn's front courtyard doors. Major and Moose were already there. The noise of the bear's roars and the screams of the horses and the alpacas hadn't died down much, if at all. I leaned close to Major and Moose and said, "You know what to do."

I opened the latch and let the dogs in, and they went right to work.

Through the crack in the door, I watched the dogs continue the harassment from earlier today. The bear was quick, but the dogs were on high alert. I needed them to keep him occupied, and the dogs were doing the job. Slowly, the dogs managed to push Goliath toward the back of the barn and out the broken back barn doors. Major was getting in some good bites, and Moose looked like he had learned a thing or two about getting too close to those mammoth paws. I needed to get in the barn, though, so I could get a shot in. I had Dad's 12-gauge loaded with three-inch magnum slugs. It was a great bear gun at short distance, and short distance was what I had. I was over five feet seven inches tall and stronger than most my age or even a few years older. But it was still too much gun for me, especially with magnum loads.

I hoped to slip inside and get in a killing shot. Goliath was at the back of the barn and was distracted with fighting the dogs. The opportunity was now. I cracked opened the door a little further and slid in. I heard Mom cry out as I stepped out of view. Poor thing.

I knelt, aimed, and looked for a shot. The big bear was a blur of movement as he dueled with the dogs. I quickly aimed as best I could. The gun roared, and I was thrown back on my rear by the instant force of the gun's backward kick.

Then, there was silence. There was total, complete silence. I watched as everything and everybody in the barn turned and looked at me. And when I say everything, I mean everything. The horses looked at me. The remaining alpacas stared in surprise. The dogs stopped what they were doing and stared back to see me. Goliath realized he had been shot at and stopped fighting the dogs to look and see who was doing the shooting. He saw me sitting there where I had fallen backward. In a blur of movement, he turned and started running back through the barn. He was coming right at me and fast. The dogs were left behind for a split second, looking confused. Then they came on. I was on my own and I knew it. I rolled to my feet and bolted.

I figured out before I took my shot where I would run if I had to. Well, I had to. I knew I missed Goliath and I didn't think getting off another shot that would actually kill him quick enough would be possible. I ran through the alpacas as they were speeding past me. They were headed out the now open doors at the front of the barn and away from the bear. There were a lot of moving creatures, and it confused the grizzly for a moment. He caught my movement and saw me run toward Peyton's stall. Running at full speed, I dropped to the floor and slid under the stall like I was sliding into home base. My chances with Peyton's crushing hooves were better than Goliath's shredding claws and sharp fangs. And I still had Dad's shotgun with me.

As I slid under the stall, Goliath crashed into the stall's walls. Missing me, he reached a massive paw under the stall to pull me back out. Fortunately, Peyton saw me coming and was ready. He watched me slide under and roll out of the way. Peyton then stepped on Goliath's beefy paw. It was a glancing blow but it had to hurt. Goliath screamed in anger. By this time, the dogs were back at work, and both Major and Moose were savagely biting Goliath's back side. Goliath decided killing me was better than killing the dogs, so he ignored them for the moment. Goliath then stood to look over the stall. I was ready for him. I pulled the shotgun to my shoulder, squeezed the trigger, and I shot him. The noise of the blast was deafening, and Goliath roared in shock and pain. I guess I was pretty shaky because my aim was a little off. The slug only grazed the top of his skull, but now he was getting hurt. Blood was everywhere, and a lot of the blood was his now. Then, I heard Mom and Libby shooting. I was not sure if they were shooting at anything in particular, but it had to bother Goliath and that would be a good thing.

Goliath gave it one last attempt. He stood again and threw a mighty right paw to kill Peyton. Peyton was ready and had reared up and towered three feet taller than Goliath. Goliath's paw met one of Peyton's enormous flashing hooves. It was like iron striking iron.

Goliath decided it was time to leave, and he whirled around and sped out of the barn. The dogs followed him, but they soon came right back. Those were two wonderful and amazing dogs. From the inside of Peyton's stall, I reached to the top of the stall and undid the latch. If Goliath was going to come back, I needed Peyton to be free to help. He was great.

I walked to the front of the barn and saw Mom and Libby racing across the courtyard. In a few moments, they were in the barn, guns at the ready. Mom looked at me. Then I did what I never thought I would do. I cried. I put the safety on my shotgun and dropped it in the straw as I fell to my knees. At that moment, I had no more fight in me. My sobs came in heaves, and I couldn't stop. I tried to stop but I couldn't. Mom came and held me. Libby and the dogs stood guard over me. After a few minutes, I was able to get a little more control of myself. It was still hard to catch my breath. I was a little embarrassed, but I just flat out needed my mom. I was shaking in rage and fear, and only my mom could fix that.

We were startled then when the dogs ran out the barn at full speed. The barking began again. When would this nightmare end?

It wasn't too long before we heard the bawl of cattle in the far pastures. Goliath wasn't done killing yet. He had run out of here and kept running north until he got to the pastures holding the cows and steers. Pretty soon, we heard the dogs. They had found Goliath again. And we all could hear it. I ran into the kitchen and got my 20-gauge shotgun. Dad's 12-gauge was just too much for me.

I ran back in the barn. Mom and Libby had been talking. This time, Mom and Libby had had enough, too. "Mount up," said Mom. "And there's no time for saddles."

The Attack – Susan

My son was a darn fool, and I was proud of him anyway. My crying would come later. I thought I had lost him to that evil bear. I will have some words with him and so would his father, but I was so proud of him. And I still needed him. We had a huge bear to run off or kill. While we had the advantage in numbers and weapons, Goliath had a few hours more of darkness as his ally. Dean wiped away his last tear. That serious look he sometimes got crept back on his face. Dean was ready. Libby looked furious. She was ready. I pulled out two flashlights from the barn's emergency cabinet and threw one to Libby. Dean told me to keep the other one.

In a flash, Libby was on Jet. I had already pulled Cali out of her stall and put on her bridle. Dean was grabbing a step ladder to climb onto Peyton. "Not riding Solo?" I asked Dean.

"No," he said. "That bear respects Peyton and is probably a little scared of him, too. He needs to be scared."

I hopped on Cali, whirled into the courtyard, and called out to Gracie. Her little face showed in the window. I told her to lock the bedroom door and stay under the covers with Kaiyo. She yelled out a quick "Okay" and ran back to the safety of the bed.

We walked our horses back through the barn. There were two dead alpacas in the barn. A few guineas and chickens hadn't made it, either. Once we got to the back of the barn and back outside, we counted three more dead alpacas. "Oh no. He got Sunny," said Libby.

He had. We looked for Rosie but didn't see her. We were all madder than good sense would allow us to be. Dean spoke to both Libby and me, "All three of us need to shoot. We don't want to miss again."

We agreed. "Keep your distance if possible," I said. "We can't see much through this darkness."

I helped Dean get up on Peyton, Libby and I mounted our horses, and we headed out into the darkness.

There are several types of twilight. Most people don't know that, but Sam was fascinated with useless facts. He told me about the different types of twilights a while back. What I remembered from the conversation told me that by this time we were in nautical twilight. That meant we could see the outlines of the mountains to the north and the silhouettes of trees off to the east. It was still dark but not ink dark and our eyes were adjusting to the dark. That was good. And it was getting lighter and that was better.

We headed northeast toward the cattle pastures. We were riding fast but slow enough to keep together. Peyton was no racer, but he kept up with us easily. The dogs had quit barking, so we were just heading to where we last heard them. We spoke in whispers. A few minutes later, the dogs came to meet us. Their tales were wagging but they looked tired. We went on alert. I heard each of us take the safeties off our guns. At this point, we were about a mile from the house and any light we received from the barn, house, or yard lights was long gone. As we rode up, we saw several cows roaming outside the fence, some cows had some bloody wounds but they looked like they would make it. We kept riding. Pretty soon, we came to a big break in the fence. Several fence posts had been smashed and the barbed wire was snapped.

We rode into the pasture, and the cows came bunching up toward us. They usually moved away from us, but they were scared of the bear and wanted protection. We rode through the cows and we came across a couple of dead ones, a cow and a steer. The steer had apparently been swatted by Goliath. It looked like he had charged Goliath and Goliath had smashed his skull. Other than the dog bites and the head wound he got when Dean shot him, Goliath was still capable of enormous damage. But where was he?

THE ATTACK – TRACKER

That bear had made a mess of things. Earlier, I noticed those people had hidden themselves in their house. With them being on high alert, there was no way I could get at that cub now. I was nowhere near the size of Goliath and I sure don't look like a bear, but I learned a long time ago to avoid nervous people with guns. In fact, I avoid people with guns in general.

I had left my hillside hideout and used the corn fields as a great place to hide. At the time, I had no idea where the bear was but I had to risk it. I needed a better view. As darkness began to settle in, I figured the father would not be coming back, at least, not by airplane. That was probably a good thing. It certainly meant less guns, but it also meant the family would be bunched up. I figured out the oldest child had a rifle and the mom did, too. The two youngest, I assumed, probably didn't know how to shoot.

I watched from my hiding place in the corn as the lawman drove with his lights and siren blaring after dark. That was a good idea. The noise was strange to the animals, and it might have caused the big bear to stay away. But then the lawman left, and the night was still young. He left way too early to do any good.

I could see in the windows of the house and was able to watch the family. They had turned on all of the house's lights, plus the lights for the porch and all of the farm buildings. Smart. I watched as they packed into the upstairs back room of the house. They were all in there. I shifted to another spot in the corn to get a better look into the windows. That put me closer to the pastures and gave me a better view of their back courtyard.

About four hours later, I smelled bear. I was on full alert. Then, I saw lights come on. The house was in my way, but I figured it was the big grizzly. I saw a flurry of movement in the upstairs room. Then, I saw the big bear stroll into the courtyard. I had an almost perfect view of it all.

I was coming to respect these people. They were brave and a little crazy. When I saw the boy and his dogs go take on the bear, I just marveled at the courage I was seeing. And he was armed. I couldn't see in the barn but I heard the first shot ring out. I figured out that either the kid or the bear would be dead. Then, I saw the alpacas bolt out of the front of the barn and I heard another shot. Somebody had to be dead now. Wrong again. Then, more guns started firing from the house. This family was tough.

That bear had lost his mind. Now, to my left and about a mile away, it was obvious the bear was trying to kill a few cows. I heard the dogs find him and lose him in the darkness. He had probably run into the forest to the east of the farm. Smart bear. The dogs wouldn't chase anything in the forest. They were well trained. The good news, though, was the family left that cub guarded by a very young child. I could hear the three others on their horses ride out toward the pastures to find the bear. I waited as they got even farther away. It was time to act. I needed that cub, and if I had to take him away from a little girl, how hard could that be? People are scared of me when they see me. I was pretty sure she wouldn't resist. If she did, well, I could deal with that, too.

I had to hurry. The family was bound to think of how foolish they were to leave a little girl alone with a killer bear out running loose. So far, they were too busy trying to kill the bear to think correctly. Unfortunately for them, he was already long gone.

I slid out of my hiding spot and ran quickly to the front of the house. It was dark, but I can see well in the dark. The house was lit up like a Christmas tree, so I was more concerned about being seen than I was about seeing in the dark. I climbed the steps and leaned into the front door. It was locked. I have many skills but locked doors were always a problem for me. I suppose I could smash my way through, but that's too noisy and I could get injured or shot. I looked in the windows as I made my way along the side of the house. When I was almost near the back of the house, I froze. The little girl had seen me!

My mind raced trying to figure out how that had happened. I stood still as a statue and leaned in hard to the side of the house. The porch roof shielded me from her view, or so I thought. I heard her yelling. She didn't sound too scared, she sounded mad. I looked but I couldn't see her. I had no clue what was going on.

I left my spot and continued to the back of the house. The little girl's voice kept getting louder. Who was she yelling at? When I came to the back of the house, one look in the courtyard told me every-thing. There stood that stinking bear, and the little girl was yelling at it to go away. Because I was still under the porch roof, it was obvious she had never seen me. At this point, I really started to hate that bear. The bear was mighty tall, but the girl was higher up, and from the window, she was taunting it. Then she threw something out of the window, and it hit the bear on the head. He roared and went into a full-fledged rage. I could see it in him. He was going to try to kill this little one and the cub, too. And that wouldn't do.

In one motion, the bear fell to his feet and ran for the back door of the house. He wouldn't have a problem with a locked door. He hit the door at full speed, and it splintered away from him. As he hit the door, I hit him. I didn't have much of a chance to get up much speed, but I'm pretty big, and that bear stopped to see what had happened. I sunk my teeth into his throat and pushed. He jumped back, and we both crashed through the railing on the porch and into the courtyard. We were locked into a battle. I got away from his grasp and lunged into his ribs and bit down hard. As he swung around, I had already let go and moved. He turned and I bit him again. And all during the fight, I heard the little girl cheer me on. I just hoped this bear had enough of fighting because he could kill me if he got lucky or if I wasn't careful.

In my case, careful meant being fast and savage. And at heart, that was what I was. Shortly after I was born, I became a savage and nothing has changed. The more I stayed away from home, the more savage I would get. That's how it worked, and right now, that was a good thing, too. I knew I had to be more vicious than the bear if I was to survive. And I would survive.

The fight moved from the courtyard into the driveway. The bear pulled away and faced me. I stood back, growling and showing my teeth. We stared at each other, sizing each other up and waiting for the other to make the next move. Our kinds were ancient ene-mies. The bear would have to be satisfied killing alpacas and cows. Killing me or anything else was not going to happen tonight.

The bear charged, and I sidestepped him. As he went past, I leaped on his shoulders and bit deeply. His hide was thick and loose so it was no killing bite, but it hurt him. The bear stood and threw me off. I rolled to my feet and dodged his swinging claws. I raced around him, and he followed me as if on a pivot. I had to keep him on the defensive. The little girl was cheering at the top of her lungs.

We continued to fight when we both heard the barking of the dogs. They were headed our way. Good, I could use some help right now. The bear instantly turned west and started running down the long driveway. I gave chase. After a quick mile, the bear turned a hard left and ran into the forest to the south. He must have thought I followed the same rules as the dogs. Hah. I have rules to obey, but they don't come from this family. I kept up the chase into the forest and got in some gruesome bites. Then, the brush got thick and whatever advantage I had disappeared. And that bear knew it. He whirled around, but I was already headed out of the forest and back to the farm. From a short distance, I watched the great bear turn and head deeper into the thick, dark forest. Good riddance.

I walked out of the forest and up the grassy bank toward the farm. I would have to deal with getting the cub later. Right now, everybody was on full alert and I was tired and hungry. At the top of the bank, the land flatted out for about twenty yards before it reached the driveway. And there in the driveway stood the dogs. They were looking fierce, and they were watching me with great interest. I was in no mood to run from dogs, and if they wanted to fight, then we would have at it. I was covered in blood. Some of it was mine, but most of it was the bear's. Soon, it would be theirs.

I didn't hesitate. I walked straight at them. They were both big dogs but I towered over them. They stood there looking as if they should attack. Then, I saw confusion. I was walking right at them and I wasn't running. After a few seconds, their tails nervously wagged a little. I kept coming, and then those tails began to wag as if I was the head of the pack. They had just seen me fight and chase the big bear, so I guess they figured I was on their side. I don't think

I was on their side, but I sure as heck wasn't on the bear's side. Dogs understand in terms of black and white; nuance isn't their strength.

We greeted each other, they licked my face, and I let them. Then, I left the driveway and headed north toward the corn fields. They started to follow me, but my warning growl told them not to. They headed back home. I was going to get something to eat and get some rest. If I came across an alpaca, well, that would just be great. They would blame it on the bear.

SAVED — GRACIE

They left me! I was so scared and they left me! I thought I would be okay, but it wasn't okay. Nothing was okay!

The window was left open and I could hear them get on their horses and run off. At least Kaiyo was with me. We had been playing under the covers. I did lock the bedroom door, but if that big bear came in the house, I would go out the window.

I remember falling asleep, but I woke up when I heard that big bear huffing and popping his teeth together. I got my courage up and looked out the window, and he was standing up on his back legs looking right back at me. He was so scary.

I started yelling at him and he just stood there. I was really just hoping Mom or Libby or Dean would hear me. They didn't hear me but the big dog did. My big mistake was throwing my dad's stapler at the huge bear's big head. It hit him right in his bloody cut and it made him really mad. I don't know why I did it, but now I know it was the wrong thing to do. Mom will probably say something like "Gracie, honey, what were ya thinking?"

Dad would say something like "You threw a stapler at a mad bear's head? Amazing!"

Dad was always happy when we did things that were brave. Still, I am thinking timeout is coming my way. But they shouldn't have left me! Dad will not like that little fact, that's for sure.

I watched as the bear decided to come in the house to get me. I couldn't move. Kaiyo stayed under the covers. I heard the back door get smashed. Before I could move, I heard the bear and the huge dog fighting. I didn't know whose dog it was. It must have been lost because I have never seen it around here before. But the bear must have made him really mad. They broke the porch and fought in the driveway. Kaiyo came to the window the second he heard that big dog growl and bark. He looked not so scared anymore. I just cheered as the dog fought the bear. He was strong and fast, and he made the bear run away. And I don't even know that dog's name.

Home – Sam

It had been a little over twenty-four hours since I left home and so much had happened in my absence. Susan called and gave me the story, and I admit to being horrified. I was also so profoundly proud of my family.

Flying over the huge Southern Forest, I was talking to Susan when I lost cell phone coverage. That was fine. We're only about thirty more minutes away. I closed my eyes, and Davey and I prayed. I peeked a look and there was my pilot of our tiny airplane with his eyes shut. I hate it when he did stuff like that! I shoved him hard, and he pushed down on the stick. The plane dove for the forest and we were already flying low. At the last second, Davey pulled out of the dive and we skimmed over the canopy. I got a hold of myself and cursed him good. I was tired and mad and worried, and Davey had nearly killed me! And his plane was a flying hunk of junk! I had real doubts it could handle the stress of a dive without its wings ripping off. Davey just sat there and laughed at me. He was enjoying himself; I was irritated.

Just before Davey and I left, I gave Lowe Brigham, the game warden, a quick call. He was already headed to the house and was planning to arrive about the same time as I should. That sounded good. I told him we had a temporary license to keep Kaiyo provided his home visitation with us went well. "Hah, no pressure!" Lowe said back to me.

I briefly told him about Goliath. He was as incredulous and as confused as I was. "Grizzly bears don't do stuff like that. They aren't like dogs but they sure don't do crazy stuff like that. I wonder if he was sick or something…"

I didn't know or care at that moment. But Goliath was definitely acting like he had rabies or something.

I had been patrolling the Eastern Wilderness for years before I ever saw Goliath. He was sort of a mystery bear. It was like he had been abandoned there. I was familiar with most of the grizzly bears that lived within fifty miles of the farm. I even enjoyed some of them. I watched many grow from cub to adult. I had never seen the enormous bear before when he just sort of showed up out there. And when he did, he was already cranky. The first time I saw him, he charged at me. Bears have a personal space issue and most grizzlies won't bother you if you stay out of that space. A few bears will let me get remarkably close. With each bear, it's different, but our general rule is that if you are on your horse, never get closer than 100 yards to a grizzly. If you're on foot, stay at least 300 yards away. Bears rarely want to kill people, and if people respected bears more, there would be fewer problems. We learned that Goliath preferred 500 plus yards of personal space. Coming any closer would invite a charge or a chase. Somebody or something had messed with his mind. And now, he had gone mad.

Lowe also mentioned there was a BOLO (be on the lookout) for Sheriff Tuttle. Susan had already told me Ellie had called around 2:45 this morning, and he hadn't made it home yet. Lowe said the sheriff's wife was still really upset. I told Lowe that Tuttle had been over to the farm to see Susan the night before. I wondered if that was the last anybody saw of him. Lowe said he would look out for any sign his car had gone off the road. That was troubling.

Finally, we came into view of the farm. From the air, everything on the ground usually has a peaceful look. The farm was no different. From a distance, it looked so nice. But a quick low flyover told a different story. We saw several dead alpacas lying near the barn and the bodies of at least two cows in the pastures. The fences looked torn up, too. At least, the house looked good. We also saw alpacas and cattle wandering around the farm. It looked messy. The good news was, I saw four people on our UTV and two dogs running next to it headed to the airstrip. We flew low, and by the looks of them, they were armed to the teeth.

Davey headed west and away from the farm in order to turn back and line up over the runway. Our runway was actually just a clean, well mowed grass strip about 2,000 feet long. Part of it was also our rifle/pistol range. That part was near where the western forest met the Northern Forest. We called that area the rifle range.

A lot of people are afraid of guns, so they keep their kids away from them. To me, that's like living in Florida but not teaching your kid to swim because of fear of drowning. America has around three hundred million guns, maybe more. A kid is mighty likely to come across one at some time or another. I would rather my kids know about guns and not be tempted by curiosity. Our kids know guns are dangerous and they have learned to respect them. From the beginning, I would take them out and teach them to shoot well and how to handle a gun. Even Gracie has used my old single shot .22 to shoot targets. She's way too young to carry a gun out here, but someday she will. My two older kids have taken several gun safety courses. This year, Dean gets his hunting license. Libby has had a license for several years. Some of the parents of Gracie's friends think I'm wrong, but I can't have any accidents out here. Still, we are mighty careful about guns. For the most part, our guns are safely stowed, or with me or Susan. But that's when we don't have to deal with a killer bear.

Right as we made the turn and lined up on the airstrip, I spotted a glare from Lowe Brigham's truck on the driveway deep in the

Western Forest. It was hard to see through the canopy but it was definitely a vehicle, and he was the only one who was visiting us. *Good*, I thought. *He'll be here shortly.*

The only thing that felt better than landing was actually getting out of Davey's plane. Still, I appreciated Davey for his friendship and for flying me back and forth from Helena. We were in Helena this morning, and then I was back at the farm and it was only 11:00 a.m. His graciousness saved me a ton of time, and it let me see the right people at the capitol at the right time.

Davey shook my hand and waited until I got off the runway. He then turned the plane around and taxied west and back to the start of the airstrip. We all watched him turn it back around and then gun it back toward us. By the time he got even with us, he was up and headed home. The plane was so loud we didn't even try to talk.

Then, I gave everybody a good look over. Kaiyo looked great and was very happy to see me. I reached out and gave him a pat on the muzzle. Susan looked tired and was very relieved to see me. Libby looked hopeful. Dean looked like he had aged a few years. Gracie was bouncing up and down and couldn't wait to tell me her part. Major was looking sharp. Moose looked beat to heck but happy nonetheless. It looked like everybody had a story to tell.

Susan handed me one of my rifles. I have a large caliber lever action rifle that was a terrific bear gun. She told me to make sure it was loaded. She was dead serious. It was. I looked around and everybody but Gracie, the bear cub, and the dogs had a gun. I was thinking this was a pure overkill, but I changed my mind when we made it to the cow pastures. We hopped off the UTV and everybody's mood changed. There were a lot of dead animals that just looked torn up. The rage of that bear was just hard to explain. We would need to clean this mess up.

But first things first. For the next forty-five minutes, I heard the stories of the night before. First Susan spoke, then Dean. Good Lord, I was proud of them. Dean walked me through his saga by taking me to the barn and going step-by-step. In truth, I cannot believe he lived. I think I might be mad at him for doing that but geez, what a kid! He would probably have to deal with some nightmares for a few weeks, but he will always remember his bravery here.

When Dean was through telling his story, Gracie grabbed me by my hand as we started walking out of the barn toward the back of the house. She wanted to tell me her story of the horrible night, too. She proudly pointed to a stapler on the ground in the middle of the courtyard. I picked it up, and the edge of the stapler had blood and some sort of animal hair in it. I must have looked confused. "It's bear hair," she said matter-of-factly.

In her wonderfully cute way, Gracie took me over to the porch and said, "Sit down. I'm gonna tell you what happened here." I was all ears.

Gracie's story broke my heart. She must have been terrified. Terror is not something a little girl should ever have to experience. I was angry with myself. I also knew better than to second guess Susan's leaving Gracie at home alone. I would have assumed Gracie was safe in the house, too. I also knew Susan felt awful about it. But we had both learned a lesson. Goliath was a far more dangerous bear than we had believed.

Still, the part she told about the big dog made no sense to me. I wondered if it were true, but thinking Gracie made that part up was even more preposterous than the story of her being rescued by the random visit of a big, stray dog. One thing I was certain of was, something drove away that bear from the back door. I couldn't imagine what type of stray dog would tangle one-on-one with a bear like Goliath. But there was a definitely some sort of fight here. The broken door, my beat-up porch, and the bear's tracks were clear. Plus, there was some blood splattered about. Dean was sitting there listening to the story and I saw him walk into the driveway. He stayed close enough to listen to Gracie, but he was looking down in the soft, crushed gravel of the driveway and courtyard. I asked Gracie what color the dog was and she remembered it to be mostly gray. I asked her if it was as big as Moose, and she laughed and said, "No, Daddy! That dog was a lot bigger than Moose!"

Well, Moose was a huge dog and there were not many dogs in the world who were *a lot bigger than Moose*. Maybe some were a little bigger, but not a lot bigger. So I was starting to believe she misjudged this part when Dean said, "Dad, you might want to look at this."

Dean was on one knee looking into the sandy bed of the driveway. He motioned me over. There next to Goliath's huge footprint was the paw print of a dog or something like a dog. But this dog's print was a whole lot bigger than Moose's print. Gracie was right. But seriously, that dog would have to be a giant. I reached in my pocket and grabbed my phone. Thank goodness for Wi-Fi. I searched for images of dogs, and went over to where Gracie was sitting on the porch. I asked her to look at the pictures and show me a dog that looked like the one she saw. While Gracie scrolled through the pictures, I went back over to Dean and those prints. We saw Moose's and Major's and the bear's and we saw the big dog prints. It looked like he and the bear were in a real fight. But why?

I looked back at Gracie and she said there was one dog that sort of looked right. I looked and she pointed out a picture of an Alaskan Malamute. That picture made me think. I showed her pictures of wolves, and she lit right up. "That's the dog!"

I looked at Dean. He looked confused. "Wolf? Dad, Moose's tracks are as big as or bigger than any wolf tracks I have ever seen. If this was a wolf, it had to be huge. And why here?"

I would have to think this one over. None of this made sense. None of it. I turned and there was Libby. She had been waiting patiently. "Dad," she said. "Do we get to keep him?

I smiled and said, "Probably."

She didn't like that answer much. "So, when will we know?" she asked.

"Oh my gosh!" I said out loud. "Where is Lowe Brigham?"

It's Not Over — Libby

Dad and I were talking, and it looked like he had been shot out of a cannon. "Oh my gosh!" He asked loudly, "Where is Lowe Brigham?"

I knew Officer Brigham. He was one of Dad's best friends, and he was the game warden for this area. I looked at Dad as Mom came over. Dean was walking down the driveway past Dad's truck staring at the ground. He was looking at wolf tracks, I guess. Kaiyo was tagging along, sniffing the ground like a dog. He would need to be fed soon. He was already bigger than when we got him two days ago.

Anyway, Dad explained that Officer Brigham was supposed to come here and evaluate us to see if we could keep Kaiyo. Everything rested on his opinion. He should've been here over an hour ago. Having him support us was necessary for us to keep Kaiyo. Dad tried to call him on his cell phone, but out here, that wasn't going to work. Then Dad called Officer Brigham's office. They hadn't seen or heard from him. They thought he was with us.

Mom came over and talked with Dad for a while. Dad called out, "Family meeting!"

Dean and Kaiyo came running back, and we all sat on the porch. Dad looked at me and Dean and said, "Libby and Dean, I need you to ride with me. We are going as far as the Road. We'll take my truck. Major will be going with us while Moose stays here with Mom, Gracie, and Kaiyo. I think something bad happened to Officer Brigham and maybe to Officer Tuttle, too."

I ran inside to get the first aid kit and the two-way radios. Those walkie-talkies were pretty handy around the farm. They say they have a range of thirty miles, but that's a bunch of hooey. We were really lucky if we could get three miles of range, but again, that range works well around the farm. I gave Mom one of them. I also grabbed a few blankets, too, just in case.

Dean was in the back seat of the cab, and I sat up front with Dad. I prayed we would not be finding them there on the driveway. If we did, it probably meant they were dead.

Our driveway is a beautiful crushed gravel road that heads west from our house a couple of miles before it heads into the Western Forest. This forest is an open forest with less brush than in the Southern Forest. The tall trees take all the sunshine, so even though there are a bunch of trees up there, we could see pretty far. Right then, that was a good thing.

About a mile down the road and well before we got into the Western Forest, Dad stopped the truck. He grabbed his rifle and hopped out. Being this far away from the house required a little more care. We had no idea where the bear was, but we had to be vigilant. "Stay here," he told us.

Hah. Like that ever worked. Dean and I hopped out of the truck. We held our weapons close, barrels down. Dean positioned himself in front of the truck. I stood to the side and looked toward the Southern Forest. The wind was coming from the north toward the Southern Forest. If there was a bear in the corn, Major would be letting us know. Major was testing the breeze, but there was nothing that bugged him. If Major wasn't worried, I wasn't worried.

We watched Dad walk down the driveway. He took a left toward the Southern Forest, walked the short field, and stopped at the edge of the grass. Dad looked over the short bank and peered into the forest beyond. Then he walked down the bank and then back up. After that, he walked back to the driveway. He kept his gaze to the ground and he followed a dim trail that lead to the corn. Dad looked back at us, and said "Back in the truck, y'all."

Dad still talks with the drawl of a Georgia boy, even though it's been years since he lived there. I liked it. The westerners out here did, too.

He hopped in the truck, started it, and said, "Gracie saw something weird."

We knew that. He kept on, "I was following those tracks and saw where the bear apparently headed into the forest. That wolf was on his heels, working him over. Then when he came out of the forest, it looks like he met the dogs and then headed north into the corn."

We looked at Major. Dad said, "Major, who and what is your friend? And why didn't you two chase him down?"

Major ignored him. After a few minutes of driving, we slipped under the canopy of the tall trees of the Western Forest. We could feel the temperature drop in the deep shade. It was nice. We kept going. Here, the driveway starts to wind around ridges and up and down hills. From the beginning of the forest to the Road, it's a little less than three miles as the crow flies. But the driveway itself is longer because it winds around the hills and there are frequent turnarounds and spots to move over if someone was coming from the other direction. Not quite two miles from the forest's beginning, Major started to get really agitated. The forest was dark here, and Major was whining and pacing. Dad told us to get ready for something. We knew what he meant when he said *Something*.

It's Not Over – Dean

I have to admit, thinking of that bear was mighty scary. But Dad and Libby were here, and we were in the truck. That was nice. Still, Major knew something was wrong. That was not fun. I looked up and I saw Libby grab her rifle. Dad had his rifle handy, but he had his right hand on the handle of his pistol. I held on to Major. I guess we were all a little scared and looking for comfort.

After a few more minutes, we rounded a tight curve and there we saw Officer Brigham's empty truck. The front door of the truck was wide open. The engine was still running, too. After taking that in, we spotted a police car to the right of the driveway, upside down, wheels up, and lodged in a gully. That had to be Officer Tuttle's car. The two lawmen were nowhere to be seen. It was quiet. Dad told me to let Major out. That was a good thing because Major was pawing me good to get out of the truck. I opened the door and Major hopped out. I quickly closed the door. We stayed in the truck and watched Major. Major stopped, briefly sniffed the air, and then he ran a beeline for the wrecked police car. He barked the whole way. Then, Dad honked the horn loud and for a good while. Dad told Libby to look out for the bear on the right side of the truck and for me to look out the left. We all rolled down our windows and looked.

One thing about Dad, he was smart about looking things over before he jumped in and did something. He was careful. He made sure there was no bear around. After a few moments, we heard the cries of "Help! We're in here!"

Dad hopped out and told Libby to get up on top of the truck bed and stand guard over the cab. Libby was a better shot than most adults and she could see like a hawk. Plus, she had a scoped rifle that could definitely reach out and touch somebody...or some bear. My 20-gauge shotgun, even loaded with slugs, was a close range only type of gun. It was good for sheer firepower, though.

Dad looked at me. "Dean, if you are up to it, could you stand guard over me while I dig these guys out?"

"Hah, just stop me!" I said.

I was always a little over confident and under prepared. But there was no other choice here. We had to save those guys.

It was early afternoon and the sun was high but the woods were all in shadow. Dad called out to the men. Officer Brigham came out first. He was a tad tussled but he still looked pretty good. Officer Brigham always looked sharp. He was like the type whose hair stayed combed in the wind and whose clothes stayed pressed in the rain. He came out of the gully and told us Sheriff Tuttle was hurt. He also said the huge bear had been pawing around the car all morning and he didn't leave until just before we got here. Yikes.

Getting Sheriff Tuttle out of the car was not going to be easy. When he crashed, he banged up his left shoulder pretty badly. He also spent most of last night suspended upside down by his seatbelts. He was in pain not only from the shoulder but he was also cut up, too.

Dad and Officer Brigham slid into the gully and broke out the back window of the overturned police car to get the sheriff out. It was slow going because he couldn't use his left arm and moving it caused him a lot of pain. Dad and Officer Brigham crawled in and started working to drag him out. Boy, Sheriff Tuttle knew some really bad words and he kept repeating them. It was slow going in there and I know Sheriff Tuttle was in pain, but listening to it was pretty funny. That sounds bad, but he wasn't like he was going to die in there. He was just banged up. So in a strange not nice way, it was funny. The slow motion rescue went on, and Libby and I were trying hard not to laugh too loud. We coughed a lot to cover up the sounds of our laughter.

Dad and Officer Brigham would move him a little bit, and out would come a stream of profanity and moaning. Then, they would all try it again. Still to his credit, he did hang upside down all night; that had to have been pretty awful. I'll definitely give him his due; that man was tough.

Sheriff Tuttle was still trying to get out of the car when Major ran past me, into the gully, and up the other side. When he got to the top, he went crazy, barking as if he were angry and afraid at the same time. Something was apparently coming our way. "What do you see, Libby?" I asked.

Libby had a good view over the truck cab and into the woods. "Nothing yet," she said.

Dad and Officer Brigham gave another heave as they pulled Sheriff Tuttle farther toward the back window of the car. Sheriff Tuttle was spitting venom and moaning like a range bull. I was trying to figure out what this scene reminded me of. As much as I tried, I couldn't put my finger on it.

Dad and the game warden were bent over, reaching into the back of the upturned car. They were tired and breathing hard, as they encouraged Sheriff Tuttle to come on out. The police car was laying there on its back with its wheels sticking up in the air like legs. Now it all came to me. It looked just like that car was giving birth to a child. Dad and Officer Brigham were acting like nurses, and Sheriff Tuttle was about to get birthed. I'm surprised Dad didn't holler out "Push!"

The two men gave another big heave, and finally, like a slip-pery wet newborn calf, Sheriff Tuttle popped on out of the broken back window of the car and flopped around on the ground. He was all helpless and dirty and sweaty, and he was cussing like a sailor. I started laughing again, so did Libby. Dad gave us warning glances.

I quit laughing, though, when Libby called out, "He's here!"

She pointed to a rock outcropping about seventy-five yards away. Sure enough, there he was. With boulders to hide behind, he was mostly hidden from view. Goliath was sitting on his haunches, watching us. He was in no hurry. Libby asked Dad if she should take a shot. Dad told her not to fire unless she could get a clear head shot. Unfortunately, that wasn't happening. Goliath kept himself behind the rocks. It was like the bear knew he was safe. And he stayed put.

The men helped Sheriff Tuttle to his feet. He was pretty wobbly, and his cussing had died down but not completely. His left arm hung from his shoulder and looked useless. Getting him out of the gully took some effort, but we got him up and out. Dad walked him to the back seat of Officer Brigham's truck. Even though Officer Brigham had left the truck running, it still had half a tank of gasoline. Dad helped the sheriff to lay in the back seat while Officer Brigham got in the driver's seat. With a few cuss words in the mix, I heard the sheriff tell Officer Brigham, "Turn on the lights and the siren. He doesn't like those!"

Dad looked at Brigham and gave a quick smile. "Wait till we get in the truck before you do that."

Within eyesight of Goliath, we strolled to the truck. I knew he wouldn't attack. There were too many of us with guns. Dad thinks Goliath is mad, like crazy mad. He's not. If he was crazy, he would have attacked us but he didn't. He's up to something. He's different from other bears. He seems to be thinking all the time. We called Major back, and we all got in the truck slowly. Officer Brigham turned on the siren and the flashing lights. Dad turned the truck around and we headed home. I couldn't wait to hear their stories. Goliath watched us leave.

8

KAIYO BACK IN CENTER STAGE – SUSAN

Once Sam got out of the forest, the walkie-talkies worked. I had been hearing the siren, too. He told me the awesome news about the rescue of the two lawmen. He did say Goliath had watched the whole thing. That was going to be a problem.

While they were gone, Gracie and Kaiyo and I ate an early lunch and we just enjoyed one another. Gracie and Kaiyo played on the floor and I watched. Dr. Cindy, the vet, told us Kaiyo could start eating other things as long as he got his bottles. Since he had been here, he had already gained a few pounds.

That bear just acted as if he was created to be with people. I knew thinking such a thing was just preposterous, but I started to believe it. Bears are definitely not domesticated animals and they are not usually as cute and cuddly as they look. This one was, though. I cannot really describe Kaiyo's personality. Even as a young cub, he was alert and curious, but he was so gentle with Gracie. The dogs even seemed to treat him as another child. It was like we were part of his family, even though he knew we were not bears.

We had so much work to do on the farm today. We had animals to round up and animals to bury. We had to repair the damage caused by the bear. The barn's back door was broken open and the cattle fences needed to be restrung. Also, my back door was destroyed. We knew Goliath was here and coming back. We also knew a tremendous wolf was wandering somewhere around the farm. And we had to deal with all that, while Lowe Brigham decided whether we could keep Kaiyo.

After Sam called, I quit my daydreaming. I first called Ellie Tuttle and gave her the good news. She was ecstatic and wanted all sorts of information. All I could tell her was his shoulder was hurt and that he was as ornery as ever. That was music to her ears. But I told her he did need medical attention and he would call her when he got to our house.

The next thing I did was call 911. The 911 call center was operated by the sheriff's department. The folks at the sheriff's department cheered when I told them Lee was safe. I told them he had a car accident on our driveway and was injured and needed medical attention soon. I also told them about Goliath, and the fact our driveway wasn't safe. They got my information and reported that a chopper would be on its way.

A few moments later, Sam and Lowe pulled up to the front door. I held Kaiyo as everyone piled out of the vehicles. Lowe and Sam helped Lee out of the car and walked him up the steps and inside. Lee was in pain and started cussing as he came up the steps but he piped down when he saw me. Libby and Dean were walking in behind them and they were doing everything they could not to laugh. Lee made it into the den and we put him in the recliner. It looked like his shoulder was dislocated and we used pillows to support his arm. It was obvious he was still in pain but the pillows helped. He then looked at me and asked if I could put Kaiyo in his lap. I was surprised at his request, but he meant it.

Once Kaiyo was in his lap, Lee's attitude changed. Kaiyo crawled on to his chest, and Lee just kept talking about what a good little bear he was. They were together for a few minutes, and Lee was petting Kaiyo's head and back. Kaiyo obviously liked Lee. Lowe was watching the whole time. Kaiyo just sat on Lee's chest and made little growly noises like he was talking to Lee. That was new to me.

Lowe looked a lot better than Lee, but he didn't spend the night hanging upside down in the woods, either. Lowe came to me and motioned for Sam to join us. We slipped out of the den and into the hall. We left Lee with Libby, Gracie, and Kaiyo. Dean stayed on the front porch with the dogs.

Lowe first thanked us for rescuing him. Then in a few words, he told us that his gratitude for being rescued would not affect or prejudice his opinion as to whether or not keeping Kaiyo was an option. He went on to explain his friendship with us wouldn't matter either. He said he couldn't consider such things because he had to be *unbiased.*

What an ungrateful clod, I thought. I understood he had a job to do, but that kind of talk just made me mad. He hadn't even started his stupid investigation and here he was preparing us for bad news. I folded my arms and bit my lip. I was beginning to think we should've left him out there with Goliath.

Sam didn't like what Lowe was saying either, but he was more diplomatic. He looked at Lowe and started the conversation. "Lowe, I hear that and I understand that we get no special favors. But you are wrong when you say that our friendship won't affect your decision, because it most certainly will."

Lowe looked at Sam and said, "I'm probably going to disagree with you, but why do you say that?"

Sam was masterful. He looked back at Lowe. "Lowe, because of our friendship, you have known us for years. You and Michelle have been here to our house many times and we have been to yours a lot, too. You and I have worked together and traveled the Eastern Wilderness together. Over those years, you have already made opinions about Susan and me, and you know whether we are the kind of people who make bad choices or good choices. You know how we farm, you know about our business, and you know how we treat our animals. You also trusted me to ride for countless hours side by side right with you when we went after poachers on more than one occasion. Back then, we trusted each other with our lives, right? So, it is our very friendship that has already told you an enormous amount about us and who we are. This isn't like you are meeting us for the first time. After all these years, if you don't think that Susan and I have the judgment or the character to take care of a baby bear, go ahead and save us the time and let us know right now."

Sam quit talking. It sounded good, but I didn't know where he was headed with this at all.

Lowe looked at him and thought for a moment and said, "Okay Sam, you have a good point. I do think that you and Susan are great people. So, yes. The same reason that we are friends is the same reason why you qualify to take care of the little guy. But the little guy is not going to stay little for very long."

Sam shot back, "Good. So now the questions are just about our capability and about Kaiyo himself, right?"

Lowe nodded. Sam continued. "Well, as far as capability, we live on a little more than 35,000 acres. Susan and I have a working farm and a number of good producing oil wells. So we can probably agree that not only does 35,000 acres keep the bear safe from people and people safe from the bear, I am also capable of building any type of enclosures money can buy, right? And since he's a baby bear, we don't need any cages right now, right?"

Lowe started smiling.

Lowe looked at Sam and grinned. "Dang Sam, you ought to be a lawyer. I think I am agreeing with you."

Oh my goodness. Did Lowe just say that? I was so excited I was about to scream. *Steady, Susan*, I told myself.

Sam then finished. "That leaves one last variable. You need to investigate Kaiyo. If you approve of him, then we are good to go, right?"

Lowe was laughing now. "Right," he said.

"Then," said Sam. "While Susan and I clean up the farm and deal with the dead animals and go about fixing the stuff, I want you to spend some real time watching Kaiyo interact with the kids and with the other animals. After that, I want you to spend a few hours with him yourself. If you do that, you will know beyond a reasonable doubt whether it is in our best interests and that little bear's best interest for him to stay with us."

Lowe looked at us both, smiled, and said, "You got a deal."

I was on cloud nine. Kaiyo could win the heart of anybody. Lowe didn't have a chance.

CLEANUP – THE HUNT – SAM

Susan and I headed back inside to see Sheriff Tuttle. He was in pain, but he was much more comfortable. Lee had been gray as long as I had known him. With his gray hair and with him being pretty beat-up, he looked like he had aged twenty years. He had been through a real ordeal. So had Susan. I laughed to myself when I thought how glad I was she didn't look like she had aged twenty years.

I saw that Lowe and Libby were out front with Dean and Kaiyo. Lowe was sitting on the steps, talking to the kids and holding Kaiyo. That was great. I just left them alone for a while. Lee looked up and said, "You do know that little bear of yours is different, don't you?"

Susan asked why he would say that. Lee looked at us and said, "I just know it, but I can't describe it exactly. It's like the bear was made for people. But not for everybody. It's like he was made for people who love him. Oh, I don't know. I guess I sound like some crazy old man."

Lee looked a little embarrassed. "Oh, Lee, you see it, too! You see what we see in Kaiyo," said Susan.

Lee perked up. Susan continued. "We saw right away how much he liked being with us. He's a magnet to the farm animals, too. They're drawn to him."

I nodded and smiled.

"Not surprised a bit," proclaimed Lee more proudly. "And oh, I forgot to tell you, Captain Stahr is on his way with the dogs. They're gonna get that big bear for you."

Captain Troy Stahr was the second-in-command at the sheriff's department. Troy Stahr was part hero, part cop, and part woodsman. He was only thirty-three years old but was respected by the entire department. He had earned his rank among many older deputies. I had known him since he was in high school. He was a good, solid cop. He was also somewhat impulsive. He had a terrific laugh, and saying no to Troy was hard. He was a little too bullheaded, but if he could kill Goliath, then we would definitely be glad to have him.

I looked at Lee and told him to get some rest and that a chopper was coming soon to take him back to the local hospital. He saluted me and closed his eyes. He had to be exhausted. Being up all night and hanging upside down while trying not to get eaten by an enormous grizzly had to be both tiring and terrifying.

Now, we had to get back to work. I called Dean from the front porch and told him to meet back in the courtyard. I dreaded this part but it had to be done. We divided the duties. Susan would get Moose and take Cali and round up the alpacas and loose cows and put them in the closest fenced pasture. I don't like mixing cows and alpacas. Cows are rough and they aren't particularly nice to the alpacas. But today, we needed them inside a fence so they would just have to make nice. Susan took her rifle, saddled Cali, and headed to the fields.

I told Dean we needed to get the dead animals and put them all together. There, we would take pictures for insurance and then we would have to dig a mass grave. I gave Dean the choice between using Peyton or the Bobcat skid loader to get the dead animals and to bring them to the gravesite. A skid loader looks like a little bulldozer. We just called it the Bobcat. Those things were mighty useful around the farm. Dean thought for a minute and said, "Dad, I don't want Peyton to see that." I agreed.

Dean fired up the Bobcat and we headed out to the cattle pasture about a mile away. We had loaded tools to fix the fence, at least, on a temporary basis. But first, the two dead cows and the dead alpacas needed to be dragged away. The herds did not need to see their dead. Death affects everybody and even animals. Seeing their dead was unnecessarily cruel, in my opinion. And I hated this part.

9

CHOPPERS – TRACKER

Last night, after the bear fight, I came across a young alpaca lost deep in the corn. It was the one I saw playing with the cub just yesterday. She wasn't much of a runner. She tried to run from me, but I quickly caught her and killed her. Then, I ate her and she was delicious. I do love tender alpaca meat.

Okay, I didn't really kill her or eat her. I wanted to, but she was just too cute a creature to eat. Yeah, I don't usually fall for that, but this time, I did. I did chase her, and I did think about eating fresh alpaca. And oh, I was plenty hungry. I just couldn't do it. Instead, I took her back to the farm. At first, she didn't understand me, but eventually, she did. The little thing had seen too much killing today, and since she was without her mother, she was probably orphaned, too. Her sadness was so thick I could almost taste it in the air. I took her under the front porch and forced her to lie down. Then I growled at her and headed back to the Northern Forest.

I was hungry and tired, so I did catch and eat a rabbit who thought it could outrun me. But that was just a snack. I crossed the field and quickly caught the scent of several deer to the north of me. It is, I suppose, hypocritical that I bestow compassion on one animal and withhold it from another. But it is my own discretion. The people at the farm wouldn't ever think of eating one of their horses or dogs, but nearly every other animal on that farm is eventually going to be their dinner or somebody else's. So, we were alike.

That night, I showed no pity on a deer and ate my fill. It was a bloody affair, but that is simply part of being savage. Like people, I like fresh meat, too. And I enjoyed it. So, I dragged the deer into the patch of willows that was the big bear's hiding place yesterday morning. I knew he would be back, and for better or worse, this would make him think about me. I also needed to blame the dead deer on the bear. The little girl saw me, and I left my tracks everywhere. I needed the big ones to forget about me.

I crawled up to my old perch and got some shut-eye. A couple of times, the bear came and fed on the remains of the deer. He probably thought he had stolen my kill. Around sunup, I saw him head back over into the Western Forest. Somehow, he was being mindful. That bear thinks ahead, and it made no sense to me how that was happening.

Today would be a busy day for everybody but me. I snoozed a lot. The farm people were busy and it was a sight to see. First, that old airplane brought in the father and then took off as quickly as it came. I could see the parents and kids walk about the place and investigate the damage. The family and the animals definitely had a rough night.

Then, I saw some of them hop in their pickup truck and head west. I watched as the father stopped the truck and get out about a mile from the house. He was walking around looking at the ground and was mighty interested in my tracks that I had left the night before on their driveway. He studied them for a while. I figured those folks were smart, and now I knew they were. I'm sure he was trying to figure me out and figure out why I did what I did. Good luck. Once I get the cub, I'll be out of here and we'll just be a fading mystery to them.

I then saw them ride into the forest. After a few minutes, I could hear the trunk honk its horn. It was far away but I can hear very well. After a while, I saw the truck come back with another police type truck with flashing lights and a loud siren closely following. When they stopped at the house, it looked like somebody in the police truck was hurt. They had to help him in the house. I didn't know what was going on down there but I was thinking the grizzly had something to do with it.

For the next hour or so, the place was pretty quiet. I saw the cub playing on the front yard with the oldest daughter. I saw the cub go under the house and bring out the little alpaca. The girl seemed to rejoice, so did the cub. That policeman type was with them, watching everything and playing with the cub. That was interesting.

I then watched the mother mount up and ride into the fields. She and her horse worked through the corn and the other fields rounding up cattle and alpacas. Most of the animals were afraid of the big bear and stayed pretty close to the farm. The mother and her horse were quick, and it was obvious she had rounded up cattle before. The alpacas herded pretty well, but the cows were less agreeable. She and her horse and the beat-up big dog did a good job of collecting them all together. She would follow the dog as he would find the hiding creatures and then she and her horse would get to work. It was fun to watch. She and the father got them all into one of the big pastures. Then, I heard a helicopter.

I saw it coming out of the south. It was headed to the farm, and by the time it got close to the house, I noticed it had a big cross on it. The people on the ground headed inside. That policeman was still holding the cub. The daughter held the young alpaca. The chopper circled and then landed on the front yard. The mom and the dad raced over as two medics left the chopper, grabbed some equipment, and went into the house. I assumed they were there for the injured one. After ten or so minutes, the medics wheeled an occupied stretcher from the house. There was a round of hugs and the injured man was loaded up. The chopper revved its engines. It lifted up, headed east, and then south toward town.

So far, the grizzly hadn't killed any people and that was a good thing. I had grown up hearing *people first*. I understood it but didn't always like it. But even in my worst moment, I could put these people first. They were solid. I was still going to take the cub away from them, but I wouldn't be enjoying it.

While the first helicopter was still on the ground, I saw another helicopter circling a few miles away. When the first helicopter lifted off and left, the other helicopter banked and quickly headed to the farm. When it got close, it was definitely coming in hot. It flared out and landed hard. After a few moments, its engines shut off. From out of the side door, I saw five heavily armed men step out. They pulled three big, long-legged hounds out of the chopper. This promised to be interesting.

THE POSSE – LIBBY

One of my parent's friends was Captain Troy Stahr. And there he was in all his splendor. Captain Stahr was tall with broad shoulders and a thin waist. He was decked out in camouflage pants that were tucked in to his combat boots. He wore a slightly too tight, short sleeved black tee shirt. His head was wrapped in a bandana and he was wearing aviator sunglasses. The captain looked way over confident and a little cocky. His men were dressed the same, except they wore green boonie hats. They held the dogs and didn't smile much. The whole thing looked silly. With the exception of the guns and the grim expressions on their faces, they all looked like they were going to a costume party.

The captain stood there and saw us looking out the window. He motioned me to come out while he was smiling and chewing his gum. Officer Brigham held Kaiyo, and we all came on out.

"Oh my goodness! What do we have here?" said Captain Stahr. "Is this the scary bear that has terrorized this poor family?"

Stahr was laughing. Gracie was scowling and about to say something to the captain when I grabbed her hand. Officer Brigham and I were not impressed either. Captain Stahr meant well. He was just too much sometimes. The captain came on over to get a better look at

Kaiyo. As usual, Kaiyo had this man figured out. While the captain stood there, he turned in Officer Brigham's arms and reached out to Stahr. I could almost count down to the moment when Kaiyo melted Captain Stahr's tough bravado. It took a second and the captain was reaching out to Kaiyo. "Take a seat, Stahr," said Officer Brigham flatly. "I think he wants to meet you."

Captain Stahr kept looking at Kaiyo, but he sat as if commanded. Kaiyo was placed in Stahr's lap. Once there, Kaiyo reached and gently pulled off Stahr's sunglasses with one of his little grizzly bear claws. Stahr just sat and played with him for a few moments. Officer Brigham smiled and went out to talk to the other men. Stahr got serious and asked me to sit with him. He kept looking at Kaiyo and said, "Tell me the story."

And I did. It took a while, too. Gracie told him her story, too. Captain Stahr looked angered and confused as he listened. He was rarely quiet. It was all worse than he first thought. The only part I didn't tell him about was what happened to his boss and what happened to Officer Brigham. I didn't know those stories yet. I told him I didn't know what had happened there. Out of nowhere, Dad walked up. "I know those stories."

Captain Stahr stood and shook Dad's hand. They were close friends and had been friends ever since Sheriff Tuttle hired him years ago. "Oh my gosh, McLeod! You look terrible!" said Captain Stahr.

Captain Stahr always called Dad by our last name. "And Susan, you look way too good to be seen with him."

Mom wasn't a believer. She was tired, and she had been up all night. On top of that, she had just spent the last hour rounding up cattle and alpacas in the hot July sun. He was wrong, though, Mom always looked good. At least, to me.

"And you, Troy, look as good as ever. Kinda like a *Jungle Ken* doll looking for *Jungle Barbie*!" said Mom.

They laughed and gave each other a big hug. They talked about Troy's parents and his children.

Dad pulled up a chair and told Sheriff Tuttle's story. It was simple, really. Tuttle had told Dad that when he left checking in with

Mom, he was looking forward to going home. He was in a hurry, and he admitted hurrying was dumb because the driveway was a winding driveway. Also, he remembered the forest being as dark as black ink. He looked briefly to check his phone when Goliath came out of the darkness and crashed into the driver's side of his car, breaking the left side windows. Tuttle swerved off the driveway to the right, and the cruiser tumbled into a steep little gully and flipped over, upside down. Tuttle said the bear reached in and tried hard to get a paw into the side window but the car was snugged too tight into the gully. When the car flipped over, the seat belt held him in, but his shoulder smacked into something and it just popped out of the socket. He sat there for the rest of the night and couldn't get out of his seat belts. Poor thing. He said the bear hung around for some time, left for a while, and then it came back around sunup.

By this time, Officer Brigham and the deputies had come to listen in. "Yeah, that's the same story he told me," said Officer Brigham.

"So," said Captain Stahr. "How did you end up in the sheriff's car?"

"Well," said Officer Brigham. "I was on my way here this morning to evaluate the McLeods' application to keep the cub here. On the driveway, I saw Tuttle's car upside down and in the gully. I got out and started walking over and I heard Lee yell out something like 'Run! Run! Bad bear.' So instead of running to my truck and calling it in, I walked over to Tuttle's car and asked him if he was okay. I really don't know what I was thinking, but when I looked back, that enormous bear had placed himself between me and my truck. I swear, I never heard him at all. He moved like a cat. So, I did the only thing I could. I ran. I ran right at Tuttle's car and jumped into the gully. I scrambled into a broken side window. And the bear was right behind me. He roared in anger. After a few moments, my eyes adjusted to the darkness and I saw Sheriff Tuttle. He was capable of cussing so I knew he would live, but he was upside down and in really bad shape."

Officer Brigham then stood up, took Kaiyo, and looked at Captain Stahr. "Take your walkie-talkies and be careful of the big bear. He's not right."

That was a signal for Captain Stahr to get busy. Captain Stahr patted Kaiyo on his head, and said to me, "Awesome little bear." Then he looked at Officer Brigham and said, "I sure hope you don't take this little guy away from this family. You know whoever else gets him would stick him in a cage, don't you?"

Officer Brigham rolled his eyes. Captain Stahr asked Dad where to get started. Dad wanted their dogs not to confuse bear scent with wolf scent. So far, the wolf wasn't a problem. Dad pointed out where the bear had hidden and watched us when he was in the corn. It was a hot day, and there should be plenty of bear scent left. Dad warned Captain Stahr about Goliath. I overheard Captain Stahr tell Dad, "Don't get all worried. It's just a bear!"

That kind of attitude was dangerous out here. Dad looked back at him and said, "Troy, it's not just a bear. If you let down your guard, he'll kill either you or one of your men."

Captain Stahr looked serious, but then he laughed. The captain turned and called his men together. He barked out some orders and they headed out on foot north toward the fields. The dogs, three big tough bloodhounds, started baying almost immediately.

Dad looked at me and asked me to go help Dean with the regular chores. I thought that was fair. Dean had done more farm work in the last two days than most of us did in the last seven. And Officer Brigham seemed not to want to let go of Kaiyo.

CIRCLES – TRACKER

The only thing I was concerned about at first was whether those dogs were following my scent or the big grizzly's scent. The two scents were mixed in a lot of places. It became obvious they were not interested in me. Twice they crossed my path, and they stuck to the bear's scent trail.

Those soldier types looked pretty tough, but looks can be deceiving. Looking tough and being tough are two different things. I would rather tangle with any one of those men with the dogs than with that horse riding mother down there. Even her foolishly brave little boy was somebody for me to be concerned about. These guys were probably sheep in wolves' clothing. This hunt would tell me if I was right or wrong.

After about forty-five minutes of walking through the corn and the fields, I watched the hunters and dogs head into the western woods. The dogs were still leashed but they were baying loudly. A quick glance over at the farm showed me the family was not going to participate in the hunt. They were performing chores of some sort.

After about an hour or so, it sounded like they had jumped the bear. The dogs were now unleashed and running hard. I was hoping against it, but I knew the bear wasn't far. He was big and mighty smelly. A dog would have absolutely no problem finding him unless the bear was downwind of a strong breeze. And these dogs were not typical dogs, they were bloodhounds. Their noses are among the best of all in the dog world. But that's a problem, too. They were bloodhounds.

Those guys probably got them from the kennels at the county prison. Most bloodhounds are trained to chase people, not wildlife. I would bet they have never chased a wild animal, even a bunny. When it comes to tracking, people and wildlife are not the same types of quarry.

I have tracked a lot of people and each of them for different reasons. When people run, they usually run away in roughly a straight line. They want to put as much distance as they can between themselves and whoever is chasing them. That's usually a good plan if the runner is in a city or in a desert but in places like out here in the woods, that plan won't work and those types all get caught by the faster dogs. Sometimes people will walk the creeks to hide their scent and that can sometimes work, but it rarely does. People chasers will go up and down the creek and they'll usually find where the runner comes out. Plus, creek walking always slows the runner down. Creeks are tricky for everybody. Breaking an ankle or a leg in the rocks and holes hidden in a creek is always a possibility. And these dogs have probably never chased a wild bear who has, so far, seemed far smarter than what I had expected. Something tells me I haven't been told everything. Something also told me those dogs were going to have a rough go of it.

The Western Forest is the best place around here to chase a bear. I am surprised the bear decided to stay there. The Southern Forest is mighty thick, and the bear would have a huge advantage in there. The forest on the east of the farm is a lot like the Southern Forest, but after a few miles, it opens up to the Eastern Wilderness. But the Western Forest is much more open, and those lawmen might to be able to get in some good shots. It's not totally open, though. There are a number of huge thickets that the bear would certainly use to his advantage. They needed to be careful. But they weren't.

My attention went back to the chase. It had started and the bear was on the run. Once again, I was pulling for the dogs. That bear would kill me in a second if it could, especially now we have locked horns. I truly didn't like him. In every way, he was making my job harder.

At first, the dogs' barking and baying was getting farther away. Then, the sound got closer again. Just as I suspected, the bear was circling. Frequently, wild animals run away from their pursuers by running in circles. They run in circles on purpose. First, they don't want to leave the area because their den is there or it's their territory. Second, it's effective at tricking the chaser. The faster they're chased the wider the circles. People hunt rabbits with basset hounds because basset hounds are slow and the rabbits run tighter circles. That way, the hunters can get good shots at the rabbits as the rabbits circle back. Unfortunately for those SWAT team wannabees, they weren't chasing rabbits.

I knew what was going on right when I heard it. I also heard the first bloodhound die. Dying dogs bring out the sadness in most anybody. I doubt he ever saw the bear come at him. Based on the sounds, the bear had run long enough to string out the dogs and he had simply circled around and ambushed the poor thing. It just made me mad at those prideful people down there. Pride has to be the most dangerous of the sins. They were leading those dogs to slaughter because they underestimated this particular bear. And it was a slaughter.

A few minutes later, the second dog lost his life. He cried out as dogs do when they are in such trouble. He had probably run too far ahead of the other dog, and they were both way too far from the men with the guns. At least, it was quick. I hated what was going on and I was getting angry. But this wasn't my fight. It was obvious, though, the bear was having his murderous fun.

Usually, calling an animal evil is a mistake. That notion easily applies to all devils and to more than a few people. But thinking that animals would have such a human-like characteristic is usually misguided. Lots of people think animals are like humans when they are actually nothing like humans. But the thing is, I was thinking this bear may actually be evil. I think he wants to kill for the sake of killing. And I have been just like those people down there. I had been misjudging him since the beginning.

I knew the hunt was over when I heard a gun go off, but it was only fired once. Either the hunter got in a killing shot or the bear circled around the whole group and got to the last hunter in the group. He probably caught the hunter from behind. He was like the other two dogs; he didn't have a chance. Either way, the hunt would be over. If the bear was dead, then that would be just fine with me. If he wasn't and the hunter was dead or wounded, then I figured the rest would lose their taste for fighting and come on out of the woods.

And that's what happened. I saw the farmers in their little vehicle coming quickly out of their main barn. They were headed to the northwest part of the farm. I had a good view from my perch. It took them little time to get the two and a half miles to the edge of the forest. They had a stretcher with them. I guess the bear was still out there. He was probably pleased.

They didn't have to wait. Just before they got there, the hunting party came in view. Three of the men carried one very injured comrade out of the forest and toward the vehicles. If he survived, I would be surprised. He was covered in blood and one of his arms looked like it was nearly torn off. His scalp was hanging off to the side of his head. He was conscious, though. They only had one dog with them. They left the other two back there, and I didn't blame them. That unfortunate man didn't need to get hurt at all. That was the worst thing. Despite being warned, they grossly underestimated this bear. That won't happen again.

CHOPPERS – DEAN

Dad came rushing into the barn to get the UTV and a stretcher we kept in case of an emergency. It was hung up in the barn. The only time we ever used it was when one of the alpacas had wandered off and got attacked by some coyotes. He was bigger, but coyotes are tough critters and they nearly crippled the poor beast. We tied down the alpaca to the stretcher and brought him back. He lived, too.

Dad told me to bring my shotgun. I had it handy. That told me the bear had jumped somebody and was still causing trouble. "Did he live?" I asked.

"Yep," Dad said, as we got into the UTV. "And he was and is mighty lucky. First, the bear didn't kill him. Second, they still have their chopper here. He'll be in a hospital in thirty minutes."

We drove out in silence with Major running alongside of us. We could see the deputies out by the northwestern corner of the farm.

Two were tending to their buddy, and the other two were facing the woods. They only had one dog with them. Too bad they didn't have Gracie's wolf when they started. So far, the wolf and our two dogs are the only things that have caused the bear to be hurt. Oh yeah, and me. I shot him in the head. I forgot that part. And Gracie hit him in the head with a stapler. I bet Goliath hadn't forgotten any of it. That thought made me shudder.

Once we got there, Dad and Captain Stahr loaded the injured deputy on the stretcher and put him on the back of the UTV. He was conscious, and he described the bear that had attacked him. There was no question that it was Goliath. It had knocked him down from behind and then bit into his left arm and about tore it off. He also nearly took off the man's scalp. In the midst of the attack, he got a good look at the bear. He even said the bear had a nasty open gash on his head. Good.

We then turned around and headed for the chopper. It was slow going since the injured deputy was in a lot of pain. Every bump caused him to cry out. The other deputies were trying to encourage him, but he was savagely mauled. They were able to stop the bleeding; that was good. About a half mile from the chopper, the ground was smoother and everybody was able to go faster. The deputies were in a fast jog and still concerned about their buddy. The chopper pilot saw us coming, so he had already hopped off the front porch and had the engines coming to life by the time we got there.

I'll give it to the deputies and Captain Stahr. They moved like a well-trained squad. The injured man was quickly secured, their weapons were stowed, the remaining dog was leashed, and they gave the signal to the pilot to take off. With a tornado of dust, they were up and headed to the hospital. That man needed some help, and I closed my eyes quickly and let God know it.

Two people would be at the hospital, thanks to Goliath. Within a few moments, the farm was quiet again. Officer Brigham was still there on the front porch holding Kaiyo. He looked at my dad and smiled. "Well, Sammy. There goes the cavalry. It's just us now. Unless you plan on running and abandoning the farm, I'm going to call Michelle and let her know I'm going to stay here tonight."

I thought about that for a second. I was glad he thought of him as a part of *us*. Even with sundown still being over five hours away, it looked like we were going to have another night with Goliath. This time, though, we had Dad and Officer Brigham with us. And for some reason, I turned around and looked into the hills to the north. Somewhere up there, I knew the giant wolf was watching us. Somehow, he was still a part of what was going to happen down here.

Our family believes things happen for a reason. The wolf saved Gracie and Kaiyo last night. I don't have a clue why he did that. But not for a second do I believe the wolf just happened to visit the farm and happened to be on our porch and then decide to take on a thousand or so pounds of angry killer bear for no reason. No, that was all on purpose. And I was thinking he would be coming back.

10

THE SCALES FALL OFF – SAM

I was baffled. Goliath had kept us busy for days now. I quit trying to wonder why the bear would want to keep trying to kill us. I quit wondering because no normal bear would go to this amount of effort to do so. We have lived among grizzly bears and black bears for many years, and none of them would have ever tried so hard to kill us. It's not their nature.

Now I'm no fool. Plenty of bears would kill us if we walked right at them and tried to smack 'em around, especially the big grizzly bears. But in general, they basically just want to be left alone. I have known Goliath for years, and other than a few tight spots and a few shots of bear spray, he usually just left us alone as long as we kept our distance. What had enraged him so? And why did I know in my gut this bear was not insane, but instead, he was frighteningly smart and seemed close to pure evil?

Lowe came out and joined me. He was bottle-feeding Kaiyo. He had been here for hours, and for the most part, he's been holding Kaiyo the whole time. I'm pretty certain we were going to be able to keep Kaiyo. But right now, that wasn't my problem. Lowe sat and asked me what I was thinking about.

I looked at him for a minute. He was definitely enjoying Kaiyo. Lowe was looking all goofy and was acting like a doting father. Kaiyo had rolled onto his back and stayed in Lowe's lap. And he was really working on his bottle. Kaiyo was probably somewhere close to forty pounds by now. He would grow about a half pound a day or more, and by this time next year, he'd be well over 200 pounds. I'm not worried about that at all.

Instead of answering Lowe's question, I asked Lowe to describe his impression of Kaiyo. I told him I wasn't talking about what he would put in his report. I wanted to know what he thought Kaiyo was about.

Asking that kind of question is always odd but it forces thought. Descriptive one-word answers like *nice* or *cute* or *fine* won't work. One year, Susan and I had a Sunday school teacher from Louisiana. When his oldest daughter started dating a mouth breathing dreg of male humanity, he asked his daughter what her boyfriend was about. She didn't like the question and she didn't want to answer it. He pressed her and she couldn't answer the question. It didn't matter. The girl broke up with the guy a few days later. She had thought about it, and as she told her dad, she didn't like what her boyfriend was about.

Lowe was a smart man, and I think he knew this kind of question was coming. He struggled with his words but I understood. All of this we were going through was new stuff. Finally, Lowe shifted his eyes from the ground to me. "Sam, words are not quite adequate but I know you have seen something remarkable in this little bear. I could say he's like a dog, and he sort of is. I could say he's like a bear, but there's more. It would almost be easier for me to tell you what he's not. And Sam McLeod, if you ever tell anybody other than Susan what I think about Kaiyo, I'll deny it. Do you understand?"

That just made me laugh, but I told him to keep going. Lowe had an odd, slightly embarrassed look. He continued. "Sam, you and I both know this little bear is not like a regular bear. There's more going on with him than just being a bear. There is no question he's one of a kind. He is smarter now as a cub than any grown bear, and he's sure smarter than any dog I have ever owned. He shows gentleness and even joy at times. Now, I am not saying he's not a bear. He's definitely a bear. He's more like a bear than other hand raised bears.

His comfort with people is as if he considered himself an equal and as if he was meant to live with people. And I can tell you this, that little bear loves your family. I truly believe he has decided he is a part of your family and he will make it happen. That makes no sense but it's true. So I guess to answer this question, I will recommend you get to keep him."

I smiled. "Lowe," I said. "I had already figured that out. I knew once you were with him alone for a while you would let us keep him. I was not remotely worried you would not come to that conclusion. But that's not why I asked the question."

I paused for a minute and asked one final question, "Lowe, you just said you thought Kaiyo was a *one of a kind* bear. Do you really think he's one of a kind?"

Lowe said nothing for a while. He adjusted his hold on Kaiyo. After a few moments, he spoke at just above a whisper level. "No, there is another. But he is as evil as Kaiyo is good. And I think we have a big problem on our hands."

We did indeed.

ALLIES – DEAN

I had sort of been listening in on my dad's conversation with Officer Brigham. I was walking up to talk to them, but when I heard them talking, I just started walking really slow and really quiet, so technically, I wasn't eavesdropping. I walked slow enough that I heard most of their conversation.

It amazed me how grown men would have such a difficult time thinking that things could be different than normal. I had already figured out Goliath and Kaiyo were somehow alike and really special. But I also knew something that Dad and Officer Brigham didn't understand just yet.

I called out a big "Hello," and they both jumped a little. Kaiyo scampered out of Officer Brigham's embrace and ran over to me. I sat and Kaiyo just attacked me. He was ready to play. As we played, I said to Kaiyo kind of loud, "Oh Kaiyo, did these big men finally figure it all out? They did, didn't they?"

Dad turned and looked at me and so did Officer Brigham but I didn't look back. I kept going. "So Kaiyo, how did you convince these sweet old folks? They aren't good learners, are they? No, they are not! And did you know they are still missing something big but they just can't figure it out, can they?"

Kaiyo was having fun. "Dean," Dad said. "Fill us in."

He had a tone. I looked at them both. "Dad, Officer Brigham may not understand, but you do. We all know Goliath is a very special and very dangerous type of bear. In fact, he's so special we haven't gotten on our horses and taken to the woods to hunt him down. I think we could pull it off, especially with Officer Brigham here. Part of that is because Goliath is really, really dangerous, right?"

Dad nodded. I went on. "But there's another part. Do we actually want to kill a bear as amazing as Goliath? I don't, not if we don't have to. Maybe we have no choice, but maybe we do."

"Dean," Dad said. "I need to think about that one. Right now, I am thinking we have no choice but to kill him. But that's only if he comes back."

"Dad. Officer Brigham. I mean no disrespect, but Goliath will come back and he will not be as easy to spot as he was last night. He's probably going to do something different. Our world has been mighty strange since Kaiyo got here. And have you forgotten one of the strangest things that has happened here?"

Officer Brigham just looked confused. Dad didn't. Dad looked at me. "Dean, I haven't forgotten. I am as sure as you are the wolf is still here somewhere, probably watching us. I am pretty sure he followed us out of the Eastern Wilderness. But I don't know what he's got in mind."

"Dad," I said loudly. "You've got to be kidding me. He saved Gracie and he saved Kaiyo and took on that huge bear! Why? That has to count for something, right? Doesn't that give you a hint that he's not trying to harm any of us."

127

I was frustrated now. "Dad, we need his help."

Dad turned his head and looked to the north. "If he's anywhere, he's probably up there watching us. But I think he wants something. I don't think he wants to help us. He's had many opportunities to do so and he hasn't helped yet."

I looked at Dad and said, "He wants Kaiyo."

I was pretty sure of it because it made sense. "Dad, think about it. The only time he got involved was when Goliath was about to kill Kaiyo. In fact, as long as we were in a position to shoot Goliath, he stayed out of it. It was only when the one thing that stood between Goliath and Kaiyo was Gracie, an unarmed little girl, did he get involved. He sure wasn't trying to protect Goliath or me. In fact, he would have let Goliath kill me in the barn. And the wolf can't have Kaiyo. But I think he doesn't want to harm him."

"Yep," said Dad. "That makes some sense. I don't know why he wants him, but I agree. He probably doesn't want to kill or hurt Kaiyo. We probably ought to go find him. We, at least, need to try to make contact."

That was Dad. And I loved him for it. "Lowe," said Dad. "I need you to guard Kaiyo and the girls. Go to your car and grab one of your rifles or your 12-gauge. Keep it loaded and with you at all times. Dean and I need to somehow have a little chat with a wolf."

Officer Brigham no longer looked confused. Around here, the strange had become the new normal. He was getting used to it. "You go get what you need, and I'll tell Susan what you two are going to try to do. Good luck!"

Dad and I headed out to the barn.

EXPOSED – TRACKER

It was an hour or so after the last helicopter took off when I saw a small vehicle come out of the farm and head north. It looked like two people and the smaller dog. I was only somewhat interested as I was just waiting for the big bear to get killed or get run off. Occasionally, I would try to catch the bear's scent but what I could detect told me the giant bear was still miles away in the Western Forest and deep in it. The wind was favorable, and if he started my way, I would know it pretty quickly. I suspected the bear was pretty tired after the chase and after killing two fine dogs and nearly killing the deputy. He probably ate one of those dogs, too. Killing and maiming can work up an appetite. That bear had to go.

My attention was brought back to the vehicle with the people in it. It headed north rather purposefully. It took about fifteen minutes but they drove right past the fields over the middle of the airstrip and then past the grassy field between the airstrip and the forest. They stopped right near the forest edge and about a half mile to my east. I had a good view, but I didn't know what they were trying to do.

The big one got out and I guessed he was the father. He got out and called the dog to him and let him smell something. It looked like dirt, because after his dog smelled it, he crumpled it in his hand and I saw the dust blow gently toward the east. He gave the dog a command and the dog got to work trying to find a scent. They must think the bear was here. But if they did, they didn't bring much of an army. Still, the father was brave and his kid was kind of crazy brave. They were also well armed. Even so, what they were doing was fool-hardy if they were hunting this particular giant bear.

That dog kept working the forest edge. After about ten minutes, they were working fast from my left to my right. The dog found what was left of the deer lodged deep in the willow thicket. There was bear scent aplenty down there, and the dog should have gone on full alert but he didn't. Several times, the dog's tail would wag because he would catch the scent of what he was looking for. I was hoping they were looking for a lost alpaca or a steer or something.

The dog went on alert. I was much higher and still a few hundred yards away, so I was not worried. Then the dog found my trail from early this morning and he was headed my way. Not good. It became obvious they were looking for me. That is not what I needed or wanted right now.

The father then looked up and tried to find me in the miles of broken forested up-country. Good luck on that. I had picked this spot because it was high, comfortable, and easy for me to get to. And it was very well hidden. He called his dog back, and when it came, he patted the dog on the side which made the dog know he did what he was supposed to do. Good man. I respected this family even though what I wanted to do was going to break their hearts.

I watched him scan the landscape with no results. That kid of his kept his eyes out for the bear. He wasn't scared; he was being smart. Just then, the father cupped his hands around his mouth and gave a modestly convincing wolf howl. What was he doing? Then he called out again, loudly. He said his family needed my help because they didn't want to kill the giant grizzly. *Why?* I thought.

Then he said something crazy. "I know that you, the cub, and Goliath come from the same place. We know you have somehow tracked our cub and you want him. You cannot have him. But we need your help."

He stood back. I didn't respond. My mind was reeling from what he had just said. What did they know about me? And as for Goliath, if he had come from my land, I should have known about it. No chance. I definitely don't know everything, but could it be? And who was he to tell me the cub was off limits? But he knew I was after the cub. How could he have figured that out?

For the first time in a long time, I had totally lost control of the situation. And they had figured out quicker than me that the big bear was not a normal bear. I missed it. Not completely, but I missed it.

Well, my cover was blown, and from now on, they would be watching that cub like a hawk. And in a year or so, the cub would be much bigger. There is no way I could force it to leave if it didn't want to, unless I was willing to hurt him. That's not my style.

The father spent a few minutes looking up at the hillsides all around me. When he realized I wasn't going to respond, he turned around and walked back. He then hopped in the cart, and they all headed back to the farm.

I should have probably just left and reported back what was happening here. Maybe somebody else could come back and get the cub. Maybe a watcher would be better suited to snatch the cub. This part about helping humans was not what I do. In fact, I am not supposed to interact with people at all. I do what I agree to do and I do it, that's about it. And I never agreed to anything like this.

Revelation – Libby

Dad, Dean, and Officer Brigham were nuts. They have over-thought this whole thing. Here's the problem—we have a nuisance bear. Period. Granted, this one is bigger and stronger than any bear I've ever seen, but so what? There always has to be a biggest of anything. I'm sure the biggest buffalo or elk or deer is out there somewhere. Big deal. Big doesn't mean anything other than big.

It is true, bears are rarely ever a real problem around here. Every once in a while when food gets scarce, some black bears will go into town and go dumpster diving but that's about it. The police used to kill them, but now, they shoot them with paintball guns, and if that doesn't work, they shoot them with bean bags. It seems to do the job and it doesn't kill them. It just hurts, and they decide town is not a good place for them to be.

Shooting Goliath with a bean bag, though, would be stupid. That bear is too dangerous. He needed to be shot with real guns using real bullets and a lot of them. That's how you take care of a gigantic, nuisance bear that wants to kill you. That bear is not special. He's gone crazy and he needs to go.

Dad and Mom and Officer Brigham had been together for about twenty minutes. They were planning for Goliath's return. It was after five o'clock in the afternoon so we would have about four more hours of sunlight, so they better get to it. They broke their meeting and all got to work. Dean was in the barn using a power drill for something, and Dad has been sawing and nailing lumber. I got the best of the jobs. Who gets to play with a fur ball made of pure, cute bear cub?

I grabbed Kaiyo and pulled him close to me. He smelled really good, but that's only because we gave him a bath. He didn't smell too good after he spent a few hours with Rosie. But he loved the bath. Of course, he did. There is no question Kaiyo is special and very different. I was the first to notice it.

It brought to mind what has happened over the last few days. There was the Elk Pen a few days ago when Kaiyo tried to warn me about the buffalos. I thought of when Kaiyo hopped in my saddle and didn't bite me or claw me or anything. I think everybody else in the family started getting it when we watched Kaiyo win over Peyton. I didn't expect him to be such good friends with us, the dogs, or with the men who've been here. Then, just yesterday, I woke up to him on my stomach and staring at me with his paws on my face. I knew before anybody he wasn't just another wild animal. Then, as people got to know him, they noticed the difference, too. Even Captain Stahr noticed the difference.

Just then, Kaiyo turned in my arms and faced me. He looked me in my eyes for a few moments and then he gave me a hug. He held on tight. He was already getting strong. When he was done, he pulled back and went back to playing with Gracie. That was about the sweetest thing ever. I watched and thought about that. Most bear hugs are not for good. Bears usually hug things to kill them, not to love them. Kaiyo had somehow turned his nature into something wonderful.

I was still in the kitchen when Dean came in the house to make a snack for him and Dad. He looked over at us and smiled.

"So, what are you making in the barn?" I asked.

He said he had been busy making some not-welcome mats. Not-welcome mats were sheets of half inch plywood that had hundreds of pointy, sharp wood screws screwed through them. Stepping on those mats is like stepping on a bed of sharp, pointed nails. It hurts and should keep the bear away from our doors. That actually was a good idea. People have been using not-welcome mats to keep bears out of their cabins for years.

From out of the blue, Dean asked if I knew if Kaiyo was different. Of course I did, and I told him I knew it before he did. I knew Dean was working me to make a point. He knows that the person who asks the questions controls the conversations. I swear he argues like a trial lawyer.

"Now, Sis, take that one step farther. Open your mind. Goliath has been hell bent on killing Kaiyo from the beginning. Why is that? Why is he hanging out over there in the Western Forest waiting to try it again? We both know that stories about bears who hold grudges and stalk humans over long distances are always Hollywood hokum. We've been living with black bears and grizzly bears all of our life. We know bears just don't ever do that. Everyone who has chased Goliath will tell you they misjudged him. Everybody from Dad to Officer Brigham, Captain Stahr, and that poor man Goliath nearly mauled to death will tell you Goliath is not *just a bear*. He thinks ahead. He plans. Grizzly bears just don't do those things. They can't. They don't think that way. But this one does. Do you really think this is a nuisance bear? Because if you do, then Goliath already has the advantage over you. As for me, the bear is an amazing bear, and there is only one other like it. That's why Goliath wants to kill Kaiyo. Until we take out Goliath, Kaiyo is in big trouble. But there are only two of these guys out there, perhaps the only two in the world. That's why the rest of us don't want to kill Goliath unless we have to."

Geez. I had to give it to Dean. That was a pretty convincing argument. Dean was just standing there finishing his sandwich. But I could tell he was thinking. I was, too. So I asked him, "What about the wolf?"

Dean looked at me, shook his head, and wiped his mouth. "Wildcard."

Then, he left toting a sandwich for Dad and went back to work. We all had work to do. I heard the backhoe start up. I think Dean had gotten busy again. Dad was out back, too. What they were doing was still a mystery.

Just then, I heard an airplane.

11

THE VISIT – LIBBY

Our family was planning something. People in planes just don't fly in unless there is a good reason. I looked out the kitchen window and saw Mom and Officer Brigham take the UTV and head to the airstrip. After a few minutes, I heard the plane land and taxi to the end of the strip. Technically, the airstrip is in the top middle of the farm. The first part of the strip is the rifle range and it goes another 2,000 feet to the east. The whole top of the farm is planted in grass, but Dad keeps that 2,000 feet airstrip in top notch condition. The grass is kept cut and deep ruts are filled in and seeded over. It is actually a nice place to have a picnic. But not today. Goliath was truly spoiling everything.

We all stepped outside onto the porch. It was easy. We hadn't yet fixed the kitchen door. The door was broken and wouldn't close. The frame was broken, too, and it and the door were basically just kind of hanging there. I was hoping somebody would remember to fix this thing before nightfall. Otherwise, Goliath could just stroll right in. Moose and Major think it's awesome to come and go as they please.

As we stood there, I looked at Kaiyo standing next to Rosie. Kaiyo was growing, but so was Rosie. Dad had called Dr. Cindy this morning and told her what was going on with Kaiyo, Goliath, and with the dead and wounded farm animals. Dr. Cindy had already heard about Goliath. She told us everybody in town was talking about it. She also asked about Rosie. Fortunately, we had formula for crias. The formula is for lambs but it is also perfect for crias. Both the cub and the cria had eaten well today, and by looking at their bellies from above, it showed. Rosie is just a precious little creature. Kaiyo seemed to know about Sunny, and he obviously made Rosie feel better. She had a terrible night and she apparently didn't want to leave his side. Hearing her little alpaca toes clip clop on the hardwood floors of the porch was a treat.

But we have raised alpacas long enough to know they need their herd. I have even heard adult alpacas that identify with humans can get dangerous. Rosie was cute but not special like Kaiyo. We all hopped off the porch and started walking up the path to the pasture that held the alpacas. It was a pretty far walk but the bear and the alpaca needed some exercise. Moose walked with me. It was amazing how he just ignored his wounds. He was one tough dog.

As we were walking, the UTV was coming our way. I saw Davey's airplane parked in the distance. That meant Davey was visiting. If he was here to help, that would be great. We could sure use an extra hand. We still had the animals to bury and some very important doors to fix. I think Dad or Dean fixed the broken fences but it would be only a temporary fix.

As the UTV got closer, I was thrilled to see Dr. Cindy riding with the others. We had a number of wounded animals and they needed Dr. Cindy's help. I had sort of forgotten about the wounded animals. I'm glad Dad or Mom didn't. And that explained why Davey was here, too.

Dr. Cindy brought a lot of stuff with her. She had her bag, she had some large animal bell style collars, and she brought some bandaging materials. Also, she had two rifle cases. That made no sense to me. I have never seen her with a gun. She also brought a small travel suitcase. So did Davey. Weird. Well, with Goliath about, the more the merrier.

They pulled up next to us, and she hopped out to look at Kaiyo. "Goodness, you have grown," she said. She looked him over and then looked at Davey and said "We have about two hours of sunlight, so let's get to it." She then looked at me. "Where's your father?"

I told her he was probably with Dean burying the animals out behind the barn. By the sound of it, the backhoe was busy digging a hole. They all went to go see them. Kaiyo and Rosie walked up the path together. Wow, they were cute. They played as we walked until we got to the pasture where the surviving alpacas were. They all crowded the fence at the sight of Rosie. I lifted Rosie up and over the fence and she walked into the herd. I lifted Kaiyo so he could watch Rosie get with her herd. One of the older males came and had a weird look. He stared at Kaiyo and then walked off. The difference between a good bear and a bad one was probably hard for them all to understand.

I saw Officer Brigham and Dr. Cindy take the UTV and begin the long task of tending to the injured animals. All the while, the sun got lower and we still had a lot of work to do.

THE VISIT — SUSAN

The downstairs of our house was a somewhat open plan with a tremendous fireplace separating the front two-thirds from the kitchen. The kitchen took the back third. Groups of furniture were placed upfront here and there to break up the open space and to create living areas. Sam did have an enclosed den he loved. It was part library, part TV room, and part game room. We put Officer Tuttle in there when he was waiting for the medivac chopper to get here.

The kitchen had been cleaned up from Goliath's attempt last night at breaking and entering. He broke but he didn't enter. That was a miracle. As for the kitchen door, Sam had taken a sheet of thick plywood and reinforced it with two-by-fours and made a temporary door. It looked both strong and ugly. Right now, I was very happy with strong and ugly. I could get a real door later.

I looked around at the faces that were staring at one another. Dr. Cindy looked concerned but not frightened. Davey was just being Davey. He made a few wise cracks but he was here. Lowe had spent the entire day here working, and he had changed out of his uniform into some of Sam's jeans and a polo shirt. Put those same clothes on Sam and he looks wrinkled and rugged. Lowe looks like he's going to the club for dinner.

Libby looked ready, so did Dean. Gracie was on the floor playing with Kaiyo. Major was inside standing guard. Moose was lying on the ground, exhausted and in obvious pain.

Sam came in, and while I loved him, he looked terrible. He was dirty and needed a bath. He wasn't joking around and he could best be described as grim and determined. But his eyes were clear and sharp. He called us to order and made sure that Davey, Lowe, and I had our rifles handy. Dean and Libby had their firearms nearby. For some reason, Dr. Cindy's rifles were still in the two cases they came in.

Sam looked at the group, pulled up a chair, and cleared his throat. He looked us over and asked each of us what we ought to do with the bear. He looked at Dr. Cindy and at Davey and said, "No offense, but Goliath hasn't tried to kill either of you or your family, so you all can participate in the discussion but no voting."

Davey laughed. "Hah, Well, he hasn't tried to kill us yet."

"Well, Davey," Sam said. "If Goliath kills you tonight, then we will keep your points in mind."

Everybody laughed, but the seriousness of everything restored the bleak grimness of our moods. Sam stood and looked us over. "Assume, for the sake of argument, that we have a way to take him alive. Then, how do you want him, dead or alive?"

After that, the discussion was lively. Libby and I wanted the bear dead, but Libby was far more certain. I was more open-minded. She spoke well and I was proud of her. She pointed out Goliath hated us and wanted to kill Kaiyo. When she said that, Kaiyo stopped playing and looked at Libby. Libby reassured Kaiyo and he looked better. He rejoined Gracie on the floor. Libby reminded us that killing a bear was much easier than catching a bear, especially a giant bear. She made it clear we were playing with dynamite, and not only were we making things harder for ourselves, but we were toying with a giant bear that was freakishly smart.

Dean then stood and stated his position. He first asked us if we had noticed that Kaiyo understood Libby. I did. I thought it was interesting. Everybody noticed. "That," said Dean. "Is why we can't kill Goliath. Goliath is just as smart as he is, and because he's older, he's probably smarter. Whatever Goliath is, he is not a true bear. Oh, he's still a bear, but he's also something else. And do we want to be the people who killed one of the two or three most amazing animals ever?"

We each looked at one another. The kids had made some very good points.

After Dean finished talking, there was movement outside on the north side of the porch. I glanced at the window and I saw we were being watched. I was filled with sheer terror, and all of a sudden, I couldn't breathe. There, a pair of glowing eyes stared back at me. Sam saw the glowing eyes at the same time. He slowly stood up. Everybody else's eyes followed mine, and their gasps filled the room. Dr. Cindy nearly screamed. I quickly grabbed at my rifle and so did Lowe. Sam stopped me and quietly asked Lowe to lower his rifle. Libby scooped up Kaiyo and ran behind me. Dean, of course, stood and started walking toward the window. I growled at him to stay put. He did. He saw I was really scared. As for the rest of us, it was like the air was taken out of the room. Major caught its scent and he started barking loudly. Moose joined in.

Sam quickly quieted the dogs and looked over at those menacing eyes. Sam turned back to us slowly and on purpose. In a deliberate manner, he calmly said to us, "I believe we have a guest. Unless anybody objects, I am going to invite him in."

Without waiting for an objection, Sam headed to the front door. I was speechless and I cradled my rifle in my lap. Sam had made more than his share of mistakes in the past, and this crazy stunt of his could get dangerous really quick.

The glowing eyes stayed on us, then turned away slowly toward the front of the house. The wolf was here. Again.

Sam opened the door, and the beast stepped out of the porch light and into the doorway. He stood there and stopped as he surveyed the scene. Goodness, that was a big animal. His shoulders nearly filled the doorway and his head was well above the door knob. Our dogs had magically changed from our defenders to total suck-ups. They ran up to lick his face, and he let them for a moment. He then gave a low, warning growl and the dogs retreated. He stepped inside and continued to look us over. His gaze ended at Kaiyo. He stared at him as if Kaiyo were his prey.

Sam then said, "Mr. Wolf, I do not know your name but you are welcome in my house. But if you attempt to take Kaiyo, well, that just won't do. If you came here for that, please leave. We still have Goliath to deal with first. And tomorrow, we will then have to deal with you."

The wolf looked at Sam for a moment, he had been challenged. If that thing was different from any old wolf, then he got the point. If he was just a wolf, then we just let an enormous carnivore into the house. Either way, this was new ground. The wolf seemed to nod and he stepped forward. "Well, good then," said Sam.

They walked over to us together. I was waiting for him to leap and try to kill somebody.

The wolf inspected each of us. He registered our scents, though in a far more dignified manner than if a dog was checking us out. As he did, we told him our names. Last was Gracie. He walked to her, and she just looked at him and smiled. "I know you! You saved me when everybody else left me alone with the big bear. Thank you."

The wolf sat and let Gracie hug him. I thought he would pull back, but he didn't. Instead, he nuzzled her and licked her face. She was in seventh heaven. And he was enormous. If he wanted to be, he could be one big, bad wolf. Moose almost looked small next to him.

Then, he turned his attention to Kaiyo. Libby refused at first, but Kaiyo wriggled free and went over to the wolf. There, they just stared at each other for a while. Something was going on. Then Kaiyo leaped at him and they rolled around as if we didn't exist. Oh my gosh, he and Kaiyo really were alike.

After a few more minutes, Sam said to him, "Mr. Wolf, would you want to join us as we discuss what happens with Goliath?"

The wolf stood and looked at Kaiyo and growled. As if ordered, Kaiyo went back to Libby. The wolf then came over and sat right next to me and listened to the plans and the debate. The dogs followed him and plopped on the floor behind him. I questioned their loyalty.

Anyway, the wolf's head was actually higher than mine as we sat. As he panted, I would get occasional glimpses of his teeth. They looked like white steak knives. This was as surreal as I could ever imagine. But the stakes were high, and the time to marvel and try to figure it all out would have to be delayed. Regardless, whatever happened tonight, I was glad the wolf was on our side.

The Plan – Sam

We all believed that Goliath wouldn't attack until after midnight. The wolf nodded in agreement. The question, really, was how we could capture Goliath. Dr. Cindy stood and brought back one of the rifles in its case. She put the case on the floor, opened the latches, and pulled out an odd-looking gun. It didn't look like much of a bear gun but I knew what it was. Lowe did, too.

Dr. Cindy spoke to the rest, "If you have a chance of stopping that bear without killing it, this is the way." Everyone stared. "If you can get close enough, then this will do it. This rifle shoots a dart that will administer a dose of powerful tranquilizer that will put Goliath to sleep for twenty minutes, at least."

Susan was impressed. So were Davey and Lowe. Dean's mind was working. Libby said, "Okay, so that bear will wake up after twenty minutes, then what? He's not going to just blow us a kiss and leave, you know."

Susan agreed with Libby, and it seemed like the wolf agreed with her, too.

So I asked the group again, "If we could safely shoot Goliath with the sleepy darts and if we could safely keep him captive, would that be better than just killing him?"

The air filled with questions from everybody, but I told them all to focus on the question. The wolf seemed to be enjoying himself. He was probably trying to figure out why we even cared. I wondered myself.

Davey raised his hand and said, "Okay, I know I have no vote but I am here and I'm not particularly interested in being a casualty and I don't want to be flying somebody to the hospital or worse. Your question, Sam, isn't fair. Before anyone can answer your question, what's your plan?"

He was probably right. Getting a commitment from anybody was too much to ask, I guess. So, it was time to reveal the plan. I told them I was assuming Goliath would come back tonight and he probably had a plan. "My guess is he thought last night would have worked but for the wolf. I think he would want to isolate Kaiyo again. I think he's going to try to lure the family away from Gracie and Kaiyo like last night because it worked."

Gracie jumped up and grabbed the wolf and said, "I'm ready!"

We all laughed. The wolf obviously liked Gracie and he licked her cheek. I even think I saw his tail wag.

I looked at the group. "First, I need to know which of us here are the best shots. Besides me."

The group looked around, and after some discussion, it came down to Libby and Susan. Everybody here was a good enough shot but Davey knew how good our girls were. Lowe objected because he was also very handy with a gun but Davey convinced him he would come in third in a shooting contest with them. That wolf paid special attention to the discussion. I told Libby, Susan, and Dr. Cindy to break off and go learn how to use those dart rifles.

I asked the wolf if Goliath would be able to figure out we had reinforcements with Lowe, Davey, Dr. Cindy, and him being here. The wolf clearly agreed. "Good," I said. "We're going to need your nose."

I looked at Dean and told him I needed as much fresh Kaiyo poop as he could find. "Lowe, get out of my clothes and put your uniform back on. Cindy, you'll have to shower and change, as well. And wolf, we'll have to talk."

Everybody looked at me like I was crazy. Kaiyo stared at me. The wolf cocked his head. Then, I laid out the whole plan. Nobody liked it, but everybody agreed it was best.

12

PREPARATION — LIBBY

Nearly every family that likes to hunt has to deal with the advantages wild game has over people. Some animals are fast; others have terrific eyesight. But most wild game is expert at catching and identifying scents. Everybody knows bears are the best at it, too. They're even better than dogs. Try going into the woods all stinky and you'll create a biological desert. Perfumes and colognes will give you away very quickly, too. Even if you and your clothes are clean, the residue of scented detergents and nearly all hand soaps and body washes are easily detected by wild animals and they look at them as human scent. So, the hunting industry long ago created soaps and detergents that were unscented. They also made sprays that were pretty good at covering up scent. They weren't perfect but they were pretty good. And we had a lot of it.

Dad said we had to get Kaiyo out of here. We simply couldn't risk letting Goliath have a shot at the little bear. At the same time, Goliath had to believe we still had Kaiyo here. It would also be in our best interest to make Goliath think the reinforcements had left, too. Unfortunately, we didn't have time to bring the farm animals into the barns. We had clothes to wash and baths to take.

We needed Goliath to think Davey, Dr. Cindy, Officer Brigham, and Dad had left. We also needed Goliath to believe Kaiyo and Gracie stayed here. But actually, they were going to leave and Dad and Dr. Cindy would stay. Oh, we also had to make Goliath think the wolf was not here, too. All this needed to be done quickly.

Dad was a blur of barking orders. First, he put his dirty clothes in a bag, and after he showered up using the unscented soap, he put on clean clothes. He had also told Dr. Cindy to do the same thing. She headed upstairs to the guest bath. Meanwhile, both Kaiyo and the wolf needed to be as scent-free as possible. We had a big mud room off the kitchen that had a shower in it. Working on a farm, having a mud room is a sweet luxury and it always came in handy. First, we washed Kaiyo. The water was warm and he thoroughly enjoyed it. He liked baths. He was scrubbed clean and we did it again. We washed Gracie at the same time. Both came out as smell-free as possible. We put her in some clean clothes, and we put Kaiyo in one of Dad's smelly tee shirts. We also sprayed both of them with some of Dad's cologne. The wolf looked like it worked.

Dad handed Davey a 12-gauge shotgun loaded with slugs, and Officer Brigham had a rifle. He also had his sidearm. Dad told Moose and Major to "Go dog patrol."

The two dogs ran out of the house and circled the house and barn. They were back in a few minutes. They showed no alarm. With the wind gently coming from the north, that meant no Goliath. At least, he wasn't in the fields. He could be in the Southern Forest but the dogs ran the edge of it, and if he was out there, he wasn't very close.

That was our cue. We quickly gathered together in a circle and held hands to pray. The wolf growled as he rushed to join us. He squeezed in between Mom and Gracie, as Gracie held Mom's hand. Everybody saw him do it. His great head lowered, as Dad prayed aloud for deliverance and safe passage for everybody. His head stayed lowered until Dad got to "Amen."

Well, I would definitely have to think that one over later when I had more time. Then, we got busy. We were in one weird world right now.

KAIYO

First, we put a bunch of Dad's dirty clothes plus Dr. Cindy's clothes in the bed of the pickup. Kaiyo was wrapped in a blanket, and then he and Gracie were put on the floorboards of the back seat of Officer Brigham's truck.

Davey got in Dad's pickup truck and started its engine. Officer Brigham stepped into his police truck. Dad looked at Officer Brigham. "Lowe, use your lights and siren, and go as fast as our driveway will safely allow you. When you get on the road, go straight to your house. If you see anything, especially if you see Goliath, call me on my landline as soon as you can safely do so. But most important, get some mileage between you and him. Call us when you get home."

The cruiser's lights lit the area in ghostly blue. The siren was so loud it could have woken the dead. And then they pulled out. About five minutes later, we watched as the little convoy slipped into the depths of the Western Forest. The lights disappeared into the far away wooded gloom, as the sound got harder and harder to hear. Then silence. Dad turned around and said, "Let's keep going."

Everybody went inside. It was the four of us, plus Dr. Cindy and the huge wolf. I looked at Dad. "Now?"

"Yep," said Dad. "It's now or never. Dean, Libby, get 'er done."

Mom and Dad were smiling, as Dean walked to the wolf and threw his arm over the wolf's thick neck. Dean seemed only slightly taller than the wolf. Dean leaned over and loudly whispered in the wolf's ear, "Bath time, big guy."

The wolf looked startled. His ears went back and he growled. But he didn't know Dean. First, Dean wasn't much afraid. Second, Dean was about to give him a question-filled lecture. No one wanted one of those.

"Mr. Wolf," said a smiling Dean. "You know as well as I do, as well as we all do, that Goliath absolutely has to believe Dad and you are somewhere else, right?" Dean kept going. "Of course, you do. You know the plan. You also know the plan depends on it. So how are we going to do that if you won't cooperate? If you don't, the plan won't work. You cannot let your pride get in the way here. See, not only do people have pride but some animals do, too. And I think we

145

can all agree pride's usually a bad thing, right? Of course, we can. So here we are with you being pretty stinky. I mean, if I can smell you, I am sure that bear can. Seriously, do you ever bathe? No offense here, but where you come from, do you folks ever get clean? I'm just guessing they don't. Or maybe you've just been out here for a while. Hey, Dad, Mom, come over here and get a whiff of this big male wolf and let me know what you think..."

They never had a chance to get that whiff. The wolf whined, threw Dean's arm off his back, and he just started walking toward the shower by himself. His head was down and he knew he had been beaten. The wolf looked like he was shaking his head in disbelief. I caught up to him and told him not to worry, it wouldn't take too long. Hah, little did he know I was going to take my sweet time. Who gets to give a wild wolf a bath without getting killed?

I got to be honest, giving the wolf a bath was a ton of fun. He just sat there and let us soap him down. A couple of times he growled, but we ignored him. Dean and I worked in tandem, each on either side of the wolf. We covered him with strong smelling straw-berry shampoo. We almost used a whole bottle. He hated it, but we scrubbed him up and down. When he was rinsed, we dried him off with some big fluffy towels. As we were toweling him off, the big wolf's attitude started picking up. *Weird*, I thought to myself. *Just like a dog.*

When we were about done, I heard Dad come into the kitchen and tell us "Times up!"

Oh my gosh! The wolf's tail went up, and he practically pranced out of the shower room. Right into the kitchen, he met Dad and jumped on his chest, knocking him down. He ran around the kitchen island a couple of times. Then he ran into the front of the house to see everybody else. He went after the nearest rug and rubbed his muzzle and neck and rolled all over it. There was hardly a part of his fur he didn't roll on. In the midst of it all, he made what we describe as *happy noises*. We heard Dr. Cindy and Mom shriek, as he got to his feet and give himself a mighty shake. Water flew off his coat and sprayed the ladies from top to bottom. They then loudly complimented the wolf while trying to hold back their laughter. All we could hear was clacking of his claws as he ran around on the hardwood floors.

Dean and I were laughing so hard it was tough to stop. So, Mr. Mighty Wolf is still just a glorified dog! Dad was leaning on the table unsuccessfully trying to hold in his laughter. The wolf then pranced back in, head high, front paws stepping out, and he was acting all happy. He was looking to see what was next. With his hair all clean and puffed out, he looked even bigger, if that were possible.

Mom and Dr. Cindy strolled in. Mom went over to the wolf and she cradled his giant muzzle in her hands. "Mr. Wolf, we know you have a name, but we don't know it. But we do know you are brave and probably a little dangerous. So, we are just going to call you by a new name. How about the name Big Bad Wolf?"

The wolf gave a low growl and shook his head from side to side. "Okay," said Mom. "So definitely not that."

Mom looked over at Dean. "Any ideas?"

Dean thought for a moment. "Dad and I think he tracked us from the Eastern Wilderness. Try something like Finder or Tracker or Catcher."

Mom looked at the wolf. "How about Finder?" The wolf again shook his head from side to side. "Tracker?" asked Mom again. I could tell she was expecting another negative response. But the wolf's tail wagged immediately and he licked Mom's face.

So, that name would do. Mom looked back at Dean and said, "That's the better name. The other two sounded dumb."

"Better than Big Bad Wolf," Dean replied.

He was right about that one.

Preparation − Sam

While Libby and Dean were bathing Tracker, I went to the barn, opened the horse stalls, and led each horse out of the barn and away from the house. I hopped on Hershel bareback, and we galloped to the pastures. The other horses followed. I opened all the gates and drove the cows out of the pastures into the open fields. They were surprised but seemed pretty happy to be released into the corn. Next, we went to the alpaca pastures and goat pastures and repeated the process. I figure as long as they could run away from the bear, they were safer than being bottled up in the pastures, even big ones like ours. The cows with calves couldn't run, so Dean and I had already made sure they and the pigs were buttoned up in their respective barns. I hopped off Hershel and took off his bridle and turned for the walk back home. He and Peyton tried to follow me as I headed home, but I turned them back. Tonight was not going to be another night of terror for them.

I made it back in time to see Tracker do the clean-dog dance. That was priceless. After that, I slipped into the shower again and washed off the sweat and lathered up with the pretty, strawberry smelling wolf shampoo. I put on some of my hunting clothes that were unscented. Then, I shot myself a few times with Susan's perfume. When the wolf came by, I hit him with a few shots of the perfume. He ignored me.

By now, it had been dark for a while, certainly since before Tracker got here. What was going to go down was going to go down in my house, and soon, too. The barn was empty. I had Dean bring me the Kaiyo poop. There wasn't much of it but it would have to do. I placed poop on three saucers, and Dean ran it upstairs and put it in the open windowsills of my room—one on the north side, one on the east side overlooking the courtyard, and one on the south side overlooking the driveway. We then grabbed anything that smelled like Gracie or Kaiyo and put it in my room, too.

Libby and Mom got Dr. Cindy to make the tranquilizer. She looked at us and repeated that the darts were made for animals as big as a grizzly, but shooting Goliath twice would be a good idea. We were told not to worry about an overdose. Just then, the phone rang. Susan took the call. It was Lowe. Susan put it on speaker. Everybody, including the wolf, gathered around. Lowe told us Gracie and Kaiyo were safe at his house. Everybody breathed a sigh of relief. He went on to say that as they drove through the woods, Goliath stood on the edge of the driveway on a hard curve. That curve slowed the trucks, and he craned his nose in the air to catch the scents while he stood and tried to look in. Lowe said Gracie and Kaiyo were on the floorboards and Goliath probably didn't figure it out. Davey chimed in he saw it all and Goliath checked out my truck. Davey watched Goliath drop to all fours and head toward the house. So, he was on the way. I was not surprised. They told us to be careful and to call when we won. I liked that.

I called the dogs in and placed a not-welcome-mat in front of the front door. I quickly screwed it into the porch decking. *He won't be coming this way*, I thought to myself. I firmly closed the temporary back door but left it unlocked. This is where he would need to come in.

We all went upstairs to wait.

THE END OF THE BEGINNING — TRACKER

Tonight was definitely an eventful evening. I made contact with the family and a few of their friends. They called the giant bear Goliath. From what I know of the story of David and Goliath, the name fit. Not without some reason, this family and at least one of their friends doesn't want to kill him. They probably should. But they think Goliath is a very different type of bear. They consider him very rare, and I guess from their perspective, he is. The truth is, bears that can think like Goliath aren't so rare. They're just not around here. But I admire the hearts of those family members. They want to do the right thing. Doing the right thing is sometimes rarer than a bear with brains.

I also learned baths were nice. Who knew? Sure, I embarrassed myself, but it felt great. Now, just looking at myself, I felt silly. I was wearing one of the mother's oversized sleeping tee shirts because it smelled like her, and they have doused me liberally with perfume. It was tight and I didn't like it. The two older children laugh every time they walk by. The only reason I hadn't ripped it off me is so I could avoid another lecture from the boy. That was punishing. I looked ridiculous and smelled terrible, too. But I do like these people. If I survived, I would surely miss them.

The plan was simple. If the bear takes the bait, then he will come in the house, stroll up the steps, and wander down the hall. He will head to the back bedroom where he will smell what he thinks is the cub and the little girl. As he passes two of the other bedrooms, he will be shot with the darts by the two females. Each will be shooting from the outside windows as they safely stand on the roof over the porch. Then, he'll go to sleep nicely. After that, I guess they'll tape his jaws shut, slap a leash on him, and take him to the pokey. No wonder no one much liked the plan.

The way in to our room will be blocked by one of those cruel boards covered in sharp nails and screws. But since it is designed to stop the bear, I think its fine. I doubt the plan will work. There are too many things that can go wrong. Before the night is over, the bear will be dead, and most likely, I'll be dead, too. I would be in the back room to stop the bear so the girls can try again to get more shots off if they miss or fail to get off shots as he goes by the other bedroom door openings. If he does come in, he'll have to deal with me, the two dogs, and the heavily armed Dad who'll be on the porch roof, too. That's a lot of opposition, but Goliath won't surrender, and he will fight savagely, probably even as he dies. There is very little room to maneuver in the room, and maneuver is my only advantage.

As we waited, the father came in the room. He sat on the bed next to me and talked. He didn't act like it was odd in the least. He told me how they had captured the cub. He was wrong on that. The cub had captured them, they just didn't notice.

He told me about the farm and his wife and about their kids. For most of their lives, it had been hard. Farming is tough. There were some near catastrophic injuries, and several times, their crops were destroyed by drought. He mentioned his parents and how the passing of his father was hard. But he talked as if it was all commonplace stuff. Best of all, he had hope and faith and gratitude for the many good things in his life. This is why this family is special. I had to keep in mind, though, that as much as I liked him, the father's hopefulness and optimism just might get somebody killed tonight, too.

The hours passed and we walked to the rooms and checked on everybody. The older girl slept some while the two other ladies paced or fidgeted nervously. They were told the moment the bear broke in the kitchen, they were to step out of the windows and on to the porch roof and get their rifles ready. All the lights were on, so seeing the bear ought to be no problem.

I kept getting whiffs of him, so I knew he was around. The dad would say "Was that him?" and I would nod. Then, the smell would go away.

Eventually, though, Goliath wandered into the edge of the courtyard. Every bit of him was suspicious, and he was ready to bolt if he felt threatened. The dad told me to keep low. He held his phone and out came the voice of his youngest child. He had recorded it earlier, but I was not there then. From a darkened corner, I and the two dogs watched. That little girl screamed at the bear to get lost and to leave and that her mommy and daddy were gonna come back really soon.

He came closer. This time, the dad told the bigger dog to start barking. The bear came closer. I was hoping everybody was now awake. Then, the dad got enough of a view to figure out where the bear was and he lobbed a stapler out the window at the bear. I don't quite know what the stapler meant to the bear, but he didn't like it. In fact, it filled him with rage. The dad didn't even hit him with it. He missed. But the bear was fit to be tied. He sniffed it, popped his jaws, and roared. And he made an incredibly fast beeline for the backdoor. We all heard the crash. He was coming fast. I heard people scramble out of windows.

The bear satisfied himself at first with vandalizing the kitchen. That made the dad mad, and he played the recordings of the little girl. Upon hearing that, Goliath charged up the stairs. His great weight caused the steps to creak and crack as he came up. As he turned at the top of the steps, he could see all the way down the wide hall into the room I was in. He suspected something. He stayed put. The dogs were staying in the room, and they didn't give chase. He didn't see the girl or the bear. It was all odd. I thought he was about to head on back downstairs. Once he was in the open, he would go on another killing spree.

To heck with it. It was my turn. I stepped out from behind the furniture, and I had the decoy. The bear saw me and was stopped in his tracks. The use of a decoy is one of the oldest tricks around. Year in year out, hunters use them because they often work.

The older girl had a big teddy bear toy that was about the same color and size as Kaiyo. The dad had brought it to his room earlier as a potential decoy. He called it Happy Bear. I grabbed Happy Bear behind the head and growled. Goliath knew I had beaten him to it. He probably figured I had killed the little girl. He knew me or my type, and he figured I was taking the cub back home. There are few things more compelling than a sense of loss. A sense of loss forces many creatures to make decisions they could or should put off for later.

Goliath felt a sense of loss, and he wanted the cub so he could kill him and me, too. He roared and raced down the hall. I kept the stuffed animal and jumped out the window. I landed about four feet lower on the slightly sloped porch roof. I quickly looked around. It was like a party back there. Nobody was left in the house. Everybody was on the roof and five guns were pointed into the room.

The bear somehow saw the board of nails and he simply jumped over it and he sailed into the bedroom. He was so quick. When he landed, he pulled up to a quick stop. He looked about. There was no one in the room. Even the dogs had been pulled out. The moment he stopped, two air guns fired from both sides. It was close quarters, and the bear was huge. Missing would have been hard. Both darts found their marks and each one sunk its venom deeply into the great bear's haunches. He had been had, and he knew it.

For the first time, I saw fear on his twisted face. He whirled around and leaped over the booby trap and he raced down the hall. The medicine was quick, though. In the few short seconds it took to get back to the top of the steps, he was already feeling the effects. He quickly became confused and groggy. His head hung low and he got wobbly. He wandered aimlessly around upstairs for a while, breaking a few things when he walked into them. Finally, he floundered to the hardwood floor near the top of the steps and quit moving.

The people cheered. The dad came to me and gave me a huge hug. "You did it, Tracker. You did it! Without you, he would have spooked. Thank you, thank you!"

The boy came by and hugged me, too. Then the girl hugged me and cried, and then the mom did the same. She looked at me and said, "I hope you know how much you have helped."

Even the doctor came over and thanked me. But in the elation of it all, I felt a deep pit in my stomach. My job just got so much harder.

Prison Builders – Dean

My granddad used to hunt a lot, but as he got older, he would usually come back with nothing. He may have missed a few shots, but I doubt it. He told me he passed up some good shots "because once you shoot a deer, you just got a bunch of new problems."

He was right. I remember him telling me, "First, you gotta gut it. Then, you gotta haul it out. Then you gotta hang it, then you gotta skin it, and then you gotta butcher it. That's a lot of gottas." Then, he would laugh.

Well, that's nothing compared to the problems you get when you have 1,500 pounds of unconscious killer bear upstairs in your house with a wake-up call that's on a really short timer! Those are real problems. But those are exactly the problems we planned on.

Dr. Cindy barked out, "Twenty minutes, people! Libby, get over here with the dart rifle and let's load you up, just in case."

She went over to the bear and checked him out. Goliath was out stone cold. Dr. Cindy checked his breathing and his pulse. Meanwhile, Dad and I lifted the dogs back through the window, and they ran over and sniffed the bear. Tracker stood guard off to the side. I darted past all of it and ran downstairs and out through the brightly lit courtyard. Just past the driveway in the dark, I had parked the Bobcat with a bucket. There was about 100 feet of rope in the bucket, and we needed to drag the beast down the stairs and out of the house. I hopped in and started it, and then backed to the house. I passed Dad who was in the courtyard. He whistled for Peyton. Dad has the loudest, most annoying whistle known to man. It's so high it hurts. But out here, he gets results with the whistle. It travels for miles. Having Peyton here would be a nice backup, too. Peyton is actually stronger than the Bobcat.

I parked the Bobcat right at the back steps and raced upstairs with the rope. Dad was right behind me. We got to the bear in time to hear Dr. Cindy yell out "Seventeen minutes!" to anyone willing to hear. Mom and Libby stood by with guns. Mom traded in her dart rifle for her real rifle. That ought to work if he wakes up early.

Dad and I quickly put a loop around the bear's shoulders. Dad also put a big blanket on the steps for Goliath to slide on. I thought that was sort of silly since Goliath actually was a living rug. He was already furry and his fur ought to be pretty slippery but the blanket thing was Dad's idea. There was no arguing; we were in a hurry.

I took the other end the rope and ran downstairs and then out the back door to the waiting Bobcat. Peyton was there watching the whole series of events unfold. I made a quick bowline knot and attached the rope to the Bobcat. I gave the word and Dad yelled for me to move out slow. I did and quickly realized the bear was already down the steps. Once we got him headed down the steps, there was no stopping him. He just tumbled on down.

Getting him out of the kitchen was a lot harder. He was so big he collected furniture around his legs and he got stopped by what was left of our big kitchen island he had trashed earlier. Finally, he got jammed sideways at the door. "Twelve minutes," cried out Dr. Cindy. We were a blur of action while we fought to straighten Goliath out so he could be pulled out the door. If he could get in by himself, we knew we could drag him out. Peyton was staring in disbelief. He must have thought we were amazing. To him, we were the mighty bear slayers. Except for Kaiyo. Peyton didn't like bears at all, so this whole scene must have been fascinating. It was definitely fascinating to me. The wolf and the dogs stood out of the way and watched.

I dragged the bear out of the house and into the courtyard. Then, I wheeled the Bobcat around and lowered the bucket. Dad said the Bobcat was rated to about 1,500 pounds so it would be close. I didn't think Goliath would weigh that much, but who knew? I didn't want to pinch his skin, so I lowered the bucket to scrape up part of the driveway. Mom, Libby, Dad, and Dr. Cindy all had to help push his torso into the bucket. He didn't really fit. The bucket was barely big enough. He went in on his back as his head, legs, and arms hung out of the bucket. He looked bigger than the Bobcat. The creepy part was, he kept his eye on me the whole time. He might have been in la-la land from those drugs, but he was awake. Fortunately, he couldn't move. Yet.

Now it was a race. "Eight minutes!" yelled out Dr. Cindy.

Behind the barn about another sixty yards is where Dad had hatched this whole plan. That's where we were all headed. I had been using the backhoe to dig a mass grave for the animals Goliath had killed the night before. Because cows are so big, Dad told me a shallow grave was not going to do. He had me dig deep. Using the backhoe, I dug an eight-foot by eight-foot pit. He came and looked at the hole. He thought for a few minutes, and told me to go six feet deeper and six feet wider. I didn't understand it until he told me it had to be deep enough and wide enough to hold a giant bear that would want out. Then, he winked at me. Dad had an antique Ford backhoe that was bigger than anything we needed out here but he always kept it in great condition. Its arm could reach out eighteen feet, so digging a fourteen-foot-deep hole was very doable. So, I did. Dad had made a simple ramp out of lumber and some sheets of heavy duty plywood. He told me the ramp had to be steep and it was. It was designed to break the bear's fall so it could roll into the hole.

"Five minutes!" yelled Dr. Cindy. By that time, I and my Bobcat and a parade of folks and animals were going double time to get to the pit. Goliath was starting to move. Dad had moved up a bank of lights so seeing was no problem. Dad ran alongside me and said, "Dean, drive to the ramp and drop the bucket. He'll roll into the pit. Then, back out of there and I'll use the backhoe to lift the ramp up and out. We have time!"

Well, if Dad believed it, I believed it. And that's what we did.

Prison – Libby

We were all jogging to keep up with the Bobcat. It looked like a little ant carrying a big beetle. That bear was so big. I watched as Dean drove to the edge of the pit while lowering and tipping the bucket full of bear. Goliath rolled out and his forward motion sent him tumbling harmlessly down the incline. I say *harmlessly* but I do not know for sure if it hurt him or not. I know there's a video out there of a tranquilized black bear that fell out of a tree and onto a trampoline put there by concerned people. When the bear hit that trampoline, the bear shot back up in the air and arced over into the yard, striking the ground head first. They say the bear had no ill effects from the trampoline launch. Once you know that, the video is pretty darn funny. And Goliath is much bigger and stronger than that black bear and he was only rolled into the pit. Nobody dropped him, he rolled. So, yeah, he was probably fine.

When Goliath hit the bottom, Dad's backhoe pulled up on the chains that were attached to the ramp. It lifted easily out of the pit and Dad swung the boom away and off to the side and delicately lowered the ramp to the ground. He shut off the engine and yelled, "And that's how it's done!"

And with that, we had a bad bear in a deep hole. Now what? "Libbers," said Dad. "If the bear wakes up and starts figuring out a way to get out, give him a dart!"

Libbers was one of his regular nicknames for me. There were dozens of others. But I liked what he said. I'll happily keep this bear all doped up. He was definitely smart enough to figure a way out, and he was strong enough to do it. The soil was fairly soft. The pit wasn't meant to keep him, it was only meant to put him at a huge disadvantage. If he tried to get out, I would shoot him with a sleepy dart. Dr. Cindy had a lot more of that stuff. And since Officer Brigham was part of this whole scheme, there would be no problems with the government if we decide to keep a drugged up bear for a few days. Finally, the backup plan is if he somehow looks like he is trying to get out, everybody on watch will use their real guns and we'll shoot him full of holes. He didn't have any good options.

Dean, Dad, and Officer Brigham, and maybe Mom, were thinking Goliath might figure out that peaceful coexistence is better than death or living his days out in a zoo somewhere. At first, Dr. Cindy didn't quite get that Goliath, Kaiyo, and Tracker were different. But after seeing more of Kaiyo and from watching the wolf, she was hoping to save Goliath. I think I was the only one who still didn't believe Goliath could be turned to see things our way. But if he can't, I am happy with the options of life in prison or the death penalty.

The sudden roar told me Goliath was awake. Oh goody. I looked into the pit that was lit beautifully by the bank of lights Dad had put up. Dad uses those lights out in the farm when we have to work past sunset. They were incredibly bright. From the bear's point of view, all he could see when he looked up was some humanoid silhouettes standing in front of the blinding bank of lights. From the pit, I imagine it looked like a scene out of the movie *Close Encounters*. He probably figured he'd been abducted by aliens. And in a way, I guess, he had.

He was still a little groggy and he wasn't steady on his feet, but his temper was unimpaired. Several times, he tried to jump but it didn't work. Bears are incredible animals, but they really aren't very good at the vertical leap, not to mention, he was impaired by the drugs. Dr. Cindy brought me a new rifle. "This one is different. It will put him into a deep sleep that will last for hours. It doesn't have the quick knock down power of the tranquilizer but it is a slow release drug. He'll sleep for another four to five hours. By then, it will be light outside."

Hitting the bear was easier than shooting fish in a barrel. I aimed at his haunch and pulled the trigger. Goliath was asleep in five minutes. Everybody breathed a sigh of relief. That bear was so annoying.

After a few minutes, Tracker wandered over to me and tugged at the tee shirt that he was still wearing. I asked if he wanted it off and he nodded. Dad and I took it off, and we both thanked him again. Dad then said that he had first watch. He told Dr. Cindy, Tracker, and me to go get some shut-eye. The three of us looked at each other and we gladly headed toward the house. I actually thought the wolf would object, but that was not the case. Dad asked Dean to fork some hay for Peyton and to take him into his stall and then head on inside and go to bed. "Can do!" said Dean. He led Peyton into the barn and was in the house five minutes later.

Once inside, Mom made a call over to Officer Brigham's voice mail. The only thing she said was "Chicken's in the pot."

Everybody chuckled at that bit of code. Even the wolf's tail wagged. I watched as Mom was a blur of action. She made snacks for the wolf, started a pot of coffee for Dad, and quickly led all of us upstairs.

"Cindy," said Mom. "We're going to put you in the guest bedroom."

Dr. Cindy gave everybody a hug and headed off to bed. Then Mom looked at the wolf and said, "Tracker, is it okay if you sleep in Dean's room? He sleeps in the top bunk."

The wolf looked surprised but happy for the offer. In three steps and a short hop, he was nestled in the bottom bunk. As we said good-night and turned off the lights, I heard his tail thump the bed.

Mom and I took the not-welcome mat that I had leaned against the wall earlier, and we put it in my closet so nobody would step on it. Then, we both headed into her room. I heard Dean go into his room, climb in bed, and say good night to Tracker. Mom and I then crawled into her bed. She looked at me in the shadowed darkness and said, "Libby, I am so proud of you that words aren't enough. In the face of terrible danger, you didn't flinch. I cannot wait to see what kind of woman you will be. As a fifteen-year-old, you have already accomplished more than most women who are three times your age."

Taking compliments is hard for me, and probably for everybody. But I have learned that simply accepting a compliment with a real *thank you* is the best way to thank the one who gives the compliment. People who try to deflect a compliment appear ungracious, but it's hard not to do. I thanked her. I grabbed Mom's face. In the semi light cast from the outside lights, she looked so young and pretty. I took it in. Then I told her, "We have an amazing family, Mom. Look what we just did."

I watched as she fell asleep. I prayed Mom would live a long time and stay with me for as long as possible, and that Dad would get to walk me and then Gracie down the aisle. I was asleep before I could say amen.

My dreams were troubled that night. I wasn't alone. Mom cried out several times, so did Dean. A couple times I looked out the window to see if I could see Dad, but the great barn hid him from view. But the sharp glow of those lights told me he was there, watching the bear and watching over us. I knew we were safe and sleep returned.

I awoke to the sound of the many song birds that live at the farm and to the smell of bacon.

13

THE TURN – SAM

No matter what I do or where I am, there is something uplifting to my soul to see the first streaks of red or yellow pierce the night's darkness. Sunrise happened quickly, and that first sliver of red sun in the east quickly turned to yellow as the sun climbed over the far distant eastern mountains. I stamped my feet and shook off the morning chill. That bear had been asleep for four hours, so the drug would be wearing off soon. I suspected he was going to wake up pretty grumpy.

It was light enough to turn off the lights and the generator. The generator is noisy, but I thank God for it. Being able to keep my eye on Goliath was more than comforting. As the sun climbed, I got a better look at Goliath. He was a truly magnificent creature. He was probably about 1,500 pounds, and when he stood, he was at least ten feet tall. His fur was a very pretty grizzled blond. Despite a few dog and wolf bites and a gash on his head, he looked to be in pretty good condition.

I had known for a while that the bear was smart. Not just bear smart. I was thinking he may be people smart. While that sounds ludicrous, I have a wolf in the house that is people smart. Goliath is still 100% bear, so he's not like a man in an enormous bear suit. For all I knew, he was a mutant. I didn't believe that, really, nor did it matter. What mattered was maybe Goliath could make a decision and stick with it.

I heard somebody open the back door. I would need to replace the door and frame soon. I looked forward to the company of whoever was coming my way. A few minutes later, Susan and the wolf came out of the back of the barn. That was another door I would have to fix. They looked rested, and Susan had coffee for me. She hugged me as I grasped the mug. Instinctively, I reached and patted the wolf. He didn't seem to mind it, and the three of us just stood there for a moment. We watched the slumbering bear, and I think we all gave thanks. I liked this wolf. He seemed to belong here. We'll see how he behaves when Kaiyo gets here. I haven't forgotten his plans and our plans are probably not the same. Right now, though, Susan and I went and sat in our lawn chairs and the wolf was between us. Both Susan and I had our hands on his back as he sat and we talked. He liked the whole thing. So did we, but it was not going to be permanent, I think.

After a few minutes, Susan stood to go back inside and make breakfast. "Can you make three batches of bacon?" I asked her. "Everybody will be pretty hungry,"

Susan laughed and said, "And it will kick off your plan, right?"

"Well, don't forget Tracker," I said. "He's a hero and heroes get hungry."

I swear, if a wolf could smile, he did. His tail wagged as he got up to go with Susan. He quit smiling, though, when I asked him to stay with me. That wolf looked so disappointed. Susan laughed and gave him a big hug. "Oh sweetie," she said. "The wait will be worth it. Hang in there, big guy."

He obviously liked Susan. He turned and sat back down with me. As Susan disappeared, the wolf and I talked. Well, sort of talked. Whatever he was, he understood English but he could only speak wolf. So, I had to rely on understanding his expressions and shakes of his head. After a while, communicating with him got easy. He knew my plan was to turn Goliath from an enemy into an ally. It was obvious he wasn't sure it could happen, but he did understand Goliath had some difficult choices ahead of him.

I was looking at him when Tracker's ears pricked forward. He saw movement. I looked, and Goliath was waking up. I had my rifle, one of Dr. Cindy's sleepy-dart rifles, and a full can of bear spray. We were ready for anything from Goliath. If he stayed in the pit, he would be safe. But if Goliath started to try coming out, I would spray him. If that didn't work, then I would try to tranquilize him. If there was no time, I would have to shoot him. No matter what, the bear was going to stay in the hole.

We watched as Goliath checked out his prison. He sniffed at each corner and he sniffed the walls. His demeanor surprised me. True, he was trying to figure a way out but his rage was not present. Finally, he stood and stared at me and the wolf. I didn't trust those eyes. I believed that at that moment, he still had malice on the mind.

So, I told him what his options were. "Goliath, you only have a few choices. We can kill you now. There is nothing you could do about it, either. All I have to do is level this rifle at you and start shooting and that would be it and this pit would be your grave. There is no place to run and you can't get out. In fact, if we wanted to kill you, you would have been killed last night or this morning. I could bring up three or four more guns, too, and we could just shoot you to pieces. And trust me, there's at least one of them in there who thinks you are too dangerous to be allowed to live."

"Your next choice is life in prison. There are probably five to ten zoos in the US and Canada that would love to have you. Look at you. You're huge and ferocious. You would be a big popular attraction. People would come from miles around to see a big bear like you that's known to have already tried to kill a man or two. You would be famous. They would stare at you and throw you peanuts. The children would mock you and the parents would laugh at the killer on concrete. The next day, it would all start over again. That would be your life until the day you die a natural death."

I let it sink in. I continued, "All we have to do is go make a few phone calls, and pretty soon, a big truck is going to pull up and some men will stuff you in a cage. The first of many cages for you. They'll shoot you full of medicine, and there's nothing you could do to stop it from happening. Several people here think that is the most humane thing for you. For whatever reason, you left your home and have had a chip on your shoulder against everyone. You have been a criminal because you aren't like the other bears, are you? They can't help who they are, but you can.

"And that leaves us with the last option. Because you can make decisions, this is the one I recommend. And by the way, not everybody agrees with me. Some think you are too evil and they may be right. But please, hear me out."

That bear stood there and didn't move a muscle. He was hanging on my every word. So, I continued. "Okay. Think of a life where you are free. You can go back to where you came from or you can continue to live in the Eastern Wilderness. But there are conditions. Your days of killing your kind and others from wherever you came from are over. Also, there will be no killing people or their livestock or their dogs. And that crummy temper of yours has got to go. It's going to get you killed. And if I am out there and you try to charge me again, even if I am only ten feet from you, I will just start shooting. No more running or bear spray from me. You may get at me, but you won't survive."

"This is your last chance. Also, I don't know how you are going to do it, but somehow, if this is your choice, you are going to have to prove to me you can live by the rules.

"We think killing you would be murder. But we also think, if we did, it would be justified. Our God, I don't know if you know him, is a God of second and third and fourth and even ten thousand chances. Because of him, that's why you are going to get a second chance. But we're not nearly as good as God is, that's why you only get one more chance from us. If you squander the next chance, you will then be explaining things to God face-to-face."

With that, the giant bear sat and faced away from us in his earthen cube. He looked stunned. It was probably the effects of the drugs, but maybe he was thinking of the choices. Dean came on out and stared at Goliath and asked, "Did you tell him?" I told him that I did. "Did he listen?" he asked.

He looked over at Tracker and said "How did Dad do? Did he lay it all out for him?"

The wolf nodded. "Well, good then. If you need me to chat with him, just let me know. By the way, Mom wants you two in the kitchen. Breakfast is ready. I got this."

With that, Tracker was already headed back through the barn. I told Dean "If Goliath does something like try to get out, then just shoot him in the head."

I said it loud enough Goliath could hear me. He was sitting on the ground turned away from us, but I saw his head turn back to me and then turn away. Yep, he heard me.

TURNING – DEAN

Our animals were suffering. For the last three days, especially the last two, the everyday needs of the farm were neglected. We still had to bury the dead cattle and alpacas. They had been laid out in the hot summer sun for a couple of days now, and by the end of today, they would be ripe. The animals all needed to be rounded up. When Davey and Officer Brigham get here with Gracie and Kaiyo, that would release the rest of us to go back to taking care of the farm.

Right now, though, I could only do one job well. Dad always told us that, for the most part, if we had a choice of doing two things poorly or one thing well, it was always better to do one thing well. And now, my job was to shoot the bear if he tried to get out. That's a job I could do well if I had to, but I sure didn't want to. Oh, I knew he was a killer, and in killing Kaiyo's mother, he became a murderer. In trying to kill that poor deputy, he became an attempted murderer. In the killing of those dogs and our farm animals, he became a vandal. In the killing of Rosie's mother, Sunny, he showed evil. His list of crimes was pretty impressive.

"You know, I said. "You are a pretty amazing beast."

The bear turned to look at me. He saw a little kid all alone. If he thought this was his chance, well, now was the time. He stood on his back legs to get a better view. I expected a charge or an attempt to frighten me. I had my 20-gauge shotgun, but it was not aimed at him. The pit was deep, but when he stood, his head came close to the edge. If he worked at it, he could easily get out of here. The only thing stopping him was me. The bear huffed a few times, but he just watched me.

"You have your choices but I know what a smart and evil bear would be doing. He'd be thinking of a way to trick us. You know, act like he was ready to turn a new leaf but go back to being the killer of the Eastern Wilderness. Why, you may even think you could pick off one of us when we go out there hunting or maybe carry off a lone hiker or two. Who would know, right?"

The bear stayed on his feet. He was listening. Now, he may have been listening just to relieve the boredom, but he was at least listening. And I like to talk. Maybe I was talking just to relieve my own boredom.

"Well," I said. "Everybody would know. See, if Dad lets you go, then he's really sticking his neck out for you. Do you think Captain Stahr is going to forget you killed his dogs and nearly killed one of his men? He won't, and that injured deputy won't forget. Officer Brigham is breaking some rules about getting rid of killer bears because he thinks you're special. And even though the Eastern Wilderness is huge, there is no place to hide. You step out of line just once, then everybody will know and they will come for you. You cannot outrun helicopters or four-wheelers or even horses. This is a man's world. Finding a bear as big as you are would be easy. So, if you are thinking of lying for your freedom, it's pretty shortsighted."

He dropped to all fours and went back to his place staring at the far wall. After about thirty more minutes, Dad and Tracker came up. Dad was carrying a bucket of water and another bucket holding about a pound of cooked bacon with him. Goliath turned around because it smelled so good.

"Goliath," Dad said. "We are not barbarians. As our prisoner, you will be treated well as you ponder your future."

Dad lowered the buckets, water first, then the bacon. Goliath sniffed the bacon. He waited. "It's not poison and it's not more medicine. Enjoy."

With that, Goliath ate. For him, it was just a snack, but it was obvious he loved it. I watched as Tracker watched Goliath. I kept watching as Tracker looked around. He went to Dad and using his snout, he pushed Dad away from the edge of the pit. He kept pushing until Dad was twenty-five feet or so away and unable to see in it. Then he came for me. I could tell he wanted some time with the bear, so I headed on back. Once I did, Tracker sat on the edge and looked into the pit. This all made me uncomfortable because the further away we got from the edge of the pit, our advantage shrank.

Dad and I watched as some sort of discussion was going on. We certainly couldn't understand, to me it sounded like growling. This went on for about an hour, and the discussion got heated at times. Several times, Dad and I started to come forward only to get *the look* from Tracker. I knew that look. Mom was a pro at giving it to me.

Officer Brigham and Davey soon came driving up the driveway. Libby, Dr. Cindy, and Mom ran into the courtyard to greet them. The greeting was pretty raucous as they all peppered Mom and Libby and Dr. Cindy with questions. Gracie was right in there. She wanted to know everything. So much had happened in just ten hours, and they wanted to know it all. Kaiyo was happy to be with Libby again. When he spied us, he wiggled free and came running. I gave my shotgun to Dad. I knew what was going to happen. Kaiyo hit me at a sprint. It was like catching a furry bowling ball. I fell backward, even though I tried not to. Everybody laughed. Then, he moved on to Dad.

After a few moments, he caught Tracker's eye. Kaiyo headed toward him. Libby was close, and she shrieked when she saw Kaiyo approach the pit. She got *the look* from the wolf. It worked on Libby, too. She got quiet and watched with her hands over her mouth.

Then, we were an audience to something special. The three of a kind—two free and one prisoner—had their time together. Libby and Mom were pretty terrified Kaiyo would fall in the pit and get killed. But I trusted the wolf. None of us were willing to cross the wolf anyway. He was in control of the situation; that was obvious.

Officer Brigham volunteered to stand watch. Mom and Dad had some rounding up to do. Dad gave Davey a walkie-talkie and directed him to the UTV. Then, Davey headed to his plane. I walked over to the dairy barn to milk the cows. Libby went over to feed the few pigs. And in hours, all the animals were rounded up with the help of Davey spotting them from the air, the cows were milked, and the other animals were fed. And during the time, the three special animals kept up with their discussions.

Officer Brigham continued keeping watch. By noon, it was time for Dr. Cindy to go home. She left us with a rifle and enough darts to take out a herd of elephants. She and Davey were taken back to the plane, and we watched as it lifted off and flew directly over us. Goliath owed his life to her. We'll see if he wanted to keep it.

TURNED – LIBBY

The whole thing was weird but we were used to it. I watched as Dad, from time to time during the day, would talk to the wolf. Dad would then look at Officer Brigham or Mom and shake his head from side to side. Then, the wolf would go back to where he was. Dad suspended a tarp over the pit so Goliath could stay out of the sun. Kaiyo and Rosie were playing in and out of the barn, and the sun moved steadily across the nearly cloudless sky. It was hot, and I wanted life around here to go back to normal. Well, not true normal. I wanted Kaiyo to still be with us and he wasn't normal.

Dad and Dean decided to butcher the cattle Goliath had killed. They hid the operation from the other animals. Dad brought a few choice cuts over to the wolf. He obviously liked that. Dad lowered a shoulder roast to Goliath. Tracker and Goliath continued to discuss things over their lunch. I prayed the bear would change. He was special and I didn't want him dead, now. The other alternative—life in prison—seemed a sad thing for such an impressive creature, too.

Over the following hours, we each took our time watching over Goliath. Sometimes the wolf would make us back off, and the two creatures would growl and chatter at one another. It was getting very late in the day and we all were talking about watching the bear during the night. Then, just when we started to get used to the situation, we saw the horror happen in slow motion. Isn't that the way it always happens? Car wrecks seem to happen in slow motion. Bad falls seem to take longer to hit the ground. And there was nothing we could do but watch in slow motion.

Kaiyo and Rosie were back to playing in the barn. She and Kaiyo were chasing each other when she ran out of the back of barn. In a few quick seconds, she had cleared the distance to the pit and she wasn't stopping. Tracker tried to stop her, but she obviously thought it was all part of the fun. We watched as she tumbled over and into the pit. Everybody ran to the edge of the pit and watched in horror as Goliath was upon her. She tried to get away, but there was no place to go. Dad reached out for the dart rifle when the wolf bit and held Dad's arm. Dean had brought his shotgun up to his shoulder, and Officer Brigham had leveled his rifle when the wolf suddenly barked. This was his first bark, so it caught us all by surprise. In fact, I didn't even know wolves could bark. Well, they can, and when we looked at him, he looked ferocious. Goodness, he was scary looking. We all just looked at the wolf. He looked like he was going to attack one of us.

Then, Gracie and Kaiyo walked from behind us to the edge of the pit and Gracie said, "Look in there. Rosie's okay!"

I expected to see pieces of Rosie. What I saw was Goliath nuzzling Rosie gently. She was obviously uncomfortable, but she was alive. Meanwhile, Mom pulled Gracie back from the edge, but we all watched. Dad grabbed the rope connected to the water bucket while Dean went into the barn and grabbed the biggest bucket we had. They feverishly attached it to the rope and lowered it. We watched as

Goliath pushed the little alpaca toward the bucket. Bears and canines differ in a lot of ways, but one of the most obvious is bears can turn their wrists. Cats can do the same with their wrists. Dogs, foxes, and wolves can't. That ability to turn the wrist allows a paw to be used more like a hand. And there before our eyes, Goliath clumsily picked up Rosie and put her into the bucket. It wasn't pretty but it worked. Dean pulled Rosie up and out of the pit.

The wolf just looked on with what seemed like approval. Dad turned back to look at us. "Maybe our nightmare is over."

What the heck just happened? Was it over?

RETURNED – LIBBY

Well, it wasn't over. It was just a part of our story which certainly was not over. Goliath had been in the pit for at least seventeen hours. Those close quarters gave him a dose of reality and a glimpse of his future. I think he feared living in a zoo more than he feared death. Bears can live a long time, and I doubt that Goliath was an old bear. If anything, he was only about seven to twelve years old. That's barely middle age for a captive bear. That meant he could live in a cage for another fifteen to twenty years. Even if his enclosure was a big one, that would be nothing compared to the vast, open lands of the Eastern Wilderness.

Goliath's other option was to be killed by us, and I can't imagine that would be an option. If he had thought he could get away, I am sure he realized he would be marked as a bad bear. He would be hunted down and killed quickly. So, the confinement and whatever Dad, Dean, and the wolf told him had sunk in, too.

Dad went over and talked to the wolf. I am not sure what was discussed, but Dad told Mom to get Gracie and Kaiyo inside. With them gone, he said, "Lowe, Dean, Libby, stand back about forty feet, stand together, and if he comes your way, feel free to shoot him. Dean, control the dogs but release them if you think you need to."

Dad looked in the pit, stood straight, but pointed his gun to the ground. He spoke slowly and clearly to Goliath. "Okay, Goliath, don't do anything stupid. Everybody's still pretty scared of you. Let me know if you understand."

With that, Goliath nodded. Dad walked over to the backhoe and used the fork like a crane boom. He picked up the ramp, rotated it over the pit, and gently lowered it. When it hit the ground, Dad hopped out, looked at Goliath, and said, "Are you ready for a change? Then, come on out."

The bear crawled out of that hole like Godzilla crawling out of the Pacific. He was so big. His great head peered around as his bulk and enormous strength propelled him up and out. The dogs started going nuts, but a bark from Tracker shut them up. Dad went straight over to the bear and looked right at him. Goodness, Dad was brave. "Okay, let's get away from this hole," said Dad.

With that, Dad led the bear past the barn through the courtyard and over to the house. We all followed. He told the bear to stay, and Dad hopped up on the porch so he could get a good view. We all stood back. Mom, Gracie, Kaiyo, and Rosie watched from the windows inside. Mom and Rosie were horrified. Kaiyo and Gracie wanted out.

Dad looked back at Mom and asked for the first aid kit. Mom shoved it out of the temporary kitchen door and then closed it quickly. Dad grabbed it and started working on Goliath's gunshot wound and the bite wounds left by the wolf and the dogs. All the time, Dad was talking to the bear. None of us knew what was being said, but they seemed to be okay with one another. I looked around. Dean and Officer Brigham were fascinated. I looked at the wolf, and he looked back at me and cocked his head. He was as curious as I was.

For the next half hour, Dad tended to Goliath's wounds. Occasionally, Goliath would bawl when Dad cleaned the wounds but Dad ignored it. He put on the medicine and kept talking. When he was done, Dad looked at Goliath. "Ready?"

The bear nodded and Dad looked over at us. "Okay. Lowe, can you come over here?"

Officer Brigham looked around and took some tentative steps toward the bear. "It's okay, Lowe," said Dad. "Come sit right here."

Dad patted the edge of the back porch deck. We all came closer.

Officer Brigham went over and sat next to Dad. Dad looked at Goliath and said, "As I told you, stay away from all people. There are a few poachers out in the wilderness, and there are hunting seasons for black bears. So, from now on, during hunting season, you should probably stay here on the farm or in the woods around the farm. The place is loaded with deer, moose, and elk, so the eating will be good and we'll help there, too. This is Officer Brigham and it's his job to protect you. If you have trouble with humans, it's up to him to make sure you are safe."

For a bear, Goliath had a "You gotta be kidding me?" look.

"Yep," said Dad. "If you ever see him out there, let him know you are nearby. And whenever you are on my land, Officer Brigham knows only a few people are allowed to hunt my lands, and we never hunt bears. Unless we have to. So, if you see him, he's protecting you, and the safest place you can be is next to him."

After that, Dad brought each of us to meet Goliath. It was very strange but it all fit in with the last few days. When Goliath met Dean, they both looked a little sheepish. Both had come close to killing each other just a few days before, so it was awkward. But Dad explained how their conflict made them respect the other because they were both warriors. It went well with them both.

I was introduced to Goliath and realized Kaiyo would be about as big in a few short years. Goliath was a fearsome creature, but I wasn't really afraid. For the first time, though, I was truly glad we didn't kill him. He was so majestic. All I could think to say was that when we see him in the Eastern Wilderness, I would bring him some treats. He shook his big beautiful bear head in approval.

Next came Mom, and they chatted for a few minutes. Last to meet Goliath was Gracie. Mom was super nervous, but you just got to know Gracie. She came up and just started talking before Dad even had a chance to introduce her. She talked about how everybody left her alone and how the bear tried to kill her. She talked about the wolf and she talked about how scared she was. When she was done, she hopped off the porch and hugged the giant bear. Mom didn't breathe. Gracie then grabbed the big bear's head, looked deep into his eyes, and said, "But I forgive you." The bear hung his head and hugged her right back.

I don't know where he came from, but forgiveness wasn't something he was used to, at least, not for a long while. It was obvious, though, he liked the idea.

With night falling, the great bear and everybody else were invited to dinner. Every human pitched in, and a feast of sorts was prepared for both man and beast. Plates were brought out to the back porch and so were chairs. Some big plastic bowls were filled with water for the animals. Then, Dad called everyone to prayer. We formed into a circle right in the courtyard. The wolf was included. Goliath hung back, but Gracie was having none of that. She left her place in the circle and brought Goliath in to stand next to her. The wolf watched it all and seemed to smile. Dad prayed and gave thanks to God for new beginnings and for inner and outer healing. And he gave thanks for the example of the thief on the cross and how we all needed and depended on that kind of grace. I don't know if bears can cry, but something was going on with Goliath. His groaning was deep but not too deep to hear. And our hearts were full.

Then, amidst laughter and some amazing stories, we humans, the bears, and the wolf ate until it hurt. For the next few hours, everybody played and stayed outside under the stars. Flying insects circled the outside lights as that became a summer night to remember. The dogs enjoyed fetch and chase, we tossed a football and Frisbees, and the three special animals roughhoused together and with us. From then on, they were known as the Specials.

As the night continued toward midnight, the inevitable fatigue of accumulated sleepless nights and fear-filled days crept up on us all. Mom started cleaning, and Officer Brigham got a call and was summoned home. We said good-bye to Officer Brigham as he hopped in his truck and left us. What a friend he had been.

Dad told Goliath he was welcome to stay on the farm that night and for as long as he wanted. We all said good night to him and to Tracker as they settled in on the porch. Gracie hung back and tried to stay with them, but Mom and Dad said no. That night, I had a baby grizzly in my bedroom and an enormous grizzly on the porch. And a wolf, too! Who could say that? My dreams were a mix of good and bad and everything in the middle. But I slept well. We all did.

The next morning, I woke up early but Goliath was already gone. And so was the wolf. I ran into the barn, but they were not there. I looked for them around the house, too, but I couldn't find them. Then I realized they had left us. I fell to my knees and wept. My heart was broken and I cried until there was nothing left in me. After a few minutes, I looked up and saw Kaiyo peering at me from the open kitchen door. As our eyes met, Kaiyo took a few hesitant steps and then galloped over to me. As Kaiyo squirmed and made his way into my lap, he gave me a gentle kiss on my cheek. In moments, my sadness melted away. And on that day, to a degree, life on the farm returned to normal. Except we had Kaiyo with us. And even though Kaiyo was a constant blessing, there would be no *normal* with Kaiyo around.

PART 2

SANCTIFIED

September — Susan

It had been almost two months since Kaiyo had come to be with us. We had seen nothing of the wolf, but Sam has heard reports that Goliath was back in the Eastern Wilderness. Even though there is no hunting season on grizzly bears yet, the hunting season on black bears was in full swing. Sam has been troubled to no end that some overeager hunter or a poacher will try to take a shot at Goliath. If the farm's harvest time wasn't right around the corner, Sam would go out there to try to bring Goliath back. Also, I think all of us missed the wolf. Dean and Gracie talk about him the most.

There is a hunting season on wolves, too. Sam isn't happy with the state's decision to have a wolf season, but he's quick to acknowledge we have not had our dogs or livestock killed by wolves either. A lot of people hate wolves, and the hatred between man and wolf goes way back to ancient times. Some others, however, think wolves are just another breed of dog. Both groups are wrong. Wolves are wolves, and they want to eat and breed just like all other animals. They are not the savage man-killers legend has made them out to be. Nor are they just misunderstood wild dogs frolicking in the snow. Instead, they are dangerous wild animals that have been known to kill people, even though very rarely. Hopefully, we will, as a people and as a great state, find more and more land for them to roam and make the wilderness just a little wilder.

Sam thinks Tracker is smart enough to avoid the hunters, but I can tell he's been worried. Tracker has to have been the most beautiful animal I have ever seen. Our human eyes are attracted to the canine form, and Tracker was the most impressive of all. He would make a world record trophy for a wolf hunter and that was always on our minds.

As for Kaiyo, he's now over eighty pounds, and his strength, even for a cub, is stunning. But unlike a normal bear, it's not usually a problem. He clearly knows he cannot claw or bite us or the farm animals. He's very gentle with Rosie, and they are definitely pals. Kaiyo has also been getting closer to Peyton. Sometimes, he and Peyton will sit in the pasture for hours. At times, they roughhouse, and other times, they just sit there and watch the world go by. They both like to graze on the lush grass around the ponds and streams. The whole thing still looks very strange.

The main reason Kaiyo could sit with Peyton for hours is because the kids were in school. Gracie was in third grade and she got home first. While Kaiyo hated the fact that Libby and Dean were gone so long, he enjoyed Gracie being with him for the extra hour. I think I saw her try to ride him like a pony the other day. He's too young for that and he shook her off pretty quick.

Lately, Kaiyo has been a participant of the Dog Patrol. His nose is far better than the dogs, and they have figured that out. Several times, I have seen him give his little roar (it's cute) and Moose and Major come running. Then the three of them will peel off and head into the fields to the north. He's not yet as fast as the dogs, and when they see a deer or an elk, they leave Kaiyo in the dust. A couple of times he has come back all alone, looking dejected. He's just like millions of other little brothers. He wants to be in the game, but he's not old enough to play.

For Kaiyo, all will change too soon for me. He's been gaining weight and strength every day. After Goliath killed the cattle, Dad and Dean decided not to bury them but they butchered them and froze the meat. That has allowed Kaiyo to have his bottles and enjoy some tasty beef and fat rich meals. That, plus the grass he likes to eat with Peyton makes for a pretty well-balanced diet.

Each morning, I take the kids in the UTV up our long driveway to meet the bus. Libby was a sophomore in high school and Dean was in eighth grade. Libby would turn sixteen in late October and she had been driving for over four months now. This was probably her last semester on the school bus. Dean turned thirteen last March. Gracie turned eight last February, and she's been enjoying third grade. Our particular school bus stops where our driveway meets the road. Our neighbor, Tracy Springs, usually meets us with her dog Blue. They live just across the road. Blue is as long as he is short. He's part Australian Shepherd and part clown. For a normal dog, he's smart, too. And he loves Kaiyo. The two play while we wait for the bus. Tracey said that one day, Blue was going to write books because he's so smart. If there was ever a dog who could do such a thing, Blue would top the list. But Blue was not special like Kaiyo.

This year, another family had joined us at the bus stop. They are the Gibbses. The Gibbs family lives at one of the old Chandler homesteads about two miles up the road. Sam had always wanted to buy the five Chandler properties that bordered the Road to our northwest. Those properties stretch for several miles. Each of those properties reached like invading fingers into our western forest lands. Some of the tracts were smallish and around ten to thirty acres. A few of them were good-sized. All of them were owned by a certain Mr. Chandler. Chandler had owned them for years and used them as rental properties and as places for his friends to hunt. That's the part that has caused us some grief. Many of the people who have lived on the Chandler properties have used our land for their trash dumps, dirt bike and four-wheeler trail riding, and for hunting, sometimes out of season.

I'm not going to lie. Sam and Mr. Chandler have exchanged some heated words about the conduct of Chandler's tenants and guests. Sam told Chandler he would buy Chandler's lands for their appraised price plus five percent. That's a bargain, but Mr. Chandler wanted too much money for each of them. Like most of Chandler's properties, the Gibbs place was a beat down farm. The house was barely suitable for anyone to live there. The pastures were a mess and overgrown, and the fences were down in a lot of places. The few functioning farm buildings needed repair, too.

Sam especially wanted this piece of property because it was about 575 oddly shaped acres that jutted into our property like a knife. It fronted the Road and then snaked back into the Western Forest. It was the closest of the Chandler properties to our farm. Our property surrounded all of the various Chandler properties, and Mr. Chandler tried to take advantage of our desire to increase our holdings and end a lot of unneighborly activities. We wanted it, but not at the price he was looking for. Sam was going to let the land return to the wildlife. The Gibbs house could be salvaged with some work, though. It was attractive and it could be a good guest house or a retreat.

Anyway, the mom is Aliyah and she speaks with a slightly discernible accent and she seems nice enough. She is beautiful and quiet, but her husband is one of a kind. He goes by the name Gunner but his real name is Steve. He's as nice a guy as they come in a goofy sort of way. He does odd jobs to support his family, and I suspect it's pretty tough for them to make ends meet. They also have two children. Jack is a little older than Dean, and the other is a sweet little girl named Kate. She's about twelve years old and she adores Libby. She's also super sweet to Gracie. They are good kids with some well-developed personalities. Jack and Dean are becoming good friends in a Mutt and Jeff sort of way. Dean is about a head taller and much bigger. Jack makes up for it in quickness and personality, though.

Gunner comes to the bus stop because he adores Kaiyo. I know because he tells me. He also tells me he doesn't like to wake up early but to see Kaiyo makes waking early worth it. Gunner even gets everybody there early so they can be first to greet Kaiyo. When we drive to the bus stop, Kaiyo will hop out of the UTV as Gunner sits crosslegged on the ground. Gunner will just laugh at how Kaiyo jumps on him and wrestles. It only lasts for a few minutes, though, because Blue joins in, and then the bear and dog go off to play together.

That had been going on for a few weeks. Then one day at the bus stop, Gunner said out loud he'd like to bag Goliath and make a rug out of him. That was not like him. I didn't know where he was headed with that comment. Libby shot a glance my way. Dean walked over, and with my look, I let him know this wasn't his time to talk. Dean looked disappointed. I then reminded Gunner grizzlies were protected by law. "No," he said. "That's not true. That bear is a known killer. Everybody knows he nearly killed a lawman and he tried to break in your house or something like that. So, anybody can shoot a bad bear."

"Gunner," I said coolly. "That is not the law. I could get Officer Brigham to drop by your house and tell you what the law is. He's a close friend. And we don't think Goliath is going to be bothering you or your family."

Tracey broke in to relieve the tension, and started talking to Aliyah. Shortly, the bus came and took the kids on off to school. As I turned around to get in the UTV, Gunner came toward me. "Susan, I need to talk over a few things with you and Sam privately."

He looked serious, and I told him we could get together some time in the next week. For the first time, Gunner's demeanor changed. "No ma'am!" he said in a very serious way. "It needs to be today."

I looked at Gunner and said, "How about first thing in the morning?"

Gunner thought about it for a few seconds, and said, "Friday morning it is!"

Instantly, his demeanor changed back into the goofy character he had always been. That was odd. When Gunner and Aliyah left, he mentioned something about looking forward to seeing us tomorrow. He looked and acted like the nice Gunner I thought I knew. Interesting.

Tracey came on over and she gave me one of those crazy looks friends make to one another and we just broke out in laughter. I'm glad Gunner wasn't here to see that. We both felt Gunner had acted oddly. Sam would need to know about this, of course, but tomorrow we would talk.

I bring this all up because that very night we got a call from Mr. Chandler. The five properties Chandler owned including the Gibbs property were all for sale. Both Sam and I were on the call speaking to Mr. Chandler. Sam and I have long learned to play good cop/bad cop when it suits our needs. We use it with the kids, too. It works great. Quite often, when the kids get in trouble, we switch off with who gets to be the bad cop. Then when the kid leaves, we look at each other and laugh. Tonight, I played bad cop.

As Mr. Chandler spoke, I would harrumph and sigh. Then, I would tell Sam more properties weren't in our budget (which they weren't) and the places were so beat up they would be money pits (which they would be.) Then I told Sam tenants are trouble and that Gunner Gibbs had even raised his voice at me today. Sam looked at me from across the room and mouthed "Really?" I nodded. Sam looked confused and a little mad.

That's when Mr. Chandler dropped the price. A lot. He admitted being a landlord, especially with a string of property destroying tenants was no fun. In fact, he said he was afraid of most of them, even Gibbs. Chandler also thought Gibbs had a whisky still running on the property, and when he had recently pressed one of his tenants for past due rent, the tenant threatened Mr. Chandler.

Apparently, the joy of owning and renting real estate had finally evaded Mr. Chandler. I still acted like I didn't want any of it and acted all afraid of bad scary tenants. Sam just grunted at appropriate times and said stuff like "Geez, I don't know..."

Then, Sam said we needed to talk and we would call Mr. Chandler back the next night. Before he hung up, Sam said he would need a copy of the leases Chandler had with the tenants and their payment histories. Chandler readily agreed.

Oh my gosh! I would pay twice that amount for those properties just for the joy of letting the land go wild again. Sam had suspected Gibbs and a couple of other residents on the other properties had shot deer and a few black bears out of season on our property, but his illegal whisky making was news to us. It made sense. Gunner didn't seem to have a regular job. That's when I told Sam that Gunner had basically demanded a meeting with him and me for the next day.

Bear View —Kaiyo

Dad and Mom sometimes forget I understand them. If I act like I don't hear them, they really do forget and they will talk freely. Usually, what they talk about is truly boring, but I do know they love me. I overhead them saying I would "probably only live for twenty to twenty-five years." To me, that seemed like a very long time but it explains things.

When I lost my real mom, I was so young. So when I saw Libby, I ran to her because she looked safe. Dad actually looked a little scary at first when he went for Goliath. I had no idea we would become family that very day. Compared to humans, I don't get to live a very long time. Compared to Moose or Major, I guess I do live a long time. Dogs just don't live long enough.

I understand I am growing up fast. Everyone can see I am getting a lot bigger, but that's not what I have noticed the most. Every day brings me more understanding.

Things I didn't understand when I was younger, I understand now. For a lot of reasons, bears have to grow up fast. I think that's why I look like a yearling cub, but I understand things even human children don't. It made sense. They get to live three or four times longer than us bears. They have time on their side. I don't.

But that doesn't mean I'm not a cub, because I am. And I love to have fun and I love this farm. First of all, this place is huge. I try to keep up with Moose and Major, but they are so fast. When I learn an elk or deer or a bear is in the corn, they will follow me until they can smell them, too. Then they take off and leave me in the dust. I hate that. But I did notice every time that happens, I can keep up with them a little bit longer.

Getting to know the other animals has been fun, too. I know I am different from the other animals and only Tracker and Goliath are like me, but I definitely like the horses, especially Peyton. All the horses are great, but Peyton and I are alike in one way and I think he senses that. He's big like I'll be. He's super strong like I'll be. He's fast but not as fast as the other horses. I understand that part, too. We also like to chomp on green plump grass. Everyone thinks grizzlies only eat meat. While I like it, it's just not true. We bears pretty much eat whatever is good, and juicy green grass is good.

The alpacas are my second favorite farm animal. Except for Rosie, a lot of them are a little scared of me but they are gentle, and when I go visit Rosie, they get used to me and treat me well. The cows are totally different. They are dangerous and they don't like anything but other cows. They tolerate the horses and even the steers don't mess with Peyton, but they wouldn't think twice about running me down and killing me. I tried to cut across one of their pastures a few weeks back and I barely escaped with my life. Gracie saw it happen, and she told me that if she was scared of any type of farm animal, then I should be, too. Gracie stays clear of the cows. She also doesn't like the pigs.

Pigs are kind of smart. I can see it in their eyes. But they don't seem to get along with anything other than pigs. When I get near them, the little ones run and the big ones charge the fence. No matter what, if I was ever in trouble, I know only Moose or Major or the horses would try to help me. I think the cows would step on me, but I am sure the pigs would try to eat me. Gracie told me Dad warned the kids to stay away from the pigs because they can be mean. That was good advice.

That all leads me to the chickens and the guineas. Those are the birds raised on the farm. They are dumb and dirty but they taste so good. They don't ever bother me, but a few weeks ago, I saw one of the roosters try to run Gracie out of the barn. She screamed and ran behind me. When the rooster decided to charge me, I gave him a quick swat. It was all bear instinct. I hit him before I even thought. But I wasn't going to let him get to Gracie and get her with his spurs. Those things are long and sharp and they could have hurt her.

Anyway, when I swatted the rooster, he flew up, fell to the floor, and flopped around and died. Gracie ran inside and brought out Mom. That was trouble. Mom and Dad didn't quite understand me. In fact, they still don't. And they cannot have a bear that kills their animals. But when Mom came out, she gave me a huge hug and said, "Don't worry, Kaiyo. I know you were protecting yourself and Gracie. Besides, I didn't really like that rooster anyway."

She grabbed the dead rooster and headed into the kitchen. I thought I was going to get in trouble. Instead, Mom fried that rooster and we ate him later that night for dinner. I do love my family.

Every day here brings new things for me to learn. I miss my brother and sisters when they go away and get on the school bus, but that left me with Mom and Dad on the farm. I know I am safe here and that they love me. I have so much to learn, and Tracker hinted that one day, he would open my eyes to who I was. I still don't know what he meant, but one day, I will.

TROUBLES – SAM

After the bus picked up the kids, Gunner and Aliyah hopped in the UTV with Susan and took the long drive back to the house. Using the UTV made the trip a short one compared to horse travel, but it still took about fifteen minutes. When they got here, I had coffee ready. I was curious about what Gunner would say. And if I had to venture a guess, he was probably looking for money. I understood. I knew he was behind on his rent and Chandler was probably going to evict him and his family.

When they got here, we went into the kitchen and sat at the table. Kaiyo followed us in. I noticed this made Gunner uncomfortable. Our small talk soon bored the little bear and he went outside to find something more interesting. Gunner was obviously pleased. At that point, Gunner spoke up. "I know Kaiyo is a special bear, at least, he's not like any grizzly I've ever seen. But this has to do with both Goliath and Kaiyo."

To add to my confusion, Gunner's whole personality was changed. So had Aliyah's. They both looked far more certain and confident. Gunner started out. "The rumor out there is that I don't work and I am operating a whisky still in the back of the property I'm renting. That may be true and it may not be true, but what is true is I meet and work with a lot of what you would call *bad actors*. Some of them are good as gold, some are pure scum. Most are okay. They may not be the types to return a cash-filled wallet they find on the sidewalk, but they wouldn't take it from you either. A few others would easily kill somebody, you or me, if it meant making a buck."

"Anyway, I made a delivery a couple of days ago to a group of folks who live and work in town. They're rough folks who hail from California. They're here working for one of the companies associated in some way with mining. I didn't know them other than as first-time customers. Usually, my first-time customers like it when I sample my own product with them. It makes them feel better."

He looked at Susan and said, "I know you will be stunned to learn that I only drink rarely."

By the look on Susan's face, he was right. "In fact," he said. "Before I make a delivery, I gargle with a PBR. The minute somebody smells beer on my breath, they start assuming I'm safe and lazy."

Susan laughed and nodded. Aliyah then said "He has an act that keeps everybody in the dark, and they underestimate him and us. Most people think we are slightly better than vagrants, but that's not how we got started. For years, we have been on the run, sort of. My family came from east Africa when I was in second grade. Where I'm from, we aren't allowed to marry for love, unless we just happen to love the person our family picks. I thought our living in America would change all that, but I guess not. Anyway, I abandoned their faith and became a Christian. That was unacceptable, and my life was in danger. So, I ran away, and after a while, I met Gunner. We did what millions of other couples do. We fell in love and we got married."

"Not long after that, I was told by a cousin that when my father and brothers heard that I got married to an American, and a Christian at that, they swore they would take me back to our home country in Africa. My family is fairly well-to-do, and I was terrified. I called my mother and she cursed me. It was awful. We think they have had private detectives following us. Gunner once found a tracking device in the wheel well of my car. Well, the mechanic actually found it. We had fun with that device but that's another story."

Aliyah took a breath and stifled a tear. She seemed a lot tougher to me than she used to. She continued, "Gunner came up with the idea of leaving in the middle of the night. He had a pension from the Air Force so we had money. It seemed like a plan. So, we did. Gunner had his parents box everything up. We stored some of it and we had some shipped to us. Since then, we had Jack and Kate. We live in fear they will be kidnapped by my family and taken back, too. Getting them out of there would be nearly impossible. Anyway, to make money, we knew Gunner couldn't hold a regular job because my family could find us. Fortunately, we have the pension direct deposited, and Gunner has a skill or two to make up the rest."

Now Gunner took over. "I have been deployed in dozens of foreign countries, occasionally for a long time. In some of those countries, alcohol is illegal and there is no way to get it. So, to make a long story short, I understand chemistry and learned how to make alcohol with ingredients that are pretty much common wherever I go. I can prepare something that tastes a little like bourbon in less than a few weeks. For scotch, it takes a week or two longer. I sold it to soldiers, airmen, the occasional sailor, and more than a few members of the top brass. Pretty much everybody looked the other way. And I made a lot of extra money. I am good at making it, too."

"So, for the last few years, we will live in a place and I will set up shop. A couple of times, we had to leave because we believed her family had found us or were about to find us. At other times, we had to leave because the Feds got too close to figuring out I was the source of untaxed spirits."

He laughed. I think my mouth was on the floor. Goodness, I did not see this coming. I had assumed something entirely different about them. Susan's eyes were wide open. Instinctively, she reached out and held Aliyah's hand. "So," I asked. "How did you come to calling yourself Gunner?"

Aliyah jumped in. "Gunner got that name because he qualified as an expert marksman. He has won his share of competitions. He's the best shot I have ever seen!"

Okay, that actually made sense to me. He had the bearing of an officer and a loyalty to his wife that was admirable. Despite their life of petty crime, I was really starting to like this couple. We talked for a little while longer before it came time to find out why they were in my house. "So, Gunner? Aliyah? What's on your mind," I asked.

What he said rocked our world. Gunner told us Kaiyo and Goliath were both in danger. "Susan, I'm sorry but I had to rattle your chain yesterday by asking you a few too many questions about Kaiyo, and I definitely needed to know if you cared for Goliath. By the way you responded, it's obvious that you do. The rumor mill said you two and the warden made a miracle out of that giant bear, and now I believe it. So, here's the problem. Those gentlemen from California were buying some of my merchandise when they asked me to sit and have a drink of my own stuff. I expected that. I sip. I never drink. But they drank. Because those fools think very little of me, they talked freely. They talked about a group of Californians who were headed this way to harvest Goliath's gall bladder and paws. They said that they would try to get your little bear's paws and organs, too."

He let that sink in.

"They talked about how bear gall bladders would sell for $10,000 to $20,000 on the Asian market. While they're at it, they'll probably try to kill a bunch of other bears, too."

"What's with the paws?" asked Susan.

I knew the answer to this one, so I told her, "Bear gall bladders and bear bile are used mostly by the Vietnamese and Chinese, but they aren't the only bear parts that are taken. Some of those Asian cultures eat bear paws because they think they'll get the bear's strength and energy. Also, some think that eating bear meat increases virility. It's all a bunch of medieval hokey pokey, but they believe it and they'll pay dearly to get it."

"And because of that," said Gunner. "The poachers will kill anyone in their way to get those bear parts. Worst of all, they are headed into town today or tomorrow."

That hit hard. I dialed and called Mr. Chandler. As the phone rang, the Gibbses looked at me quizzically. As the phone was ringing Chandler's line, I asked them if they were behind in their rent. They looked me and nodded. "One month or two months?" I asked.

Gunner held up three fingers sheepishly. I looked at him and smiled. Mr. Chandler answered. We spoke briefly, then I said, "You got a deal but only if you can close in two weeks." Chandler stammered and said we had a deal. I told him my lawyer would call him shortly.

I then called Mike Williams, my lawyer. Everybody makes fun of lawyers, but I sure liked mine. During all of this, the Gibbses still looked confused. Mike answered and I said "Mike, this is Sam McLeod again. Susan and I are all in. Chandler and I reached a deal. Draft the contract at the price we discussed and get it on over to Chandler as soon as you can. I want to close in two weeks. Make sure you throw in an assignment of leases and transfers of security deposits. And can you update the titles to those properties?"

Mike said he could, and we hung up. Maybe I'm in the minority, but I love my lawyer.

I looked at Gunner and Aliyah, and said, "Don't worry about paying rent. And if you want to continue to help me out, you can forget about rent until at least after Christmas."

Aliyah burst into tears, and Gunner just looked at me and Susan, still confused. Aliyah grabbed Gunner's confused face and looked at him. While pointing to us, she said, "Gunner, meet our new landlords!"

Gunner was obviously a tough man, but he got all mighty misty-eyed. Susan and I understood financial hardship. People say that because I have oil wells, all I think about is money. That's not remotely true. I thought about money all the time when I was broke. I don't think about it nearly as much as I used to.

Anyway, the Gibbses were going to be useful allies and they had a perfect cover. I needed them. And they sure needed us McLeods right now. Best of all, they warned us about the poachers, and they had no expectation Susan and I would be able to help them out. It's fun to see good things happen to those who deserve it.

That brought me back to the poachers. What I have learned over the years is that poachers hate to be shot at. They're used to being illegal hunters, not to being hunted. I put in a quick call to Lowe Brigham and said that poachers were coming. That was enough for him. He was on his way. He lived for this stuff.

This poaching problem is dangerous stuff, but we deal with troubles as they come. And trouble came quickly enough.

The doorbell rang.

2

POACHERS — SAM

I had forgotten I even had a doorbell, but it rang anyway. UPS and FedEx come by frequently, but I know the drivers and they always drive around to the kitchen door in the back of the house. That's where we usually are, so it made sense. Our letter carriers visit from time to time, but they come around back, too. We are too far from the road for Girl Scout cookies, sadly, and almost no one else comes unannounced. Susan looked and said it was two men she had never seen before. Gunner looked from a concealed position, and whispered, "Uh oh. One of them is one of the gents I met to deliver the merchandise."

I looked at the group, and told Gunner and Aliyah to lay low. I then looked at Susan, and said, "Cover me, I'm going in."

Then, we both laughed. That line comes from some movie, and it always made us laugh. I also knew if I needed help, she would have my back.

Meanwhile, the men at the door had their own problems. They were facing two enormous dogs and a bear cub who was capable of doing some real damage. They could go nowhere. Major blocked the steps, Moose blocked them from going right, and Kaiyo blocked the left. They looked so relieved when I opened the door.

At this point, I had to control my anger. They were here to figure out a way to kill my precious bear and scout my place out. I knew all that, but I couldn't let on I knew. I put on a big smile. "Hi there. Can I help you?"

That was hard. I actually wanted to tell Moose and Major to go at it and eat them for dinner. The first thing I did was to tell them to be still. I took out my cell phone and took their pictures. They were stunned. I told them "We had a robber come to the farm once. The robber threatened us, and one of the dogs leaped at him and practically bit off his gun hand. Then, the dogs chased him into the corn and killed him."

I told those two that the next time somebody came here that I didn't know, I would have to take a picture of them first. "You see," I told them. "After the dogs got through chewing up that robber, there wasn't nothing left of his face. It made identification tough. I don't know why you're here, so if you aren't on the up and up, then I have pictures to identify you for your next of kin."

Then, I shut up. Of course, none of that was true, but the dogs and the bear were on full alert. The men looked horrified and they asked to come inside. "No, I don't think so," I said. "I don't even know who you are. If you're tired, then how about you sitting on those steps."

I had trained the dogs using a few German words and a lot of English words. I used German because it sounded so good, and with the language being guttural, the dogs seem to respond better. "Gegenteil!" I barked out. I even said it with the right accent, like I was born in Bavaria. The two dogs and Kaiyo backed up about five feet. Kaiyo was a lot smarter than the dogs but he responded to my command, he didn't just mimic the actions of the dogs. That surprised me. Surely, Kaiyo wasn't bilingual. Well, that's not true. He speaks bear perfectly, and he seems to know whatever I say to him in English. That he may somehow understand German was intriguing. I would have to think about that later.

As for the German word *gegenteil*, I looked up that word and several others a few years ago when we got the dogs. I'm not positive it means what I think it means. I am convinced it means something in German, though, and I like the way it sounds. It didn't matter. The poachers here didn't understand German, either. It all made me look mysterious to them. They came to my house expecting to be in control, and they were totally not in control. And they knew it.

Still, I had to be careful. These guys were smugglers and poachers and maybe killers. At this point, though, they looked silly and mighty uncomfortable. I was standing and they were sitting. "Again," I said a little more seriously. "What can I do for you?"

They lied from the moment they started talking. The one who knew Gunner started speaking first. "My name," he said. "Is, uh, Jim…Jim Anderson and this is Glenn Taylor." I quickly assumed these two jokers were lying about their real names. I didn't let on, but I wanted to laugh.

Anderson continued, "We are hoping you'll give us permission to hunt on your property. You see," he said, as he grabbed his hat and tried to look sincere. "we are both unemployed and we need to put meat on the table to feed our families. A deer or an elk would sure help us out."

I wanted to hit him. I looked at them and said, "I only let people hunt on my lands if I know 'em. And I don't know you two gentlemen. So the answer is no, Mr. Anderson."

I looked at Mr. Taylor "Do you live around here? I've never seen you before."

He was quick in responding. I'll give him that. "There's a reason for that," he said. "I have been looking for work and I was hoping to get a job with one of the oil crews around here."

Now, I was really mad but I stuffed it and put on a smile. I looked at them both and I pointed at the Southern Forest. "You know, even if I knew you two, it wouldn't much matter. See that forest?"

The two men looked past the driveway and south at the miles of dense forest. I kept on. "Those woods used to be full of elk and deer and moose, too. That's all changed. A while back, a particularly vicious, big grizzly decided to live there. Not only that, there are other grizzlies that live there, too. There are also still plenty of black bears. They ran most of the game right out of there. I think the bears are out there because my part of the forest goes for miles and there are berry patches everywhere, especially on the roads to the oil wells. I can take my four-wheeler back there and the bears pretty much ignore me. Well, except that giant bear. He's grouchy. And the last thing I want is for anyone to get hurt."

They no longer looked disappointed. They thought they knew where their payday was. Then, I told them a hunter had gotten into my forest and he wasn't prepared for bears and he had the scare of his life. Glenn then asked casually why I let him hunt there. "I didn't," I said. "He took the back entrance about seven miles down the Road toward Radford."

They stood to leave, and I spotted Kaiyo out of the corner of my eye. He was standing on his hind legs and he was focused on them both. *He's really getting big,* I thought. I just stood there and acted like I didn't notice. Kaiyo dropped to his feet and started walking toward them both. His ears were pinned back and he was growling like a dog. He was definitely cute. He must have learned from Major. The dogs acted as if on cue. They took a few steps toward the two men. Kaiyo stopped by my side, but he was definitely not happy with them. The two men flashed glances from bear to dog to bear to me. That's when I said, "You ought to slowly ease in your car and get on out of here. I don't know if I'll be able to hold them off much longer."

The two men said their good-byes and they tiptoed past Moose and went straight to their truck. They left quickly.

Nobody knew it then, but Kaiyo would soon be having the first of his many big bear adventures.

Susan, Gunner, and Aliyah came on out and were laughing and enjoying themselves. They brought me a cup of hot coffee, and we settled into the rocking chairs on the front porch. For a few moments, we just watched as Kaiyo and the dogs went back to roughhousing in the grass of the front yard. The corn looked like a wall of green that extended from right to left. We could hear the cattle lowing in the distance. The temperatures here in September were truly terrific.

Mornings are usually in the mid-forties, and today was no different. As the sun rose in the crisp blue sky, the temperature had climbed to the high sixties. This was God's country. Well, three seasons out of four.

Gunner broke the silence and said to no one in particular that Glenn Taylor was a pretty rough character. "Sam," said Susan. "You obviously have a plan. What is it? And where did that crazy act of yours come from?"

"Did y'all like it?" I asked.

By the looks on their faces, they all did. Then Aliyah asked why I sent them to the Southern Forest. And that, I told her, was a good question.

I was about to get started, but Susan shot me *the look* and I held back. That was a good thing, too. The Southern Forest was not really something I could explain over a cup of coffee. As long as we have lived here, that area has, for lack of a better expression, given us the creeps. Our property is higher in the north and lower in the south. Our farm benefits from being a flat valley that interrupts the fall of the land and is well watered by the higher lands to the north and west. The fall of the land continued to our south to the area we call the Southern Forest. It is dense and riddled with creeks and gullies and a number of low hills that direct the rainwater into often flooded hardwood lowlands. Some parts of the Southern Forest are mostly pine and some parts are low scrub. The hills are usually thick with oaks and aspen. Much of it is swampy, and beavers have dammed a number of creeks. Waterfowl love it in there.

The western edge of the Southern Forest is the Road, and it extends to the east for at least twenty to thirty miles until it rises to the Eastern Wilderness. I own part of it and that is where our oil wells are. Except for game trails, the only way to easily enter in the area is on the few gravel roads the oil companies bulldozed in to drill and install the wells. With the exception of the one entrance off the Road, the only way to get to my other wells was from our driveway.

A few years back, we had to place a steep berm and a gate at the Road entrance because the gravel drive was like a magnet to four-wheelers and to dirt bikers. We also had a number of uninvited hunters and poachers come on the land, and that was not acceptable, either. But for the last few years, the berm had pretty much eroded away. We don't much need it anymore.

I believe in hunting, and we love the tradition. I have no problem with letting people hunt on parts of my property, but I need to know them first. For a couple of years, I leased a tract of over a thousand acres in the Southern Forest to a hunting club. I knew many of them, and the relationship with the club was a good one. They would keep the area clear of four-wheelers and dirt bikers, and by their presence, they kept the poachers out, too. They put in food plots and cleared out areas to let meadow habitats flourish. I loved having them keep a camp there. And I was sorry when they left. I was even sorrier when they said they would never come back.

I also leased other tracts to some other clubs but they all pulled out. In the fall, they would bring in their campers and trucks and make a camping area complete with outhouses and cleaning stations. Then, they usually would leave in some degree of haste. After about five different hunting clubs, nobody ever came back. Even the four-wheelers and the dirt bikers quit trying to sneak in. Except for the occasional poacher, no one who knows about the Southern Forest will set foot on it.

I bought the property because I wanted to have a buffer between my house and somebody's future housing development. The trend out here is to turn open land into ranchettes of ten acres or so. I understand why people like them, but the wildlife takes a whipping as their habitat disappears. The larger animals are especially affected. I didn't want that.

In the distant past, even though the land wasn't all that good for farming, a number of homesteaders tried it out. They all failed.

I have explored the Southern Forest and even camped there. On several occasions, I have walked up to old beat-up homes and small structures that had long ago been abandoned to the elements, the animals, the vines, and the trees. These old homes and farm buildings are like seashells at the beach. Once abandoned, something else, like a hermit crab, moves in. The same is true here. These old places are filled with creatures. Birds, bats, raccoons, and bears like these places a lot. Walking up on one of those abandoned buildings is not something to do without being noisy enough to let the residents head out the back door.

There is no doubt this forest is a creepy place, but I imagine the old homesteaders fought a few too many fires, a few too many droughts, and far too many blizzards and finally had to call it quits. I did lie to the crooks who came to the house today. There is a ton of wild game out there. Deer, elk, and especially moose are abundant. Wolves are not unusual. There are also some grizzlies and black bears, but not in the numbers I said were out there.

As for the creepiness of the Southern Forest, it's a problem. It wasn't always like that, though. The old homesteaders never complained about anything like what's going on in there now. I think it's getting worse, too. The oil company workers always said they felt watched and they hated to stay after dark. Even now, when the wells or the pumps need maintenance, they refuse to come out alone. And despite some misguided company regulations to the contrary, they are always armed.

The hunters, some of them friends of mine, said their time out there was often terrifying. They complained of ceaseless nightmares at night and strange cold spots even on warm days. Some of the hunters told stories that, while hunting, they would see strange creatures dart in and out of the brush. Some of them were even chased out of the woods by things unseen. And those hunters were, for the most part, seasoned hunters who had spent years in the outdoors.

I admit that when I had camped out there, the nights were usually pretty sleepless. The woods there come alive at night, and at times, it sounded like Hershel, Major, and I were entertainment for several *somethings* that crept close and truly didn't like us being there. Poor Major would be up, growling all night. I rarely slept.

Even on our farm, there is something that, from time to time, comes close to the farm but just inside the Southern Forest. It watches us. Whatever it is, the dogs are scared of it, and they stand their ground and growl. It is something to see. Several times we have watched as the dogs caught something, maybe a sound or a scent, and then run past the driveway and skid to a stop short of the forest and stand guard, hair raised, growling the whole time. One time, whatever it was came to the edge of the forest behind the house, and then it walked to the west just inside the tree line. I watched as the dogs paralleled it for over a mile. Then, whatever it was slipped back deep into the woods and the dogs came running home.

I am tired of it, so the last time it happened, I walked straight past the dogs and yelled into the woods. I was answered by an unusual utterance that is hard to describe. It was close to a loud growl but it wasn't quite a growl. That's when I raised my Winchester and pointed it at its direction. In a second, I heard it running like a line-backer back into the woods. Sticks snapped and branches crashed. I think I heard something like a howl/growl of anger. That actually disappointed me because that meant it was smart. Smart things can bring problems. The part I did like was it feared bullets.

It concerns me Kaiyo may choose to investigate whatever it is that's out there. It scares me even more Dean will choose to go see what it is. So far, he's been pretty fearless, and that makes me both proud and uneasy. Having a grizzly that will have his back is going to make him even braver, and that will be a problem. I suspect Kaiyo will embolden the kids to do things they wouldn't do otherwise.

With all that, answering Aliyah's question was easier said than done. But neither Susan nor I wanted a bunch of monster hunters, demon worshipers, or ghost busters invading the Southern Forest. So far, we've not actually had a problem with the residents of the Southern Forest, and I liked it that way. So, my answer to her was simple. "Aliyah, there's only one way in from the Road and that means there's only one way out. Once they're in, we can bottle them up."

Just then I saw Lowe Brigham driving out of the Western Forest and into the sunny part of the rest of the driveway toward my house. I think it made Gunner uneasy, but I told him Lowe needed to hear this. Gunner agreed, but I could tell he didn't much like it. Gunner had good reason for concern but he knew how to look cool.

Lowe came to a stop and hopped out of his truck. Once again, Lowe somehow managed to look good in his government spec uniform. His pants were ironed and creased, his shirt was without wrinkles, and his hair was combed. I half expected a star-like twinkle to flash when he smiled. Kaiyo heard the truck, and when he realized it was Lowe, Kaiyo charged, leaped, and knocked Lowe down. "Oh my goodness," said Lowe. "What happened to our baby bear? Geez Kaiyo, you're huge!"

Like all children, Kaiyo seemed to take pride in getting older and growing up. Kaiyo and Lowe just wrestled on the ground for another two or three minutes, and it was obvious Lowe was disappointed when it was over.

After he got off the ground and wiped away the grass, he bounded up the steps and looked us over and said, "Well, Samuel, it's been two months without an adventure. What's on the plate for today?"

"Poachers are coming and they want to kill a few bear friends of yours. It's possible they are dirty enough to kill a few human friends of yours, too."

Lowe morphed back into all lawman. I introduced him to Gunner and Aliyah. Lowe was cordial, but I could tell he knew who Gunner was. Susan filled Lowe in on how she knew the Gibbses and how nice a family they were. "Gunner," I said. "Can you give Officer Brigham here a version of what you told me earlier today?"

To his credit, Gunner didn't hold back. I expected him to just mention he had heard through the grapevine there were poachers around, but he and Aliyah told Lowe the whole story. It took a while to finish the story, but Gunner was as honest as any outlaw could be. Then I told Lowe about the visit we got today from the likely poachers. I even showed him the pictures of the two of them.

Needless to say, Lowe was taken aback. He didn't expect the high level of candor he got from Gunner and Aliyah, and he sure didn't expect the poachers to be so stupid as to let a picture be made of them. I could watch Lowe's attitude about Gunner change while Gunner was telling the story. He had thought poorly of Gunner and his opinion changed greatly after hearing the story.

Then, I told Lowe I was buying all the Chandler properties and Gunner would be my tenant. Lowe looked pleased, but he asked if we could talk privately. We left for the kitchen.

Once in the kitchen, Lowe stopped and leaned back on the counter. He paused for a minute and then said, "Sam, Chandler has been talking to the folks over at ATF."

The ATF is the federal police force that enforces taxes on alcohol among other things. They are serious about their jobs and they happily arrest and prosecute moonshiners. Gunner was a moonshiner. Despite sounding sort of cool, for the most part, moonshine isn't a good bet. Sometimes, moonshine is as dangerous as poison to drink. Sometimes, it's pretty good. But the real appeal of moonshine is that it's a lot cheaper than what's sold at a liquor store. It's cheaper because shiners don't pay taxes. The states and the Feds heavily tax alcohol sales.

In addition, *shining* has a long history in America. From before the American Revolution, John Hancock of Boston, a signer of the Declaration of Independence, was a known smuggler of molasses to make tax-free rum. NASCAR even got its start from moonshiners in North Carolina souping up regular stock cars so they could outrun police cars. But history or not, I couldn't have an illegal still operate on property I intend to own.

"How much time does Gunner have before they raid his place?" I asked.

"Chandler convinced them to wait until he sells it. I think the ATF agreed. But Sammy, if I were you, I'd tell Gunner to get rid of his still, and if he doesn't, then you will have to turn him in. And if you don't, I will."

I turned around and headed back out to the others. Lowe stayed back. I looked at Gunner and Aliyah, and said, "A little birdie told me your operation is about to be visited by the Feds. How soon can you break everything down and get rid of the evidence? And I mean all of it."

Gunner gulped. Aliyah's face went white. "Gunner," I said. "I will own that property in the next few weeks, and I wouldn't let you have that still on my land anyway. Go home and get rid of that stuff. Get rid of it for good. If you want, after you're done, then you and I can talk about replacing your income with more legitimate means. I have a few good ideas I think you'll like. As for the still, how long would it take you to break down?"

Gunner chuckled and said he could break down in two hours. I told him to break it down, and then run a tractor over it all so it didn't look like a still, and then sell the metal at the recycling center in town. Gunner's jaw dropped. "Trust me," I said. "If you do, you'll be glad you did."

Aliyah looked at him and nodded nervously. "This has to be done today," I said. "Because tomorrow it will look like cop land around here."

I looked at Gunner one more time. "By the way, Gunner, are you still a good shot?"

Gunner looked at me and smiled. "One of the best there is."

"Good," I said. "I may need your skills. But as for the poachers, I need you out of this. Take the kids to school tomorrow and go shopping. Be seen in town. And if anybody asks for your merchandise, tell them you don't know what they're talking about. From now on, you two are going to walk the straight and narrow. And don't tell anybody or admit that you ever made moonshine or say anything about the still. I think the ATF boys and girls, if they come, they won't like coming up empty-handed. Keep your nose clean. If they're going to search your place, they will do it with a fine-tooth comb, and they might tap your cell phones if they haven't already decided to do so. Don't fret too much, though, the ATF has much bigger fish to fry than one dude with a still. The heat will blow off in a week or two."

With that, we said our good-byes. Susan and the Gibbses got back in the UTV, and Susan took them back to the bus stop and to their car. Lowe came back out and sat next to me. "Well, Sammy. What's your plan?"

My plan was about as weird as they come. And it might not work at all.

The Ploy – Sam

Before we got started, I needed Lowe to focus. "Okay," I said. "First, let's start with you. You're a lawman. What do we have on these guys? What could y'all do to stop them?"

Lowe rubbed his lower jaw and thought for a few moments. "Not much, to be honest. All we have is a reliable tip and two guys from California who came to ask your permission to hunt on your property. Knocking on your door to ask to hunt is neither unusual nor is it illegal. The only thing we have is a reason to believe that they want to kill Kaiyo and Goliath, and sell their parts to feed the Asian black market, but that's not much to go on. California Fish and Wildlife is a top-notch group of lawmen. We could call them to see if they recognize the two guys who came by here yesterday. If they do, there might be some outstanding warrants on them. Also, our office would create a file to initiate an investigation. Then, we might follow some of them and try to find probable cause to make a stop. But that's about it."

"Exactly," I said. "We got nothing. If they have already poached around here, nobody knows about it yet. But we cannot just sit around and wait for one of them to take a shot at Kaiyo, right? So here is where my plan comes into play. The reason I think it will work is because if I were a bad guy, I would do it, too."

Lowe looked interested. "Sammy, your last crazy plan worked. Let's hear it out."

"Okay. Here it is. I will need you and at least two other officers. I am hoping I can get Troy Stahr to donate his time and the time of a couple of deputies. That probably won't be hard. Both your groups have jurisdiction over this type of thing. And Troy loves this type of stuff. If you think this is a plan, then I'll call him today. Hopefully, he can come over tonight."

"Anyway, I expect five to eight poachers to be dropped off early tomorrow morning at the Road entrance to the Southern Forest while it is still dark. That's all McLeod property there and I have it well posted for no trespassing. There is no way anyone can get on my property or stay on my property without knowing they are trespassers. Because of that, the minute they step foot on my land, they're guilty of criminal trespassing. That's enough to lock 'em up for a half day, but it won't stop them from trying to kill our bears at a later time. Catching them that way will just make them smarter."

Lowe jumped in and said, "Hold on, Sam. I'm not willing to let these guys take a grizzly just to make a legal case against them. And they can legally shoot a black bear, and we wouldn't know if they harvest his parts and sell them unless they're stupid enough to leave the entire dead bear in the field minus paws and gall bladders. They're probably willing to risk a criminal trespassing charge in exchange for some bears."

"You're right about that, Lowe," I said. "In fact, that's unacceptable. My plan doesn't involve any of that. What it involves is teaching some of them a lesson they will never forget. If they survive."

Lowe's eyebrows shot up.

I continued. "So when they get dropped off in the morning by one of their coconspirators, I'll be watching from a short distance away in my ghillie suit in the woods. They'll never see me. After they walk down the gravel road about a mile, I want you to drive down the gravel road and light it up with your blue lights. Maybe Stahr can bring a dog or two to bark it up. My goal is to block their way back to the Road and force them to head east in the forest until they either turn themselves in to you or Stahr, or they will have to deal with whatever or whoever it is that lives there. At first, they'll think they can head east and simply walk the twenty or thirty miles out of the forest to some of the roads that lead into the Eastern Wilderness. I suspect that after a few days, they'll come running out of there and beg to be saved. At that point, you will have criminal trespass and evading arrest to charge them with."

Lowe looked at me for a few moments and played with his pen. "Yeah, that's actually a good plan. Let's do it. Call me tonight if you need me to talk to Stahr. But if I know Stahr, he'll be chomping at the bit."

Lowe then looked at Kaiyo, and whispered out loud, "I do hate poachers. This ought to be fun."

A few years ago, Lowe had tried to camp in the Southern Forest and he had basically been chased out of it by things that came to his campsite. They stayed in the shadows, but they screamed and threw a bunch of rocks at him. He knew what we were planning was neither nice nor safe. But the poachers were free to give themselves up. The poachers' futures would lie in their own hands.

THE ORDEAL – DEAN

Dad was on the phone with Captain Stahr last night for about a half hour. I knew what was going on and that's why I got up early. Dad was up before me, and he, Officer Brigham, and Captain Stahr were in the kitchen having a cup of coffee. Kaiyo was there with them, and he and the lawmen were messing around. Dad was quiet and in the bottom half of his ghillie suit. He looked serious. The other two looked like they were playing with a bear cub. Kaiyo does that. He makes us forget about our problems.

Dad looked up and asked me why I was up so early. I went over and hugged him. I knew this was one of those things where he could get hurt. Dad was never one of those dads who held back his love for us. He hugged back and held on tight. He whispered that it would be all right. Kaiyo spotted us and he instantly quit playing and came over and put his paw on Dad's knee. It was like he knew we were serious.

204

To my surprise, Gracie and Libby came downstairs and went over to Dad. I think my mouth was wide open. Libby looked at me and said, "I didn't wake her up. She woke me up!"

That made sense. Nobody wakes Gracie up unless it's absolutely necessary. Even Dad leaves her alone unless it's time for school or church. Mom changed her chores to afternoon chores. It just wasn't worth trying to wake her up. And here she was. I also saw Mom come down the back steps. I guess we were all pretty worried about Dad. We worried about Dad for good reason, too. That man attracts pain. He's strong but not much of an athlete, and physical coordination is not his strong suit. If you look at him, he's a mess of scars. Some people have tattoos, Dad has scars. He is truly accident-prone. But it never stops him.

It was three in the morning and the moon was only a sliver in the sky. That meant it would be darker than dark. Dad and the two officers said their good-byes and went out the back door. Dad was armed with some bear spray and his 12-gauge pump shotgun loaded with buck shot. Buck shot was the right thing for this situation. It would work against either bears or men. He put on the upper part of his suit, and he looked like he was made of grass. He took off his grassy hood, waved us a kiss from Officer Brigham's truck, and he was gone. I had a bad feeling about this one.

It was 3:10 in the morning and it was quiet. A coyote yipped to our west. The stars were out, and Mom said it was time to go back to bed. We all sort of stared at each other, and we trudged back into the house. The dogs curled up on the porch. But Kaiyo didn't come. He stood there on his back legs and watched the lights of the vehicles disappear into the darkness. He whimpered for a few moments. Mom had to go get him and bring him in. He didn't want to come, and it took some coaxing to get him inside.

I couldn't sleep very well so I got up super early. Well, super early for a Saturday morning. Dawn was around 6:30, and it wasn't dawn yet. I couldn't see much outside so it was still dark. Kaiyo came downstairs with me. When it got light, I went ahead and dressed and got started on my chores.

Around noon, Captain Stahr came driving up the driveway. He was followed by one of his deputies who took a right turn down the oil company gravel road. That gravel road came off our driveway about halfway between the house and the Western Forest. Coming behind Captain Stahr was Officer Brigham. They were coming in fast. Their cars raised a cloud of white gravel dust that drifted slowly away from the road bed.

Captain Stahr was the first to hop out but he waited for Officer Brigham. Kaiyo and the dogs watched from the back porch. So did I. Mom stepped out of the barn behind them. They immediately turned and went to Mom. They spoke for a few moments before Mom let out a moan. For the first time, she looked a little panicked. She spotted me coming her way and she straightened up.

I knew it had to be Dad. "What happened to Dad?"

Captain Stahr and Officer Brigham didn't answer, they just looked at Mom. "What happened to Dad?" I asked a little more forcefully.

I didn't look at Mom when I said it. I was afraid she would cry. I looked from Stahr to Brigham. They squirmed. "Damn it! What happened to Dad?"

They looked surprised. Finally, Mom said, "Dean, they can't find him."

I looked at Officer Brigham. "Did you find any blood?"

Captain Stahr nodded and said "A little."

"Did you see where he went?"

Officer Brigham then said, "Okay, let's not play twenty-one questions. Let's go inside, and we'll tell you what we know."

I needed to hear the story, but no matter what, this was going to be terrible news.

Once inside, Libby joined us. The dogs stayed outside, but Kaiyo followed us in. Gracie was still asleep, of course. The lawmen spoke and we listened. Libby cried while Mom held back most of her tears. I was just confused. But I truly believed Dad was alive.

Officer Brigham spoke slowly. "Your father's plan had worked like a charm. They all saw the poachers get dropped off about an hour before dawn and slide past the entrance into the Southern Forest. There were seven in all. We were communicating with Sam. He followed them until they were about a mile from the entrance and deep into the forest when he told me to come with the siren blaring and with lights flashing. I did, and by the looks of things, the poachers ran into the forest past the oil well at the end of the road."

I didn't have to use my imagination like Libby did. I knew that oil well area because I had been there many times with Dad. It was definitely creepy back there.

"Several times," said Officer Brigham. "Your dad reported that something had been hanging close to him since he got situated in the woods while he waited for the poachers. We kept in touch, and he mentioned that whatever it was, it was close. He said he was looking forward to morning. Stahr and I both told him we needed to call the operation off and get him out because it might be a big bear, but your dad didn't want us to do that. He also said that whatever it was, it wasn't a bear. How he knew that, I don't know, but he was sure of it."

"Wait," I said. "You told us the poachers did come and that you were still in contact with Dad, right?"

They both nodded. "Okay, then you were talking to him as he followed the poachers down the road from a distance. Did you find his tracks? If you did, what did the tracks tell you?"

Libby was sitting on the floor holding on to Kaiyo and she was paying close attention. Captain Stahr raised his hand. "I'll answer that. It appears your dad was staying just off the road. We did find where he crossed several times to stay in a position to keep watching the poachers. In fact, Lowe must have driven right past him before he disappeared. We found his boot prints in the tracks of Lowe's truck. Your dad crossed into the south side of the woods from where it appears he was crouched as Lowe drove past. It looked like he ran back across the road, and then we lost his trail a few yards into the forest."

"Were there other tracks that looked like something was following my dad?" I asked.

"Yeah," said Captain Stahr. "There were. Most of them were covered by the tire tracks from other cars driving there to look for your dad. Whatever it was, it was heavy and probably big."

"Was it on four feet or two?" I asked.

Officer Brigham and Captain Stahr looked at each other. "Well," said Officer Brigham. "It looked like it was on two."

Everybody just took it in. I thought that was terrible news, but I didn't show it. "Did you find his gun?" I asked.

"Yes, we found his shotgun about ten yards from where we lost the trail. It looked like it had been thrown," said Captain Stahr. "And it appeared there was a struggle. That's where we found a little blood on some leaves."

"Did you find his pistol?" Mom asked. "He had it on him when you guys left this morning."

I was going to ask that, but I'm glad Mom did. She's smart and I needed her to stay engaged. The two officers looked at each other and looked back at Mom. "No, Susan. We sure didn't," said Officer Brigham.

Well, that was some good news. But that was about the only good news. As the day went by, more police cars were parked on our driveway, and they came and went up and down the service road that went to some of the other wells. Several times, a helicopter flew overhead, landed, and took off again. Two of the poachers had been caught already, and they had no information about Dad. They said that they hid in the *forest of hell*, and they were terrified. They confessed to the plan to kill bears and sell their parts. They just wanted out of those woods. One of Officer Stahr's deputies picked up the driver of the car who dropped off the poachers. They found a set of black bear paws in the car. He confessed, too. It looked like Dad's plan was working for everybody but Dad.

Libby and I did our chores, but it was becoming obvious to both of us that if Dad was to be found, it would be up to us. We agreed we would give the police types until dawn tomorrow. If Dad wasn't back, we would go try to find him. That day, Kaiyo never left our sides.

Around midnight, I slipped into Libby's room. She winked at me, and I held up five fingers. She nodded. We planned to wake up at five in the morning and go find Dad. I went to Mom's room. She was strong, but to say she was worried would have been a gross understatement. Gracie was hugging on to her like she was hoping this was all a bad dream. I hugged them both. We called in Libby. When Libby got there, Gracie, Libby, Mom, me, and a small bear, who seemed to understand what we were doing, prayed for protection. Libby prayed Dad would be armed in every way possible and that we needed help not only against flesh and blood, but against the powers and the spiritual forces of evil that patrolled the Southern Forest.

There's more to the Southern Forest than just scary animals. I guess we have always known that. Right now, Dad and the four or five remaining poachers who were on the run were each having to deal with the evil things that come in and out of those lands. Dad was better prepared; those poachers were not. The poachers may not survive. Our prayer was that Dad would. Then, except for Gracie who stayed with Mom, we all headed for bed.

When I woke up Libby at five, I noticed Kaiyo wasn't with her. That was unusual. Kaiyo usually slept in her room. Libby and I quietly searched the house, the barn, and the back and front yards. He was gone.

3

HELP – KAIYO

I loved them, and they were in trouble. Especially Dad. We needed help, and since talking it out doesn't work for me on this side, I had no choice. It was up to me.

I have been traveling in the Eastern Wilderness for about two hours now. The sun still had not come up, but I have already learned that lots of animals don't like grizzlies and they enjoy chasing around cubs. My time of strength would be coming but it wasn't here yet.

Some people say grizzlies can't climb trees, but I can, so can most other young grizzlies. In fact, us young ones usually can climb pretty well. And it's a good thing, too. I wasn't but a few miles into the wilderness when a coyote chased me up a tree. He came at me hard, and I ran for my life. I was able to make it up a lodgepole pine just in time. For the next ten minutes or so, the coyote wandered around the base of my tree and acted like he was some sort of wolf. As I looked at him, it dawned on me. I had sharp teeth, he had sharp teeth. I had really sharp claws. The coyote? No, not really. I could stand and fight. The coyote? Not really. He weighed about fifty pounds. I weighed about ninety pounds. I know this because Libby weighs me about every day and writes it down. She's serious about it, too.

Anyway, the only thing the coyote had on me was speed, age, and experience. Since I didn't intend to chase him, that meant he only had age and experience on his side. That was not enough, I hoped. And I couldn't stay in the tree all day. So, I started coming down the tree. I was busy and I couldn't let a stupid bully coyote hold me up. When the coyote saw me coming down, it confused him. He had lost his edge. I dropped from the last eight feet and whirled around to face him.

He came at me and he got a face full of paw and claw. My swat rolled him over. That was all he had. He turned and ran. His face was bloodied, and he learned a lesson. So did I. I learned that one coyote is not a problem. Unfortunately, there are more problems out here than one coyote. And it seemed I was destined to find them all.

As the sun rose, I kept heading east. I drank from a few streams, but I was pretty hungry. My hunger would have to wait.

Ever since I was adopted by my family, I knew the Southern Forest was not just a forest in the south. Tracker warned me about it. He said the forest was home to a lot of regular animals, including some big grizzlies and some wolves. I'm just a cub, and even though I'm getting bigger, it's not safe being off the farm. Moose and Major are like my incredible bodyguards. But they won't go in the Southern Forest at all. Tracker also said that an unnatural oppression haunted the Southern Forest. He didn't go into much detail but that was probably because I was just a cub and didn't know what an unnatural oppression was. I didn't ask him what he meant. It did sound bad, though. I knew, as long as I stayed out of the forest, I didn't have to worry about it. Now, I guess I do have to worry about it.

He also told me there were creatures that he called watchers that came in and out of the Southern Forest. Tracker said "You don't want to mess with a watcher."

He said some were good like us and that some had gone wild and some had become friends with the Oppressor. He told me to stay away from all of them. He said there wasn't enough difference between a good one and a bad one to risk it. Right then, I wished that I had asked Tracker a lot more questions. But back then, I was just so glad that Goliath wasn't trying to kill me anymore that I forgot some of the things Tracker wanted to teach me. Then, he left me.

But he left me with a beautiful family that protects me. And now that I am all alone, I know I have been blessed to have all the instincts of a natural bear. That made sense. I am a real bear, of course.

The sun rose in the sky and it was hot. I held to the creeks and avoided anything that lived. Late in the afternoon, I caught the sweet scent of a dead deer. Moose and Major have caught and killed a couple of deer that came too deep into the corn. The deer know better, but sometimes even deer get greedy. Anyway, I knew what deer smells like and tastes like. It's good and I like it.

So, I followed my nose. I tried to stay hidden, but I wasn't used to being a wild bear yet. I've learned that everything out here either runs from me or wants to kill me. There seems to be no middle ground. About an hour earlier, I stumbled into a small herd of elk. I won't do that again. Goodness, those things are huge. Peyton is bigger, but Peyton is bigger than nearly everything. I miss him, too.

So, about that dead deer. The Eastern Wilderness is really pretty. At times, the grass goes for miles. Then, there will be occasional patches of timber—some are small, some are big. Creeks meandered throughout all of it. The farther south I went, the more trees and brush I encountered. So, as I was headed east, I stayed to the south so I could hide. Unfortunately, the dead deer was out there in the open. I hid and watched it for what seemed like forever. It was probably only for a few minutes, though. The deer had some crows and magpies on it and a couple of coyotes working it over. They looked nervous. They kept eying a patch of timber off to the east. That was my first clue—the dead deer was trouble. Unfortunately, my stomach was screaming at me to eat. I was a growing bear, and being hungry was no fun.

My second clue that the dead deer was more trouble than it was worth came when I puffed up and moseyed on over to the carcass and took a few bites. I acted all big and fearless and grouchy. I acted like a bear. I was on one side of the deer and the two coyotes were on the other side. We were eating, so I guess we had a truce of sorts going on.

Then, the coyotes turned together and ran out of sight. The crows and magpies flew over into the trees and started calling out. I kept eating. I didn't smell anything unusual and I didn't hear anything unusual. I learned from that day that I needed to protect my back side. Because when it came, I didn't hear it. Then I heard it. I heard something like *rarrh*. Yes, it sounded like *rarrh*.

I whirled around, and there standing behind me was this cute little cat. I knew about cats, but we didn't have any on the farm. We did have a problem with rats on the farm, but Dad said cats kill too many song birds and not enough rats. Dad likes birds. I started to wonder why a cute little cat lived out here when I realized he was as big as a regular cat but he still looked like a kitten. Then, I knew.

In less than a second, I whirled around again, jumped over the deer, and started running back the way I came. I got about ten to fifteen steps when I felt a sharp pain in my backside and I was tumbling headlong as the kitten's mother was in a full-fledged attack. I saw her coming at me as I tumbled. I thought this was the end of me, but when I landed, the force of her blow to my backside twisted me around. Now mama mountain lion was facing my teeth and my claws. I swung right at her face, and I hit her faster and harder than I had hit the coyote. Her claws were sharp but so were mine. I hit her solid in the head, and blood leapt from her ripped nose. Now she was furious but so was I. She stopped, crouched, and screamed at me in rage. I stood to look as big as I could. We stayed there for a few moments, eyeing each other. She finally turned away, content that she had protected her kitten and her kill.

"Oh thank you, God! Thank you, thank you, thank you!" I said to myself.

I watched her go back to her stupid, precious deer carcass and her really cute kitten. I growled at her. "This time next year, try that again and I'll kill you!"

Well, I didn't actually say it out loud. Not that she would have a clue what I was even saying, though.

I checked for wounds. She sunk a claw in my butt, but that was about it. It hurt and I was a little bloody. I actually got the best of her. Who would've seen that coming? I was so proud of myself. Still, I had to be careful. If that was a big male lion or a bear or wolf, I would've been toast. I gave the lion a ton of room and circled around her to the north and continued heading east. I was still hungry and I had a sore rear end, but at least, I wasn't lion food and that was a good thing.

After a few more hours, it was getting late in the day, and by that time, I was so hungry it hurt. I had to cross a wide creek, and when I did, a school of fish scooted past me. They weren't really big, but a couple of them would make a nice meal. For the next ten minutes, I chased fish up the creek and back. They were so fast. I finally realized I was wasting time and it was getting to be dark. I clambered up the creek bank and into a wooded area with some cover. I found a log with a big hollow in it and started to climb in. As I learned, good shelter in the wild is rare and animals fight for it. This log had a badger in it, and he was as mean as a snake. He caught me on the shoulder and gave me a big bite before he went back into his log. It didn't really hurt because I'm so furry. But it could've. There was plenty of room for both of us in the log but he wouldn't budge. After the lion, I just didn't want to fight anymore.

Sure, I thought. *Go ahead and pick on the baby bear. Next year, you'll be my dinner.*

If there is a next year for me. For the first time, I was thinking I might not live long enough to get help for Dad. I found a good tree and climbed high on its boughs. Up and out of reach of everything but a small black bear or a small mountain lion, I curled up in the crook of some branches and finally fell asleep. I was hungry and dreamed of my bear mother and of that terrible day. I dreamed of my Libby. I dreamed that Dean had come and rescued me, and Gracie and me and the dogs were playing in the thick grass of the front lawn. Each time I woke, I remembered that I was dreaming and I cried some. I also knew that something was circling my tree, but I could tell it couldn't climb. I also smelled a familiar scent, and then I knew I was dreaming again.

I woke as the birds were chirping in full swing. I breathed deeply and the familiar scent hit me again. *No,* I thought. *It can't be.*

I poked my head over one of the branches and looked at the ground. Nothing. I turned in my little perch and looked the other way, and when I did, I was staring into two of the most beautiful eyes staring right back at me. And I saw a wagging tail to go with those eyes. Moose! I bawled and hurried down the tree. We tumbled into one another. He was as glad to see me as I was him. He had found me last night and waited for me.

At first, I was thinking maybe Dean had come to the rescue. The way it works is, Major looks after Dad, and Moose looks after the rest of our family. I checked the air for sign of Dean. Dean would do something like come out here for me. But the only scent I caught was of Moose. So, Moose has been following me since yesterday morning. I sure could have used him against that mountain lion. And the coyote. And those elk. And the fish. But I did learn a lot of helpful lessons.

Today was going to be a different day. I had the biggest, strongest, meanest dog in Montana with me, and I felt stronger than ever. Now it was time for breakfast, but we would have to get breakfast on the way. With Moose, breakfast was a lot more possible. I have seen him chase down deer and break their necks. What a great dog!

I had to admit, though, I didn't really know the way. I was guessing. Having Moose here, though, meant everything. I think the only thing that would challenge Moose out here would be a pack of wolves or an adult grizzly. And I was looking for one of those in particular. And I was getting closer.

I remembered Dad saying that when I was first saved from Goliath, it was about twenty miles away from the farm. I don't know how far that is but I bet it's a lot. I did understand I had to keep going. In my heart, I knew Dad had not been found yet and I had to get back there quickly. It was still mostly dark but we had to keep heading east. Moose was all in. I loved his attitude.

And so, we got started. I was so hungry. I've been growing fast but I wouldn't be growing much today. It was hard not to think of my milk bottles, my meat meals, and the juicy, green grass with Peyton. Being a cub, I missed my mom and my brother and sisters. They take such good care of me. But I had to be a bear. Dad was in real danger.

Darkness – Sam

I didn't even know what day it was. I remembered hearing helicopters go overhead from time to time. So I figured I missed a day or two. My head was still sticky-bloody on the right side and my hair was crusty with dried blood. I was super sore, and my head wound kept bleeding. I guess oozing is a better word than bleeding. Anyway, my headache had reached and surpassed my all-time personal record for a terrible headache. Quite frankly, I didn't know my head could throb so bad. And almost worse than the headache was the awful smell of this place. When I woke, my sense of smell was assaulted. The best way to describe it was it smelled like ripe sewage mixed with wet dog hair. Living on a farm, dogs routinely roll in the nastiest of stuff. They are so proud when they do that. The stench of this place was a lot like that, but there was no escape from it.

Whatever was nosing around me a few mornings ago sucker punched me and knocked me out. It had been sneaking around me for hours, but I couldn't use my flashlight or I might have alerted the poachers. Hopefully, Lowe and Troy have been able to keep those poachers in the woods. Right now, though, it seemed like I was getting the worst of it. Whatever took me was big and strong and light on its feet. I don't know if it knew it was me or if my being in the ghillie suit freaked it out. I have to admit that when I was in the suit, I didn't really look like a human. Maybe that thing was just trying to protect its territory. Of course, maybe it wanted to eat me, too.

The good news for me is that I was fully conscious, and because of that, I found out I still had my .45 pistol, my knife, and my flashlight. With that, I had a degree of control that it isn't aware of. That was an advantage. I took the ghillie pants off and that left me with jeans and a shirt and a light jacket. The top of the suit was gone somewhere. And for some reason, my boots were gone. My feet were all scraped up but I was able to wiggle my toes and feet. I had heard about this type of strategy before. If a prisoner is barefooted, he can't run far and he can't run fast. Whatever took me had a nice pair of my boots and I wanted them back.

I am pretty sure I was stuffed underneath one of those old houses decaying deep in the Southern Forest. A cave-like crawl space had been hollowed out and it was pitch-black dark. I flashed my light and saw there was only one way out and it was blocked by a small boulder. I saw a number of bones on the dirt floor. Most looked like deer bones but a few of them looked human. The skull resting about twenty feet from me definitely looked human, at least, mostly human. That just couldn't be good. I guess that answered whether my kidnapper wanted to eat me. I was thinking it probably did. But it could've killed me pretty easily, and for some reason, it didn't. Right now, I was just a prisoner. But that brought me a bit of a smile. I was a prisoner with a gun.

I had to think. My dad taught me a long time ago to follow the rule of the apes. Not real apes, of course. He used acronyms because it made things easier to remember. The *a* part is that where ever we go, we need to be aware of our surroundings and aware of moods. A good mood can make somebody complacent; a bad mood can make somebody think poorly. And our surroundings tell so much. From threatening people to tense situations, we need to be aware of where we are.

Then, we always need to be in a posture that allows for peace. That was what the *p* stood for. He told me being a man doesn't mean being some sort of cocky macho man. Survival with honor is the goal. Not every insult needs to be escalated into a situation. Peace has a tremendous value, and it may save a life.

The next part was escape. Just because I carry a firearm doesn't mean escape isn't an option. Often, it's the best option. The last part is to strike. If you can't escape and peace is not available, then strike.

We have always been told our typical primitive responses are fight or flight. That's not true, and the untrue part gets people killed. The truth is, our primal responses are fight, flight, or freeze. And freezing is often a problem. Unless you are facing a grizzly bear, freezing is usually the worst response. I was taught that if there is going to be a fight, then go ahead and attack. Anything else is giving the advantage to the enemy. There are numerous stories of people who remain seated in crashed airplanes even when told to get up and get out of the plane. They froze, and because of it, they died. If they knew freezing was a natural but primitive response, they would understand that it didn't make for a good plan.

So with all that being said, I was fully aware I was stuck in some disgusting, smelly crawl space, and peace would be very unlikely. I sure couldn't count on it. And my head hurt a lot. My feet hurt but nothing like my head. I needed to figure out how to escape. But first, I needed to pray.

We don't believe in some crazy superstition or that some arrangement of words acts like magic. We believe that for whatever reason, God has chosen, among other things, to work through our prayers. We don't know why. He sure didn't need our prayers to create the world or even to feed the birds each day. But he still wants us to pray. So, I prayed. I prayed for safety. I prayed for my family, and I prayed for victory.

I had always thought these woods were infested with something spiritually evil and I was right. I'll save for later the story about what happened as I prayed. But I can say that while I was praying, it got scary noisy. Prayer was highly unwelcome here. After I prayed, calm returned to the area. They were gone. I then left the spiritual warfare in God's more than capable hands.

That was important because whatever it was that knocked me out and brought me here was no spirit. And it was time to get out of here and strike back if I could.

A PLAN – LIBBY

We were guessing Kaiyo went after Dad. If he was just any old bear, we could assume he ran away. Bears do things like that. But not Kaiyo. Dean thinks he and Moose are probably together, but that made no sense to me. When we started looking for Kaiyo, both dogs were here. But Moose's absence just made things weirder.

It had been two full days since we last saw Dad. The police were all over the place, and they have been flying over the Southern Forest during the daylight hours. The Southern Forest is vast and easily over one hundred thousand square acres. The canopy is thick, and flying over the trees isn't very helpful. But I loved they were doing it. Captain Stahr was hoping Dad would make it to a clearing. Davey also had been flying over the farm and the forest, and he has taken Mom up with him a few times. She scans the forest with her binoculars.

Dean is actually pretty confident, and that gave me confidence. I don't really know why it did. Dean is just a thirteen-year-old boy. But I liked his logic. He told me Dad had to be alive, because if he were dead, Stahr's dogs would have found his body by now. That was hard to think about, but it was a very logical statement.

Yesterday, Dean and I were going to look for Dad but we got way off track when we lost Kaiyo. We searched everywhere and figured out Kaiyo had, for some reason, probably headed into the Eastern Wilderness. We all cried, especially Gracie. By the time we quit looking for Kaiyo, sneaking into the Southern Forest to go try to find Dad was impossible. Last night, we all sat out on the porch. Major had approached the Southern Forest and growled. With his hair standing on end, Major then started barking furiously. Dean grabbed his shot gun and walked out to Major. Mom didn't try to stop him. She knew he would be careful but we had about had it with the mystery creatures of the Southern Forest. After a while, Major relaxed and they both headed back to the porch.

We also had heard the scream of a poacher off in the distance. Sheriff Tuttle had taken over the search. He was staying here with us. He and a deputy left the house and drove out into the forest on the service road to see if they could find him. Another Deputy went in from the Road, but they all came back empty-handed. Sheriff Tuttle said they could hear the poacher but he was too far off and sounded like he was headed east. They also said they heard a different type of scream and it sounded like it was racing to intercept the poacher. I actually felt kind of sorry for that poacher. It was all very strange and terrifying. Dad's plan was getting out of hand. Sheriff Tuttle thought it was already out of control.

At least it was daylight and with daylight came new hope. Davey had landed early this morning and he brought his wife Lisa with him. Except for Gracie, we were all awake when we heard Davey fly in. Dean shot from the kitchen table and ran to the barn, started the UTV, and headed out to go get them. Sheriff Tuttle, Captain Stahr, and Officer Brigham sat out on the front porch with a few maps on the table. They were competent men, and I knew they were trying hard.

I stepped outside and waited for Dean. It was Monday morning, and for us, there would be no school today. I headed over to the barn and absentmindedly fed the guineas and the chickens and placed hay in the horse troughs. Jet seemed to know what I was thinking. Solo, Dean's horse, was ready to go, too. Dean had brought back Davey and Lisa and dropped them off at the back door. When Dean came in the barn, I already saddled Jet. "Good call," he said. He then saddled Solo. "Now," he said. "We need a good story."

We both hated to just sit and wait, and Mom was distracted. "Who's to say we can't go looking for Kaiyo?" I said.

Dean laughed. "Yeah, and who's to say he isn't lost in the Southern Forest?"

Dean and I went in and said hello to Lisa. Davey was out front talking to the lawmen. Miss Lisa is one of the nicest people I know. She was there to help Mom in a way only good friends can. We chatted, and then I casually told Mom that Dean and I were going to give the horses some exercise and maybe see if we could find any sign of Kaiyo. Mom was lost in thought, and I didn't wait for approval. Dean ran upstairs to get dressed in riding clothes. I was wearing my cowboy boots and jeans and a light jacket. Dean and I knew that to find Dad, we had to go into the vastness of the Southern Forest. That couldn't be done on a four-wheeler or an SUV or flown over in a helicopter. We had to go in it.

When Dean came back downstairs, he grabbed two walkie-talkies and ran out to the front porch to Davey. He handed Davey one of the devices and said "Channel four, and don't try it until you are in the air. Don't forget it, Davey."

Davey laughed and stuffed it in his pocket and went back to talking to the lawmen. The lawmen gave Dean an odd look as he ran back in. I stayed in the kitchen and threw a flashlight, some apples, and a few waters in my backpack. Dean did the same. We each grabbed a can of bear spray, and I grabbed my rifle and some extra ammunition. Dean had his shotgun, and we headed out to the barn. When we got to the horses, they were almost giddy, they were so excited. At least, we were doing something.

REUNION — KAIYO

Since just before dawn, Moose and I had been walking toward the rising sun. It was another beautiful day, but I was so worried about Dad. And I was so hungry. I was running out of energy, too. I was thinking Moose could go on forever. I envied his blissful ignorance. After a few miles, we had to cross a swollen creek, and both Moose and I barely made it. We both had to rest for a few minutes. I think Moose was really shaken up. I left Moose to finish catching his breath, and I climbed the low hill bordering the creek. When I got up and over the top of the small hill, I came eye to eye with two wolves fussing over a few scraps of dead rabbit.

I'm dead, I thought.

Those wolves looked at me like I was their breakfast, and had I not acted, I probably would have been. They came at me, and I did what I had to do. I attacked. They expected me to run; running is natural. But by attacking them, they were taken completely by surprise. Had I run, they would have been on me almost immediately. I growled as loud as I could and bowled the first one over. He outweighed me by thirty pounds, but I had the momentum. The second one pivoted and tried to sink her teeth in me, but I and the male were all balled up. Then, Moose was upon them both. Moose was enormous, and his presence had them so confused. I was standing and was ready to swat one, but they were having to deal with Moose. I didn't like two against one, so I jumped on the back of the big male as he faced Moose. That was just more than the two of them could handle. He shook me off his back, yelped, and they ran off. I did get to sink my claws in his ribs and that was nice. To the wolves, it was all pure weirdness. To me, it was all about being family. Yep, Moose McLeod saved Kaiyo McLeod. It probably wouldn't be the last time, either.

We kept heading eastward when I caught a slight scent. The scent was right, and I caught it before Moose. I was hoping the owner of that scent would be nice. If he wasn't, it would take ten dogs like Moose to save me. Moose finally caught his scent about the same time I spotted his gold fur standing in a shallow creek. Moose barked and he heard it. He lifted his head and tried to find us out in the grass. He spotted us, probably just Moose, as he heaved his bulk out of the creek. I forgot how big he was. Goliath was either going to kill me or help me. He came at us running.

The distance disappeared as we ran at one another, and in just a few seconds, he was almost on us. Even as a bear, it is surprising how fast we bears are. And Goliath was fast. I was scared. I knew he had tried to kill me a few times before. But Moose went right to him and they greeted each other like long-lost pals. Goliath looked at me and winked, while Moose jumped with pure joy. I forgot Goliath had tried to kill Moose a couple of times, too. But not today. Goliath fell to the grass, and Moose just went in for some serious play time. Goliath obviously knew we came out here to contact him. He let Moose play to burn off some excess enthusiasm.

After a few minutes, Goliath came over to me. He was so big it was intimidating. It was comforting to know I would be maybe as big as him some day. Goliath gave me a hug because that's what bears do. He asked me why I was out here all alone. I barely got the words out when I just started crying big bear tears. Not enough people understand bears can cry, and I have cried several times on this trip. And this was one of those times. I told him about Dad being missing and about the creepy Southern Forest and I told him about leaving everybody without saying good-bye and I told him about the other mean animals and especially the wolves and the mountain lion and how Moose came and rescued me from my loneliness and then from the wolves. By the time I was done, I was totally out of breath.

Goliath put his enormous arm over me. "That's all my fault, you know. But I am so proud of you, Kaiyo. You are going to be a great and strong bear. You will make all of us bears proud. Well, at least, the bears like you and me will be proud."

I looked at him through my bleary eyes and stammered, "But how is it your fault?"

Goliath hugged even tighter. "Kaiyo," he said. "A cub like you shouldn't ever be left alone. Ever. In my evil madness, I killed your bear mother because she was like me. For years, I had been listening to the wrong things. They fed my hatreds and my pride. Your mother would have never left you alone until it was your time. She fought so hard to protect you. I think about that horrible day often. I also think about how your human father and your big brother decided to give me a chance. They gave me the chance I never gave to your bear mother."

Goliath just sat there looking off at the horizon. "Yes," I said. "But you're nice now."

Goliath got stern. "No, Kaiyo. I am not nice, and I probably never will be. That is not who I am, and it is not what I was made for. I think I will be satisfied with just trying to be good."

Goliath shifted to look directly at me. "Kaiyo, never forget. Nice and good are not the same things and they never, ever will be. *Nice* masquerades as good all the time, but sometimes it is just the pretty face of evil. *Good* is always trustworthy. Nice is just a behavior that deserves no trust. It can be welcome and you can appreciate *nice*. I guess, we all do. But trusted? Never. The Master understood it even though too many of us think of him as a nice man. He's not really nice at all. He never was. He is wonderful and completely full of love, though."

"Huh. A master? Who's your master? Goliath, you don't have a master. You're too big and strong. No one tells you what to do."

I was so confused. "Hah," said Goliath. "Don't you believe it. Everybody has a master, even if they deny it. I used to serve a very different master. In fact, sometimes we have lots of masters that compete for our affections or our wants. I didn't know it until your father became my master the day he caught me. He could have killed me at any time. Or he could have sold me into the slavery of a zoo. Anyone with that kind of power is the very definition of a total master. Sitting in that pit forced me to think about it. It forced me to think about everything. And when I was in the pit, my old master had no voice and no power in there. I was left alone with my own thoughts. And it dawned on me that the Master, the real Master, was the one my old master feared. It was obvious to me I had a choice and my eyes were opened."

"By the way, Kaiyo." Goliath asked, "Have you noticed that we're different? Take a look at Moose over there."

We both looked at Moose wandering around, sniffing the ground. He looked up at us and saw us both looking at him. His tail immediately started wagging, his ears dropped, and he came our way to play. Goliath nuzzled him, and then Moose caught another scent or something and wandered off. "As you grow older, Kaiyo, you will figure out we are far closer to humans than the other regular animals and yet we are still animals. We are blessed in ways even I will never quite understand. But it is a blessing. Did you notice how much you are drawn to those humans who serve the Master? That, my favorite young bear, is all by design."

I nodded. It was true. It was attracted to some people and not at all to others. I started to ask another question and Goliath stopped me. "Kaiyo, I know you have questions but I am not the right teacher to teach you. I am still learning myself and I fear giving you too many wrong answers. Now, let's focus on saving your dad. I owe my life to him and I haven't forgotten it. I never will. By the way, have you eaten?"

I told him about how hungry I was and about the mountain lion's deer and the fish.

"Then," said Goliath. "We shall eat on the way! Let's go get your father."

With that, the three of us headed back toward the west.

It was obvious I was slowing down the group. Goliath asked me to crawl up on his back. It wasn't a typical *bear thing*, but I tried it. We might have looked silly, but we covered a lot more ground. What took me an hour of travel the day before took us only about twenty minutes. Of course, with Goliath and Moose, we had no interruptions. A herd of elk ran away and the wolves just watched from a distance. Goliath had a reputation, and it wasn't a very nice one. Right now, that was handy. Nothing came near us.

In no time, we had crossed the deep creek and now we were at the one with the fish in it. "Want some?" said Goliath. "You need to eat."

"Yeah, but they're impossible to catch. They're too fast."

"They are," said Goliath. "But we're smarter, right? This is a trick even the ordinary bears probably understand. Watch this and you'll never be hungry again."

I hopped down and watched Goliath. He walked into the creek and the fish raced away. But he didn't chase the fish. He pawed at the creek with his claws and made it totally muddy. One end of the creek was filled with cloudy water. Then, he told me to go upstream where the fish were and scare them back down the creek. I did and they went right into the dirty water. It was really shallow there. They swam right in and couldn't see. Goliath easily flicked two out of the creek. He motioned me over, and I was able to flick one out. That was great. "Lunch!" he said.

He gave one to Moose and one to me. We all ate quickly, and for the first time, I wasn't so hungry it hurt.

We then headed west again. I finally had some energy, and we all moved fast. After another thirty or so minutes, we smelled the mountain lion's deer. It had started rotting, and that just made it smell even better. After another ten minutes, we came to the carcass. "You and Moose need to eat. Don't worry about anything. Take ten big bites. That's all you need. We can't get slowed down with a too-full belly."

We'll see about that, I thought.

I was first over the little hill, and there was the mean mountain lion sitting by her precious deer carcass. The moment she saw me, she didn't hesitate. She obviously remembered our fight and she came for me fast. She was within an easy leap of me when she saw Goliath come up and over the hill. That stopped her. Her eyes got really big. Then she saw Moose, and she turned and fled. Yep, I was back and I had reinforcements!

Moose chased her but not far and he came right back. There was still plenty of meat left, and Moose and I ate our ten bites. They were big bites, too. Moose actually ate more, but it was okay, he couldn't count. I could've eaten twenty bites but I trusted Goliath. I looked at Goliath and asked if he was going to eat. He said something about him being full because he had just eaten an entire camper. Then he laughed. I was pretty positive he hadn't really just eaten a camper but I was not positive he hadn't done it a few times in the past.

It dawned on me I didn't know Goliath's real name. Goliath was just the name my dad named him years ago. Between bites of deer, I asked him what his real name was. Goliath looked at me kind of sad like, and said, "It has been a long time since anyone has asked, but that makes sense. I haven't been very friendly. So except for you, Tracker, and the McLeods, I have had no friends and it is friends who make your name sweet to the sound. Because it has been so long since I have heard my old name, I have decided I only want to go by the name Goliath. The people I love gave me that name, so it is precious to me. So Kaiyo, Goliath is my real name."

My mouth was full so I just nodded. It made sense.

Goliath then looked over to the south. "We're close to the eastern edge of the Southern Forest. There are some gravel roads out here that go all the way to town. We need to head south, so when we go into the forest, we can be as close as possible to the point where your father was last seen. We animals use roads all the time, but usually only at night. It's really the best way to get around. The wolves are pretty smart and they use logging roads all the time, day or night, to get at the moose, caribou, and elk. Roads put the prey animals at a disadvantage. I use roads, too, for the same reason. Anyway, we're probably going to see some humans, but don't get friendly. Act like a regular bear. We'll stay off the road in the grassy shoulder, and people will think we're a mother and her cub. Having Moose with us will just confuse the heck out of them, but we can't send him home. Besides, we need him."

We headed south and found a gravel parking lot at the end of a long gravel road. On either side of the road, the trees had been cut way back and it was open and grassy. The parking lot had a few cars in it but we saw no one. It was hunting season so we had to be careful. I heard Dad say that we grizzlies were protected, but that didn't mean somebody wouldn't try to shoot us anyway.

We had made about five or six miles down the road and left the openness of the Eastern Wilderness a while back. It was still wild country, though, and thick forest was on both sides of the road's wide grassy shoulders. That gravel road pretty much marked the eastern border of the Southern Forest. It was thick and dark in there. We saw numerous game trails that went in and out of the woods. Then, an airplane came over pretty low. The plane passed us and circled around and came back for a closer look. We knew that plane so we weren't worried for our safety. That was Davey's plane. As he passed us a second time, he waggled his wings and headed on south. That only meant Dad was still missing. I already knew it in my heart and so did Goliath. We both gave each other concerned looks.

We were getting close to where we should enter into the forest when we spied several police cars and trucks parked on the road. They were still about a mile or so away, but Goliath stopped us. I thought it was time for us to go ahead and enter the Southern Forest. Goliath wasn't happy that our way south was barred. He didn't want to deal with people in general and especially the police. He was pretty sure a few of those deputies that he had terrorized might have been carrying a grudge. He had a point. Goliath had nearly killed one of those deputies and he also killed some of their dogs. They probably still thought of Goliath as a bad bear. I guess I couldn't blame them.

All of a sudden, one of those police trucks came barreling up the road toward us pretty fast, raising a big cloud of dust. We had been spotted. We started to head into the forest when we heard the truck honking its horn. Goliath told me to wait. We were right at the edge of the forest and the road was pretty far from the forest edge so we felt safer. Goliath said, "If you see a gun come out of the window of that truck, we have to run into the forest as fast as we can. But you go first Kaiyo. The innocent before the guilty."

I had no idea what he meant by that, but we were both ready to bolt into the woods. I looked over at Moose. Instead of sticking with us, he was running toward the truck and his tail was wagging.

Sometimes a dog's trusting nature is a bad thing. We thought we might have to leave him. I didn't think a policeman would shoot him, but he was definitely a scary-looking dog. Goliath and I had already started drifting into the woods and we were ready to run if we needed to. "Try to keep the big trees between you and that policeman if he starts shooting. We'll be home free after about twenty yards. These woods are dense. And they won't follow a bear in the woods."

"Moose! Is that you, big boy?"

Wait! I knew that voice. Goliath knew that voice. It was Officer Brigham! Wow. That was great news to me. "Wait," said Goliath. "Wait until he gets out of the car. We need to be sure."

The truck stopped and out stepped Officer Brigham. Moose was thrilled. I started running to the truck as Officer Brigham walked toward us. "Come on, Goliath. You're family, too," said Officer Brigham.

I looked back and Goliath was right behind me. We had to be careful not to knock Officer Brigham down even though Moose was giving it a shot. All of the other cops were standing in the doors of their vehicles watching us with binoculars. I think they were waiting for Goliath to take him out. But Goliath and I stopped short. Goliath told me to. We let Officer Brigham come to us, and boy, did he! He was a hugger. That was fine because we bears are known for it. He first hugged me, then he went straight for Goliath. Officer Brigham wasn't scared at all. Goliath was still surprised at the grace, but he soaked it all in.

After a few minutes, Officer Brigham settled down and told us what was going on with Dad. The news was both good and bad. First, they were pretty sure he was alive. That was good. But he was on the run and he was headed our way. The bad part was, he was being chased. Goliath looked confused at that, and Officer Brigham explained. "The helicopter pilots have been able to use their thermal imagers to detect Sam's heat signature and the heat signatures of several other creatures. When the trees are thick it doesn't work too well, but there are enough openings in the canopy to give them something to work with. The pilots believe that something big is helping him, but they're being followed by several other big things. They seem to have been keeping their distance, but it looks like they're gaining in numbers."

Goliath pointed a paw at himself. "No, Goliath," said Officer Brigham. "They're definitely not bears. But they're big."

Goliath looked ferocious. He looked at me, and said "Did Tracker ever tell you about watchers? I'll tell what those things are later, but this is bad news."

I knew enough about watchers to be a little scared.

Officer Brigham also said they had captured three more poachers. "They had made it to this road earlier this morning. They were all scraped up and their clothes were in tatters. They were babbling about all sorts of horrors. One of them seemed to have gone insane. All of them practically jumped in the police cars. None had seen your father, but they were all in fear. We heard things in the woods as they came running out. It sounded to us like some sort of laughter. It was really disturbing."

Then he told us something that probably wasn't good. Libby and Dean had slipped past everybody, and they were in the Southern Forest looking for Dad. Now they were missing, too. Officer Brigham looked at us and asked if the deputies could say hello to Goliath. "Please? It won't take but a few minutes," said the lawman.

Goliath nodded. Officer Brigham gave a sign, and those deputies popped down in their trucks like prairie dogs ducking in their holes. In a flurry of spinning tires and flying gravel, they came flying up the road. When they got even with us, they skidded to a stop, parked, and out came four deputies. One of them limped and had his left arm casted and hanging in a sling. His scalp was covered with fresh red scars. That was the one Goliath had almost killed. They all came down and each greeted Goliath. I went over to Officer Brigham and left them to talk. They stood, and the deputies talked as Goliath sat and nodded from time to time. The wounded deputy was laughing and talking along with the rest. I guess it made sense. They were all warriors and all warriors share the war part in common, even if they were once enemies.

It quickly became time to go get my dad. Everybody put on their serious face again. One of the deputies told us the plan was simple. Goliath was to head west into the forest and intercept Dad who had been running to the east toward us. Hopefully, Goliath could get to him before those other things did. They told Goliath to protect Dad from his chasers and to get Dad to a clearing. There, they would try to helicopter in and get him on out. Goliath would then have to fight his way back out. It seemed like a good plan. I turned to head into the woods. "Not so fast, Kaiyo," said Officer Brigham. "I was told to keep you with me. This work is too dangerous for a cub. In fact, we're all worried about Goliath."

I was just a young bear, but that just brought up my natural grizzly bear rage. It was like I was dealing with those stupid wolves again. I stood and growled and went toward Officer Brigham. He looked stunned. So did Goliath. The deputies stepped back and a few laughed. The injured deputy then said, "Lowe, take it from me, you don't want to be messing with an angry bear. No offense, Goliath, but they don't like to be told what to do."

They all laughed, even Goliath gave out a bear laugh. I didn't think it was funny at all. I had fought wolves, coyotes, and a mountain lion. Who was he? I dropped to all fours and turned toward the forest. Goliath and Moose followed me. "Well, at least, be careful," yelled Officer Brigham. "Your mom is going to kill me!"

I didn't look back. I was already in the Southern Forest and we had work to do.

SOUTHBOUND – DEAN

Libby and I got on our horses and we left through the back of our barn. From the back of the barn to the northern edge of Southern Forest, it was only about seventy-five yards, and for a good part of that distance, the barn hid us from the view of anyone at the house. Mom and Lisa were still probably talking and wouldn't notice us for the few moments we were visible from the back porch or kitchen windows.

Solo was a true mountain pony. He was a slate blue dun mustang. His mane and tail and stockings were almost black while most of his body was a gray-blue color. In Spanish, he would be called a grullo instead of a dun. It's all the same and both terms are used in the west. Solo was part mountain goat and part cheetah. He was fast as lightning, but perfectly comfortable tiptoeing along a thin trail halfway up a near vertical cliff. He was perfect for this.

Libby followed as I turned Solo onto a game trail that led into the forest. In moments, we were out of sight and swallowed up in this mystery forest. Dad never wanted us to explore this area because it was just too strange. We had explored the north lands all the way to the mountains and the Western Forest all the way to the Road. Both Libby and I had taken trips with Dad out to the Eastern Wilderness. It was odd that this forest, literally right at our back door, was avoided by all of us. When Dad told us to stay out, we really didn't have a problem obeying him. The forest was creepy, and we all knew about people getting run out of there. One time, when I was a child, several young campers went in the Southern Forest south of our property line. The story is, they were never seen again. Their campsite was found and it was ripped to shreds but they were gone. Some people blamed grizzly bears, some said it was a crime scene, and some said it was all a hoax by the campers themselves. Others noticed some of the campers' stuff was tossed up in the trees and they blamed watchers. I know one thing, though, bears can't do things like that.

We all knew those watchers were part of the creepiness, but not all of it. Both Libby and I had been in and out of the Southern Forest, but we had always stuck to the oil company gravel roads and we were always with Dad. Getting older, the forest was becoming less intimidating to me. I actually looked forward to the day when Dad, Kaiyo, and I go in and clean that place out.

We did know there was a lot of wild game out here. The forest couldn't have been all bad. It's not like there were vampires or such running around because that would be ridiculous. But there were things out there that were still mysterious, and they were not at all good. Dad and Mom always said that nobody had all the answers and that we were still in the age of discovery. And now we needed to go discover Dad.

About twenty feet into the forest, we passed a trail that looked like it ran east to west and parallel to our long driveway. It was hidden by the dense trees and brush, but it went west for as far as we could see down it. I pointed. "I bet that's the path that those watching things use."

"Gross," whispered Libby.

We kept going, saying little, only the sound of our creaking saddles giving up our presence. After about a half mile, the forest canopy got thicker and the undergrowth wasn't so thick. That allowed us to encourage Solo and Jet to pick it up. We flushed several deer and we saw a moose crash away. Horses usually don't like moose and are frightened of them. But ours have seen plenty of them so they weren't very scared. Moose are huge and potentially dangerous, though.

Our goal was to head due south about seven miles to where a few of our wells were. Dad was abducted near those wells, and that's where we had to start. We were going faster than a walk and slower than a trot. Both horses were super strong, and this kind of travel was no problem for them. After about a mile, we came upon an old homesteader's driveway of sorts. It was somewhat grown over, but because of it, we were able to go faster. We didn't know where this path was headed, but it went south in the direction where we wanted to go and that was good enough for now.

Libby and I rode side by side and we both figured out that, by now, the police would add us to the list of people who have been swallowed up in this forest. After about another forty-five minutes of hard riding, we knew we were getting close to a place where a home was or used to be. It's not hard to tell if you read the clues. We passed a few boxwoods and those are not natural out here. Dad taught me if you saw something out in the woods or in the grassy areas that didn't look natural, it probably wasn't. People will plant things around their house that live long after the house burns down or falls apart.

The further down the lane we went the darker it got. "Oppressive," said Libby.

"Yeah, keep your eyes peeled, Big Sis. This place is definitely a dual threat. There are regular flesh and blood things that are bad enough, and there are some spiritual things out here that are bad, too. Remember Dad telling us these woods were haunted?"

"Yeah," said Libby. "But I always sort of thought he was kidding."

I had an idea of about where we were. Libby and I had been headed south for a while and we both believed we ought to be a few miles due east from the oil well that was reached by the one driveway that came off the Road. Not only did that mean we had to keep our eyes open for poachers lost in the woods but it also meant we weren't too far from where Dad was first taken. If Dad was taken, the thing that took it would not head north toward the farm or west toward the road. Both areas were crawling with police and law enforcement.

That left east and south, and because the forest was thickest to the east, searching to the east just made more sense to us. Still, we really didn't know much of anything. That would soon change.

Within another fifty yards or so, the outline of an old, beat-up brown house started coming into view. It was dreary-looking being stuck out here in the middle of nowhere. It was well camouflaged, too. To be honest, we were more scared of the flesh and blood stuff than the evil spirits that were all around. Still it was obvious there was an unnatural oppression that was here. If people only had a clue how common this situation was, they'd be pretty surprised. But we didn't come unarmed.

Everybody who knew us knew we followed Christ. It wasn't a secret. We learned early on that when anybody asked us about who or what we believed, we had an answer for the hope that we had. I think Libby loved the beauty of Christ. I was attracted to the power and the reason. We were both right, I guess. So, right there on horseback, Libby and I prayed. It made a lot of sense at the time.

When we were done, I looked at Libby and shrugged. Whatever oppression we sensed had left us and it left us quickly. She laughed and we rode to the old house. I grabbed my shotgun, hopped off Solo, and handed the reins to Libby. I walked over to the house and started looking around. I turned back to Libby. "Now, don't lose sight of me. We need to cover each other. And get your rifle out and ready."

As I inspected the outside of the house, Libby and the horses stayed about twenty-five feet away. They followed me, so we never lost sight of each other. That slowed me down but it was essential. We made our way to what was the front of the old house and the front door was wide open. The place had experienced a lot of traffic. Whatever lived there tracked in a lot of mud and leaves. The place smelled bad, too.

Then I saw the top of Dad's ghillie suit just inside the front door. "Bingo!" I called out.

Libby saw it, too. I called for Dad but there was no answer. The dilapidated house wasn't very big so I screwed up my courage, looked back at Libby, and headed in. Libby covered me as long as she could. I pretty much ran from room to room and saw Dad wasn't in any of them. That place was just flat scary. I half expected to see anything from Dad, dead or alive, to a kidnapper, a rabid raccoon, or a grizzly bear using the house as his personal cave. Fortunately, nobody and no creature was home. But something had been. In one of the rooms, I found Dad's boots next to a bloody spot on the wall. That was good, actually. Dead people don't bleed. But I knew Dad was in deep trouble.

I also noticed each room had evidence that something had been living here. Mostly, there were pine tree branches thrown on the floors and piled together like uncomfortable mattresses. And really big mattresses, too. It was time. I grabbed Dad's stuff and got out of there.

I walked outside and shook my head to indicate Dad wasn't in there. I showed her the boots and ghilli suit top. I then started to walk to the next side of the building when Libby pointed out the crawl space. It wasn't a standard crawl space. It looked more like it had been dug out a while back. Now some people say that, for a kid, I'm pretty brave. If they knew how creeped out I got with really dark, spidery places, they might think again. And that's what I saw—a dark, terrible-looking, spidery, cave-ish space. Libby was first to notice a big rock that looked like it had been moved. I walked over and saw it had been dragged away from the crawl space. I went back to Solo, stuffed Dad's things in my saddlebags, and pulled a flashlight out of the pack. "I'm just going to stick my head in that hole and look around."

Libby smiled. "Enjoy the spiders."

That was cruel. As I walked to the hole, I saw an encouraging sign. "Tracks," I called out.

There in the drag marks left by the removal of the boulder, I clearly saw the imprint of a man's foot. If I had to guess, it was my dad's track. I still had no idea why he wasn't wearing his boots, though. "Libby, I think it's Dad's footprint."

Then, I walked a few steps to the dark hole, got on my knees, turned on the flashlight, and looked into the crawl space. The first thing I noticed was the rotten smell. Then, not ten feet away in hole, were the pants part of Dad's ghillie suit. I scanned the rest of the crawl space but there was nothing else there except some bones. "There are some bones in here," I told Libby. "And one of them looks sorta human. The others look like elk or deer bones."

"So, he's either on the run or whatever took him still has him," said Libby.

"Yep, and that also means he's still alive," I said.

I hopped on Solo again, and took the reins from Libby. From there, we were able to see a hint of a trail headed east. It looked like it was new.

Just then from a hundred or so yards behind us, we heard what can only be described as a piercing howl and a roar ending with a growl. That put shivers up our spine, but it was intended to.

"That would be a watcher, Libby. And I think he's bluffing. He or it or whatever it is over there is just trying to scare us."

"You sure about that?" asked Libby.

"Yeah, pretty sure," I laughed.

But I was worried. This was the type of thing that had run off countless well-armed hunters and poachers, plus riders and hikers that were here in the Southern Forest. Watchers probably deserve the blame for the missing people, too.

Libby and I headed east, while that thing kept howling and breaking trees and huffing and puffing and stomping around and such. We never saw it, but it was making so much noise it didn't even know we had left. After riding quickly for about ten minutes or so, we heard a small plane fly overhead. That was Davey's plane. I pulled out my walkie-talkie and called out to him. Davey responded to me immediately. "Dean, you're in deep trouble but I am so glad to hear you. Is Libby with you? Over."

"Yep," I said. "Is she in trouble, too? Over."

"Yes, but not as much as you are. Over," said Davey.

"Great. What's the story on Dad? We found his ghillie suit. Over."

Davey responded, "We think your dad is on the run. He's being chased by several big creatures, but there is at least one big creature that may be helping him. The police have some thermal images that are really helpful. That much we know. Goliath, Kaiyo, and your dog are headed west to save him. I saw them earlier. Over."

Libby squealed at that news. "Well," I said. "Then we are going after Dad's chasers. Do you know where Dad is? Over."

"Yeah," said Davey. "We think he's about ten miles due east from the oil well. Over."

"Headed that way," I said. "Oh, and Davey, tell Mom we ought to be home for dinner. Over."

"10-4," said Davey.

Libby was ecstatic. "We are going to get to save Dad and Kaiyo, too!" she said.

"Yeah, right," I said to her. "And Goliath is just along for the ride? Something tells me he's going to probably save all of us."

I put the walkie-talkie back in the bag, looked at Libby, and just then, that screaming thing found us. He tried the howling thing again and was darting in and out of some thick cover. Occasionally, some sticks would be thrown our way. He was big, too. "Okay Libby," I said. "We can't have this thing following us. I think they're far more dangerous at night and we still have plenty of daylight left. He thinks he and his kind can scare us away like they do to most everybody else. Let's charge him and scream while we're doing it. He'll never expect it. I think this will throw him way off. When I get near him, I'm going to shoot over his head. He thinks he's scaring us. That's got to change."

"Well," said Libby, smiling. "There's a first time for everything. Let's do it."

Libby's smart. She doesn't need a whole lot of explanation. She understood me and I understood her. With a look, we spurred our horses and we went to a full gallop right at the area where the watcher was acting up. We were screaming at the top of our lungs and our horses screamed out, too.

We must have looked deadly serious because that thing saw us coming and it screamed like a baby. He ran backward, reversed himself, and started running from us. He was big, tall, powerfully built, hairy, and very fast. I got close and placed a shot over his head. He ducked and screamed again and he ran off even faster.

As this story is being told, I wouldn't doubt if that thing wasn't still running. His screams of terror continued until we could barely hear them.

We stopped. Libby looked at me, and in her deadpan way she said, "Sissy."

We laughed hard as we turned our horses due east. There was more danger to come, but Dad was finally going to have some help.

TIME TO GO — SAM

I was making some headway with the small boulder keeping me stuck in that nasty place. It was the only way out of this dank, stinking, dark hole, and I wanted out. I would lie on my back and push with my feet. I was getting the rock to move back and forth when I heard walking upstairs. No matter, I still wanted out. I kept at moving the rock. At this rate, I was confident I would be out soon. I had to get out. I was so thirsty my mouth and throat were on fire. I was hungry, too, but that could wait. I also knew it had to be daylight. I had heard a helicopter fly over twice.

Then, I heard something come by the rock. With a quick easy tug, the rock was pulled free and some crazy looking creature that was downright ugly poked its head in the space. All it probably saw of me was the glare of my flashlight. Whatever type of creature that thing was, it was a mystery to me. It reached in for me.

"No, I don't think so," I said.

With the brightness of the flashlight, it didn't see my .45 leveled right at its head. I was ready to pull the trigger when it clearly said "Go dogs!"

What in the heck? I thought. I was incredulous. But I knew he said it the first time because he said it again.

"Go dogs!" it said.

For a second, I convinced myself I was hallucinating. But then it grabbed his lips and squeezed them as if telling me to be quiet. He motioned me to come out. I holstered my .45 and started coming out, but I was moving slower than it wanted me to. Apparently.

That thing sort of helped me out. Yanked me out was a better description. Its hands were huge and it pulled me out faster than I could crawl. But I was out. At first, I was surprised at how good fresh air smelled and at the brightness of the day even though we were shaded by the thick canopy. I had been in that hole for at least two days and there was very little light in there. My eyes took a moment to adjust. When they did, I found myself staring at a giant…something.

It was human-like, tall and hairy, and not attractive. It looked sort of human, but it was incredibly muscular. It also didn't have much of a neck. I had heard about these creatures for years, but I didn't really believe they existed. I guess they did, though, because there he was. And I also guessed that he or his kind were those watching things that came close to the house from time to time and caused the dogs to get upset and growl.

I had my hand on my holster and was seriously ready to start blasting if he got rough with me, but the thing was looking behind us. Off about 400 yards away, I heard some loud, apish whooping sounds. *It* started grunting and it looked nervous and looked like it wanted to leave. He pointed to the east and said "Go dogs!"

That was good enough for me. East, we went.

It walked while I jogged through the woods. I had to ignore being barefoot, he seemed to be in a hurry. I was starting to fade when the beast found a spring at the base of a boulder strewn hill. I scraped away the leaves and drank. I pulled in the crisp, cold water and could feel my tissues rejoicing. Yeah, I may have to deal with parasites, germs, and dysentery later, but just then, the water was clear, cold, and wonderful. I drank freely from the spring and enjoyed, but not for too long. It was in a hurry.

We had made it about a mile from the house when we found the spring. Then, we heard all hell break loose again back at the house. The fact that the screams were also screams of rage and anger was obvious to both of us. Whatever those things were, they must have realized I was gone. And they didn't approve.

"Go dogs," it said.

It pointed to the east again. I realized we were on the run and that I was in some real danger.

Now I have to admit here the whole *Go dogs* thing had me totally confused. I knew what that meant and so would a lot of other people but they didn't live in Montana. "Go Dawgs" is a cheer for the Georgia Bulldogs and for a number of other teams with a bulldog as their mascot. There's more to the overall cheer than that, but not much more. In the world of college sports fans, people will some- times say things like "Go Dawgs" "Roll Tide" "War Eagle" or "Go Blue" to one another instead of saying "Hello" or "Nice day." When somebody says something like that, then the proper reply is to say the same thing right back at them but with a slightly different tone.

Still, I had no idea what was going on here. But it got my atten- tion. I looked back at that thing. "Go dogs," I said tiredly back to him and we started running east.

The fact we were being followed was no secret. Whatever was chasing us was noisy, and they probably looked just like my rescuer. He seemed to be helping me but it was for a totally unknown reason. Unless he was a rabid Georgia fan, it didn't make any sense. If he really was a Georgia fan, then the world was just too strange for me.

As we were running, I realized I needed to give this guy a name. Calling him *it* or *the beast* was a little demeaning, especially since he appeared to be helping me. Since he was a Dog fan, I decided to call him Rimmy. That was short for old friends Rob and Jimmy. They were truly rabid dog fans.

A helicopter hovered over us out of sight but just above the trees. Rimmy would look up from time to time. He stayed under the trees and low cover and never showed himself. My feet were bleeding, my lungs were on fire from all of the running, and I felt like throwing up, but I didn't miss making that observation. He didn't seem to like being seen by people. Rimmy forced me to keep running.

After another two miles, I had nothing left. Rimmy could have gone another fifty miles. He didn't even look tired, but I was done in. Off to my right on a hill, I saw a low cliff face that had an open view into the woods. I made my way to it. I was too exhausted to keep running, so it was there where I would make my stand. To his credit, Rimmy didn't leave me. He was mad as heck we were stopping, but he didn't leave me. He kept pointing to the east saying "Go dogs," but at this point, I was tired of hearing it. He really needed to expand his vocabulary. Anyway, my head hurt so bad it was hard to think and it was bleeding again. My feet were bloody and torn. I was in pain, I was exhausted, and by then, I was in a really bad mood. And I still had my gun. I didn't think our chasers knew that, either. I had enough of them.

Within three or four minutes, they came in fast from the west and were almost upon us. I could see their forms moving in and out of the brush. They were screaming and headed my way. I was resigned to the fact they were probably going to kill me, but those things were just ridiculous with all the whooping and hollering. Had they ever heard of stealth? I was hoping Rimmy wouldn't leave me. He looked like he'd be a good one in a fight, and a fight was surely coming.

Then they were there. Four of them. And yes, they looked just like Rimmy. Tall, hairy, built like trucks, and ugly…just disgusting. They all stunk, too, just like the awful smell of the crawlspace. They saw Rimmy and that stopped them for a second. Even though the situation was pretty bad, I did notice that Rimmy didn't stink like they did. Also, I couldn't even tell if they knew him.

After a moment or two of screaming, one of them cocked his arm and hurled a softball size rock at me. It came at me like a rocket.

If I hadn't ducked, it would've killed me. That guy was a terrific shot. And that also explained my still oozing head wound. If those guys decided to all throw at the same time, I was going to be stoned to death. I didn't like the idea. Rimmy stepped forward and stood in front to protect me. That was nice, and I appreciated it, but it was my fight, not his. And of course, I had a gun. That definitely made me braver.

I was angry and exhausted. Those things needed some push back if I was to survive. I grabbed Rimmy's enormous arm and swung it around me and I stepped in front of him. In one move, I un-holstered my .45, raised it quickly, and shot the one who threw the rock at me. He was quick but I got him. The bullet apparently hit him in the ribs, but unfortunately, it was not a killing shot. But geez, did I just earn some respect from those hairy giant cannibals. Next time, they will have to learn to frisk their human prey. Rimmy stood there with a look of total satisfaction. He looked my way, smiled, and then turned back to face the attackers.

Anyway, the shot knocked that hairy thing down, but he was up in a second and hid behind a large tree. He was roaring loudly as he left his bloody handprints on the tree. I liked that. I suspect the bullet had carved out a pretty deep furrow in his ribs and had probably broken a few. It had to hurt terribly. The other three things fanned out to try to surround us. I could hear one of them climbing the hill behind me. He was trying to get above us. That one bothered Rimmy.

The worst part was, they had more of them on the way. I could hear more creatures coming from the east, and some others coming from the west. Whatever they were, they weren't trying to sneak up on us. They were crashing through the trees. Rimmy put on his ferocious face. I was ready to start blazing away. I had seven more slugs in the gun and another seven in my spare magazine. I was definitely under gunned. These guys were truly big. Strangely, I was afraid of shooting Rimmy if we mixed it up. He really looked just like the others.

Then, the screaming started again. I got ready to shoot when the two watchers to my left and the one to my right, the bloody one, started running toward each other into the center of the clearing in front of us. Oddly, they were looking behind them. Each of them were looking very confused. I was about ready to pull the trigger when I heard humans whooping and hollering "Don't shoot! We're coming in!"

Just then, two beautiful horses with their screaming riders exploded into the open area to my left. I knew those horses! They literally ran over one of the watchers. I saw Dean as he took a shot at the other one, hitting him and forcing him to stagger backward while clutching his left arm.

At the same time, an enormous wall of beautiful, roaring, brown, grizzly fur rocketed out of the dense forest brush to my right. It savagely tackled and proceeded to brutally attack the beast I had shot. I recognized that roar. It was Goliath! The two huge animals fought savagely for a few moments, but Goliath was clearly the stronger one. The ugly beast finally got a break, and he rolled free and ran off at enormous speed. He was a bloody, clawed up, chewed up, shot in the ribs mess. The creature the horses knocked down ran off, too. All three were pretty torn up, especially the one that fought with Goliath. I even saw Moose chasing the bloody one. The watcher that had been sneaking up the hill behind us was mighty lucky. He vanished unhurt into the dense forest.

Then, the little clearing filled with my rescuers. Libby jumped off Jet and ran to Kaiyo. Moose came back and was acting like a happy dog. Dean stayed on his horse and was talking on a walkie-talkie while he kept his eyes on the woods. Rimmy started to wander off and I grabbed him. "Hold on, Rimmy, you need to meet my family. You saved my life. Wait here."

I think he understood me.

I called Libby and Dean, and Kaiyo and Goliath over to meet Rimmy. After a solid round of hugs and expressions of my gratitude, I briefly told them what Rimmy did for me. Dean tried to shake his hand but Rimmy didn't know about that tradition. Then Rimmy smiled and said "Go dogs," and pointed to me.

Libby and Dean dropped their mouths. After a few moments, I looked at Libby and Dean and said, "I have no idea what that's about, but apparently, he's a fan. I'll fill you in later."

I gave Goliath a big hug and told him that we were even. He had saved my life. Then, Kaiyo came and practically knocked me down. It was so good to see him. He hugged and wouldn't let go. I think he was crying. Libby told me that Kaiyo had gone out into the Eastern Wilderness all alone to find Goliath. That he managed to survive surprised me and made me so proud of him. What a brave little bear he was.

I heard Davey fly over a couple of times, and then a helicopter came and hovered above the trees nearby. Dean was on his walkie-talkie bringing it directly over. After a few minutes of positioning, a steel stretcher came through a slight open spot in the canopy and was lowered on a cable to the ground. Libby grabbed the stretcher and said, "Daddy, you're going to the hospital, so enjoy your ride."

Despite me being thrilled at being rescued, I was actually feeling awful. My feet were filthy and bloody, my head was oozing blood, and the pain made it hard to think. The thought of riding a horse home and then enduring a long, bumpy ride in my truck to the hospital was not a good thought. A smooth, quick helicopter ride seemed so much nicer. Before getting in, I thanked Rimmy. He acted like he understood. Then, I gave another hug to Goliath, and then to Kaiyo. "Goliath, please stay for a few days," I said.

I hugged Libby and Dean, and they belted me in. I was finally safe.

When I woke up, I saw Susan looking back at me. She flashed the smile that I loved, and then she kissed my chapped, cracked lips. It wasn't heaven, but it was mighty close.

EPILOGUE

A Prince Goes Home

The End — Libby

The helicopter pulled Dad up and in through its big side door. It hovered for a few moments longer, then its nose dipped. It moved forward slowly, then picked up speed and it was gone. While it was hovering above us, the noise from the chopper was not only deafening, it was everywhere. Then, it was just another sound competing for attention in the forest, quickly disappearing in the distance. And the forest fell silent.

Kaiyo, Goliath, and the watcher Dad named Rimmy sat on the ground and seemed to talk together. Rimmy was enormous. He had a body like an eight to nine-foot-tall body builder. His face was slightly apelike and slightly human. He wasn't as big as Goliath, but there were no grizzlies who would mess with him without a mighty good reason. I was glad to finally know what a watcher actually looked like. Even though Rimmy was on our side, he was still frightening to look at. But I will always remember he had kind eyes when he looked at us. Kaiyo liked him. While they chatted, Dean had his last discussion with Davey. He told Davey to tell Mom we would be headed home shortly.

I went over to the three Specials and told them we needed to head back home. I took Rimmy's big hand and looked into his big face. I asked him to join us tonight. At first, he shook his head from side to side. I told him that his answer was unacceptable. He still seemed to refuse, so I told him I would have Dean talk to him about coming over. Immediately, Goliath and Kaiyo started making noises directed at Rimmy. Dean looked our way. Rimmy listened to Kaiyo and Goliath, and then he turned to me and smiled. Then he nodded. I'm pretty sure the bears warned Rimmy he didn't stand a chance against Dean. Rimmy gave out a big laugh, and I finally let go of his hand. Then Rimmy stood up, looked over at Dean, and put his finger to his lips as if to tell Dean to be quiet. I think Rimmy understood he had just avoided losing to Dean's brand of interrogation.

It was time to go. I asked Kaiyo if he wanted to ride Jet. He shook his head as if to say no, just as Goliath lowered his giant head and allowed Kaiyo to climb up and ride him home. Dean was already on Solo, and I climbed on Jet. "Okay, guys," I said. "Keep alert. We aren't out of the woods yet."

Dean laughed and blurted out, "Well, obviously! We're actually still in the woods."

"What I meant," I said. "Is that those creatures are probably still around and we need to get home. The only way is to go back the way we came. If anybody gets too tired, let me know."

And off we went doing double time.

It didn't take too long before we got back to the old creepy house where Dad was kept as a prisoner. We stopped. "Is this your place, Rimmy?"

Rimmy shook his head from side to side. "Do you want it to be?" I asked.

No again. "Great. Rimmy, can you and Goliath tear this thing down?"

Within five minutes, there wasn't a wall standing. Those watchers were going to have to either move away or sleep in the rain. After that fun, we got home without another incident, and well before dark. Unfortunately, Rimmy wouldn't come out of the woods. He has a strong concern about being seen. That's fine. To each his own, I guess. I asked him to stay around until after dark. He smiled and nodded. That was good enough for me.

We must have been a sight as we rode out of the Southern Forest and up onto our grassy back lawn. I came out first on Jet, then Kaiyo came out riding Goliath, then Dean followed on Solo. Lisa and Davey, Gracie, and the three lawmen were waiting for us on the back porch. Davey walked over and took Jet's and Solo's reins. "Don't worry," he said to us. "I've got this. I'll take care of the horses. Go call your mom and tell her what happened. She's so proud of all of you."

That was nice. Officer Brigham and Captain Stahr each went to talk to Kaiyo and Goliath. Lisa came and gave us hugs. She was kind of our second mom, and she had made an amazing dinner. And then we called Mom. Davey was right, she wanted to hear the whole story. She gave us good news that Dad would be patched up, shot up, stitched up, and cleaned up, and then he would be coming home. That was the best news.

For the next hour, until sunset, we ate and played. Moose and Major roughhoused with everybody. Gracie had a field day with Goliath. Kaiyo had three milk bottles and two slabs of beef. Lisa was also ready for Goliath. She had defrosted and lightly cooked about thirty pounds of beef with buttered potatoes and apples. She made an entire pie for him, too. It was all a lot like the last time, back when Goliath turned and became one of us.

Lisa had also heard about Rimmy, and she didn't forget him either. She figured Rimmy would eat about the same thing as Goliath, so she made a wonderful and equally huge meal. She put it in a large cooler and Dean took it into the edge of the Southern Forest about twenty-five steps from where he last saw Rimmy. He called out to Rimmy but Rimmy wouldn't come out. Dean said it was okay and took the cooler back in the woods. When he got to Rimmy, he opened the cooler. Out came a steamy hot aroma causing Rimmy to smile in wonder. Dean told me when Rimmy saw what Lisa had made for him and his eyes got bigger than dinner plates. Rimmy quietly whispered "Go dogs," as he looked it over. Then, he laughed big. We all heard that laugh.

Just before dark, Sheriff Tuttle, Captain Stahr, and Officer Brigham came to say good-bye. They told Goliath that they and the four deputies swore to one another they would never tell anybody about Goliath, Kaiyo, or Rimmy. They also told me the last of the poachers had crawled out of the forest and was a scratched up, scraped up, whimpering mess. He went straight into a police car.

They actually had to pull him out of the car to frisk and cuff him. He then went back in the car and straight to jail. He and all the others confessed to trying to poach bears and a lot of other awful things. They would also probably need counseling for years for what they went through in the Southern Forest.

After the lawmen left, and when it got a little darker, Rimmy finally came out of the woods. He and Kaiyo and Goliath again sat together and sort of did what appeared to be talking. Rimmy obviously felt far more comfortable in the darkness. And he was full. Whatever they were talking about, they all laughed out loud several times.

Dean and I sat on the back porch, and we told Davey and Lisa our part of the story. Gracie listened, too. The good news was, Dad had been treated and released from the hospital. The story everyone was told was that he was assisting the police with the poachers and had a bad fall, got knocked out, and then when he woke up, he was lost and in a state of confusion. And because of that, he had to be rescued by the Sheriff's deputies. That ought to work. There was some truth to the story, though not much.

Thirty minutes later, we saw Mom's truck come driving down the long driveway. She was bringing Dad home. They pulled into the courtyard, and Dad slowly stepped out. His head was bandaged and he was on crutches but he actually looked okay. The dogs greeted him first and Kaiyo came over to say a quick hello. He then ran back to Rimmy and Goliath. Dad looked over at them. They were sitting in the wide grass strip between the barn and the Southern Forest. Dad waved and said loudly, "Go dogs."

Rimmy responded in kind. Dad came over to us and said, "Someday, I'm gonna figure that one out."

I lived in a magical world.

For the next two weeks, Dad healed and Goliath stayed at our farm. The farm animals never got particularly used to him except for the horses. He preferred to sleep in the barn, and he and Peyton became close. I think it was the warrior thing again. Then, one early

Saturday morning in early October, he came through the kitchen door. He came in and gave Kaiyo a hug. He was leaving, again.

I knew this day was coming. I tried not to but I cried. It was so sad. Dad tried to talk him out of it, telling him he could spend the winter here. Mom just gave him a hug. So did Dean. So did Gracie and I. And that was it. He went back to his home in the Eastern Wilderness. I couldn't blame him. He was a king out there. And we missed him terribly.

With the fall season, life fell into a pattern that included school, chores, and Kaiyo's latest adventures. Dad had bought Gunner's property and the others from Mr. Chandler, and Gunner was hired by Dad to help around the farm. We needed him and he worked hard. But for the most part, life was pretty regular. Dad worked the farm nearly every day, and he watched his football on Saturdays. Dad loves Montana football, but he still adores the Georgia Bulldogs. In fact, he's pretty partial to all of the southern teams.

One Saturday night, we figured Rimmy out. When it's nice, Dad likes to record a game or two and sit outside and watch the games while cracking peanuts and drinking a cold beer. Kaiyo sits with him when he does. Dad swears Kaiyo understands the game. Personally, I think he just likes the peanuts.

So it was a tough game and Georgia scored and pulled ahead. Dad yelled out "Go Dawgs!" A second or two after that, from just in the Southern Forest, we heard Rimmy loudly say, "Go dogs!"

Dad broke down laughing, and Mom hearing it from inside, laughed, too. They had wondered over and over how Rimmy ever knew to say "Go dogs." Now it was so obvious to us. Rimmy had probably heard Dad say that cheer a lot over the years, though maybe not nearly as often as Dad would've liked.

Dad went inside and grabbed the leftovers and some apples and walked out to the edge of the farm. There at the edge of the forest, he and Rimmy hugged and they just sort of talked to each other. Basically, Dad talked and Rimmy would nod his head and grunt a little. Rimmy would get more vocal, but Dad didn't understand any of it.

Every once in a while, Dad will call out the cheer to see if Rimmy is there, but he's been back only a few times. The problem is, Kaiyo and the dogs still alert us to the presence of a watcher from the woods. They know Rimmy and often they will eagerly disappear into the forest to say hello to him. Lately, though, it's back to the growling. Dad said next time Goliath comes over, we're going to have to clean out those woods. I think he's right. Those woods could also use a spiritual cleansing, too. We could do both.

So, things were good.

Then one day, Tracker showed up. I didn't know where he came from, but he trotted into the farm like he owned it. Gunner might have shot him had Moose and Major not gone nuts over seeing him. Tracker was definitely the alpha dog around here. Gunner figured out he was a special when Rosie the alpaca jumped the fence to go see him. Rosie had grown and leaped the fence with ease and raced to get to him. Gunner went out to meet the wolf and he walked back in with him. Mom and Dad stopped everything. They were thrilled with the wolf's return. Tracker's being here made Dean's day. They liked each other. Gracie was the happiest ever. Kaiyo seemed okay with Tracker, but he was as not ecstatic like the others.

After a few days, everybody got used to Tracker being here just like we got used to Goliath. Every day, the wolf and Kaiyo would go explore and sometimes just walk the farm. Tracker avoided the people he did not know, and he warmly greeted those that he did. Tracker is a wolf and he has all the air of royalty. He even has great posture when he walks. Everyone is glad he's here. That is, everyone but me.

I don't think Tracker does anything without a reason. He's a thinker. But why he was here remained a mystery to all of us, except probably Kaiyo. Then, it happened. One morning, Tracker came in from the back door just like Goliath did the last time we saw him. He came into the kitchen and stood there. He looked at each of us. It was obvious he was leaving. Dad gave him a big hug and talked, while Mom hurried and made him a quick breakfast. Gracie barely let go of him. Dean was on his knees with his arms around the wolf.

Dean even cried and that was rare. Kaiyo, though, didn't hug the wolf. Kaiyo hugged me instead.

At first, I was confused. I looked at Mom as she turned away with eyes filled with tears. She buried her face in Dad's shoulder, and I saw her start to weep deeply. Dean was confused, but then Kaiyo went to him and gave him a nuzzle on the cheek. It dawned on me what was happening. Gracie wanted to know what was going on. I was so hurt that, in the midst of my tears, I said, "That wolf is stealing him! He is taking our Kaiyo away."

By this time, I was just getting started. I looked at the wolf, and between tears, I said, "Everything was great until you got here! You're just like all wolves, you're a thief! Please don't do this. You don't have to take him. He's ours!"

I knew immediately what I had just said was definitely not the right thing to say. I also said the last part about Kaiyo being *ours* a little too possessively, I guess. Maybe I said it way too possessively, because that's when Kaiyo left my side and went over and stood next to the wolf. I half expected the wolf to stick out his tongue at me. I was shocked, though. The fact Kaiyo decided to leave hurt me even more. All I could say was, "I didn't mean it that way Kaiyo; I didn't!"

I kept crying. Dean looked at me and gently said, "It's done, Sis. They're both leaving."

The two of them turned and walked out the back door, then down off the porch and up the cart path that headed northeast toward the entrance to the Eastern Wilderness. Poor Gracie, she was a basket case. After a few minutes, Dean looked at me and said, "Let's escort them as far as we can."

We both ran out and hopped on our horses bareback and went after them. We ran down the path but they were gone. Kaiyo wasn't all that fast and we should have found them easily, but we couldn't find them anywhere. We guessed they circled back into the Southern Forest to keep us from following.

And that was it. We searched for tracks, we even tried to get Moose to find them; he had found Kaiyo once before. Nothing was found. And so, we headed back to the barn, released all the horses out to pasture, and went back into the kitchen.

Gunner, Aliyah, and their daughter Kate had come over. Gunner was distraught. He loved Kaiyo deeply. Kaiyo often joined him as he worked on the farm. It wasn't unusual at all to see Gunner driving by on the UTV with Kaiyo sitting right next to him. Aliyah was consoling Mom while Kate ran over to Dean and gave him a big hug. She was only twelve years old, but I'm pretty sure she thought a lot of Dean. Watching her put her arm around him confirmed my suspicions. In my despair, I still noticed there was something there between them.

I walked to the front to where Dad and Gracie had gone. They were sitting on the front porch and Dad was explaining things to my little sister. He told her Kaiyo was a gift to our family and the adventures that we experienced with him made each of us and our family so much stronger. "Gracie," he said. "You got the chance to throw a stapler at a killer grizzly and then cuddle with him all in the course of a few days. Who in the history of mankind has ever been able to do that?"

Dad pointed at me with his thumb. "Libby here was able to give a wild wolf a bath, and rescue me from the watchers. Dean, too. Shoot, I bet we could write a book about all the ways we have been blessed by that amazing little grizzly bear. So, yes, we will all be really sad Kaiyo is gone, but I am so glad he was here with us for the time we got. And who knows, Gracie, maybe we will see him again someday."

"So, where did he go?" Gracie asked.

Dad rubbed his chin, looked at Gracie, and said, "You know, sweetheart, I have been wondering where he came from since we first figured out he was so different. That day he tried to warn us about the bison when he was just a cub, that was when Libby and I started to suspect he wasn't a normal bear. Tracker and Goliath proved it because they were so different. Anyway, I'm pretty sure wherever he's going to, it's not in Montana."

Dad looked at me and winked. I thought that over. Those were wise words. And Dad was right. Kaiyo was a blessing. And I had been truly blessed. So was everybody else who knew him. And we all knew Kaiyo had gone home, wherever that was. And as Dad said, it probably wasn't in Montana.

And our lives continued on.

That's not to say we didn't long for that cute little bear because we did. Several times from out of nowhere, I would be overcome with grief and cry. Something as simple as a sound or a random thought could trigger a wave of sadness. At other times, we could talk about Kaiyo and feel no grief at all. We all had our moments. Mom told us grief was a mugger. She was right. The grief usually came at me without warning when I was not prepared.

But in the midst of it all, the cows needed milking, the alpacas and all the other animals needed feeding, stalls and living areas needed cleaning out, we had homework to do, school papers to write, and the dogs had a farm to patrol. Life pretty much went back to normal because it had to. Fortunately, that was still a wonderful life.

Several times, Dad, Dean, and I went hunting in the Eastern Wilderness. On one of those trips, we saw the huge tracks of Goliath next to a creek bank. We gathered and stopped just short of the tracks and stared at them for a while. Everybody missed Goliath, too. We didn't say a word as Dad took us back into the hunt.

My sixteenth birthday came and went, as October slid into November and the colder weather settled in for the duration. The memory of Kaiyo was a big part of our Thanksgiving remembrances. We had all come to miss Tracker, even me. I think Dad never held a grudge, and probably Mom didn't either. But we all figured out that Tracker was never really for us. He was friendly and he obviously liked us, but he never would have come to know us if it hadn't been for Kaiyo. For some reason, Tracker's aim always was to protect Kaiyo. From the time he got here, he helped us only when we were protecting Kaiyo. We don't know why he came for Kaiyo or where they went, but we all eventually came to the conclusion the wolf did what he did only because he thought it was good for Kaiyo. And we were okay with that.

The snows of December came and that always made farming tough. Our winter goal each year was simply to keep the livestock healthy. The milk cows had their own barn, and the horses had their stalls. The pigs were safe inside, and so were the chickens and the guineas. The few sheep and goats we had were hearty, and we kept their pasture free of too much snow. The cattle were super tough, and as long as we kept them fed, they did just fine. We had built a few barn type buildings in the pastures that broke the force of the wind and were dry, and that was about all they really wanted. With cows, ice storms were killers, but this year, that hadn't happened.

The alpacas looked like walking mops so they were warm enough. They actually looked absurd, but in a cute way. We cut their coats in the early summer, so by winter, they were covered in the best wool in the world. Since alpaca fur is second only to polar bear fur in warmth, their only problem with winter was not the cold but the depth of the snow. So, Dean, Gunner, or Dad would plow as much of it away as reasonably possible. They were fine.

We all looked forward to Christmas because we were still kids, of course. We had our lists, and Dad and Mom got the house looking beautiful. Mom, Gracie, and I spent a lot of time in town and a few days in Bozeman. Dad and Dean hunted some, practiced at the rifle range, and generally kept themselves busy. Dad and Dean also visited the Gibbses a lot because Dad had hired a builder to fix up their house. It started out as a beat-up place, but when the work was completed, that house was beautiful. The Gibbs family was so happy with their new home.

Occasionally, like at dinner, we would pray for Kaiyo. The wolf, Goliath, and Rimmy got prayed over, too. But that was about all we could do. We sure couldn't go get them. Goliath was probably hibernating, Rimmy was super elusive, and Kaiyo was somewhere with Tracker. So, we planned for the holidays. And we were all excited for Christmas, and as it approached, the excitement built.

We had parties to go to and we had several at our home. School finally let out for the holidays, and the absence of tests and themes to write brought peace to all of us school kids. Dean and Jack Gibbs spent a lot of time here and at Jack's place. Jack's little sister Kate was a tagalong, but I don't think she bothered Dean nearly as much as she bothered Jack.

Our life was good.

Christmas morning finally came, and as usual, Dean and I woke up early and waited on Gracie to wake up. I'll give it to her, she tried hard. Gracie slept like she was in a deep dark pit, and waking up for her was like trying to climb out of that pit. She finally woke up, and the three of us headed downstairs together. Mom and Dad were downstairs nursing their coffee. They looked terrible but in a cute sort of way. The truth is, parents don't get a lot of sleep on Christmas Eve and that was true here. Finally, they led us into the front, and there under the tree were our gifts. We attacked our packages like pirates. And through it all, Mom and Dad smiled.

After an hour or so, we all sat back to breathe. Mom and Dad were always over generous, and this year was no different. They were amazing. Eventually, Mom and Gracie made their way to the kitchen and brought back a plate full of hot sweet rolls and sausage biscuits—our Christmas tradition. And we followed another tradition. We each gave thanks to God and thanked him for the sacrifice of Jesus. Eternal life is a pretty sweet gift, and our family didn't take it for granted. Outside, the sun was just coming up. The sheer beauty of the snow-covered landscape made all the old Christmas postcards come true. It was so nice.

And a wolf howled.

It wasn't all that far off. The dogs stood up, stretched, and walked over to the windows. Dad looked at Mom and said, "That's not good. The alpacas are out."

We heard another howl. This one was a little closer. I knew this interruption to our otherwise awesome Christmas morning wasn't welcome. Our livestock was in danger. Still, the howl of wolves was and is a beautiful thing, and we have always enjoyed the sound of wolves. A wolf's howl has to be the best reminder of wilderness there could be.

Dad and Major went in the mud room where Dad kept some coveralls, a parka, and his rifle. Dean was usually the first to want to go, but it was Christmas and Dad told him to enjoy the morning. Dean was also in shorts and a tee shirt, and Dad was in a hurry. Dean definitely did not look disappointed. "I'll be back in twenty," Dad said.

We heard the door open, and with it, we braced for the guaranteed blast of frigid winter air that was sure to shoot across the floor all the way to the front of the house. The cold hit us like a hammer. Dad was always good about opening and closing the doors fast. Out here, it's a necessity. In the summer, we battle the heat and the flies. In the winter, we fight the ever present wind and the cold. An open door invites both problems and a yell from somebody. With all that cold air, Dad got yelled at by everybody.

"Come on! Close the door, Dad!" yelled Gracie.

We all chimed in. It was so cold. But Dad didn't close the door. He just calmly but loudly, said, "I think y'all might want to see this."

We all got up, wrapped our shoulders in our blankets, and wandered into the kitchen. As expected, Dad had the back door wide open. Major was at his side and his tail was wagging. We all looked out the door. There just beyond the steps and in the driveway stood a very big wolf. He was looking right at us. It was Tracker! Gracie ran out of the kitchen, down the stairs, and into the snow even though she was barefooted. Mom tried to stop her, but stopping Gracie was always a difficult task. She ran over to the wolf and hugged his giant neck. His tail wagged. We were confused but so glad to see him. Then, we heard another noise.

Tracker was looking to our left at the north corner of our house underneath the porch roof. We followed his eyes and there stood a bear. We all froze for a second. The bear was taller than Moose and heavier. But a look at that face and we knew. It was Kaiyo! Wherever he had gone, he had obviously eaten well. He was bigger and even more beautiful than I remembered. We knew then that Kaiyo had come back!

Well, there was complete pandemonium. Everybody forgot the bitter cold and the wind. As a group, we raced over to Kaiyo. Everyone talked a mile a minute, and even Kaiyo gave his bear version of a loud, joyous greeting. At the same time, we all had a complete group hug. Gracie went and dragged the wolf into it, too. When we took a breath, Kaiyo pushed past us, strolled down the porch, turned, and went into the kitchen. Tracker was second and the dogs followed. We were all left standing on the porch in the freezing cold. We were still stunned as the frozen winds whipped around us.

Kaiyo came back out, looked out at us all, gave us a little bark, turned, and went back in the kitchen. We got the message and we all piled inside. And when we did, we walked into another book or two of amazing adventures.

And best of all, Kaiyo had chosen. And he chose us!

The End

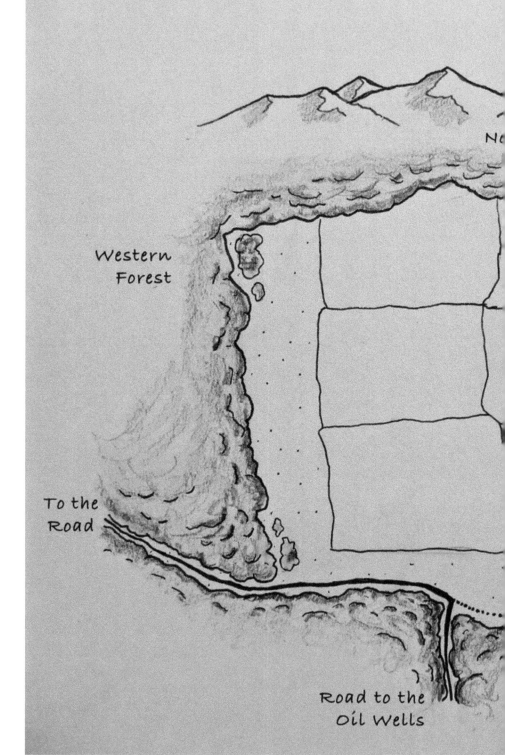

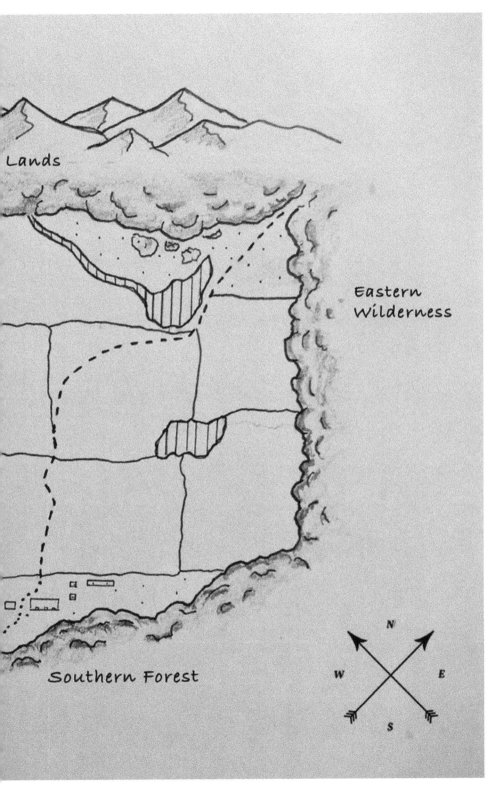

Lands

Eastern
Wilderness

Southern Forest

N
W   E
S

ABOUT THE AUTHOR

Author Cliff Cochran sees life as a collection of countless sagas that somehow weave themselves together to form God's plan for creation, redemption, and completion. From Jesus's parables to Shakespeare to modern theatre, the draw is always the story. He focuses on the power of story as an attorney, as a husband, and as a father of three because life is often best learned that way. *Kaiyo/The Lost Nation* is the result of the many requests from his now adult children to preserve years of fascinating bedtime and campfire stories. Those stories were told to strengthen their faiths, feed their limitless imaginations, provide insights to their own potentials, and to encourage them to see life as an adventure.